PIECES

OF ME

By Eisley Jacobs

PIECES OF ME
http://www.EisleyJacobs.com
All Rights Reserved
Original Copyright © 2013 by Eisley Jacobs

ISBN-13: 978-1479272914
ISBN-10: 1479272914

Cover art by Big House, Little Room Designs and A. Porter
Cover model: Danielle Bean
Cover photographer: Iona Neff

Edited by Kristen Yard and Jacob Neff.

Pieces of Me is dedicated to my
mom and dad.

Words cannot begin to describe my
appreciation and gratitude for
all you have done for me. Thank you for
believing in me and encouraging me
to always follow my heart.

I love you!

I hunch over my knees in the middle of the room, hugging them as tightly as my arms will clamp. I rock back and forth, praying this nightmare will end. The cold floor sends shivers racing through my body, competing with the heavy thumps of my heart against my chest.

My eyes search the unfamiliar surroundings as I fight the urge to throw up.

Where am I?

The alarm resounds in the small room, but I don't dare touch it. Instead, I will it to stop. I will myself to wake. To remember everything.

No. Anything.

Why can't I remember?

A headache lingers at the rim of my consciousness. My fingers find my temples, massaging in rapid circles as I pinch my eyes shut.

I force myself to suck in a slow breath, tears tumbling

down my cheeks.

What's wrong with me?

My fingers dig into my temples, reminding me this is no dream. This, whatever it is, is real.

I press my face into the flannel pajama pants I wear, stifling the sob.

A sound echoes behind me in the hall outside the room, causing me to flip around so fast my head spins. Light floods from under a door, and a shadow passes through. Instinct tells me to take flight, but the terror in my body won't allow my limbs to move. My chest collapses as if a four-hundred ton weight has been set upon it.

I can't breathe.

Desperate to inflate my lungs, I push myself to all fours and concentrate on the cold floor, tracing the patterns of the wood with my eyes.

Where. Am. I?

A breath catches in my throat.

I can't remember my name.

The alarm grows louder, and the constant beeping is grating on every nerve in my body. I yank the cord from the wall, finally thrusting the room into silence. The clock tumbles to the ground, narrowly missing my head, and a sticky note flutters into my vision.

One word is written on it.

Amnesia

Pain sears every cell in my body.

Panic attack.

I grasp at the bed, heaving myself up to sit on the edge. I fold myself in half, tucking my head between my knees, coaxing my mind to calm. I don't know how I realize this is the right thing to do, but it helps. The pain eases, and the haze in my vision lifts. I allow myself only another moment before I push off the bed.

I stand motionless in front of the mirror, numb from the words on sticky notes plastered to every available space within arm's reach. It's like I've done this before and knew I'd do it again. One of the yellow ones shakes me to the core, and I want to release the scream building in my chest.

This is how your day
begins every morning.

The sooner you accept it
the better you'll be.

Anger sizzles in my chest, and I resist the urge to rip the words from the wall along with every other note that papers the small space. I want to tear them to pieces, but the desire to read them is even stronger.

Notes on the mirror remind me who I am, why I'm here, and who this person is staring back at me, the red hair flowing in wisps over my shoulder with a chunky blonde streak in the front. And those piercing blue eyes.

Have I always had blue eyes?

I feel like I've just woken from a nightmare I can't shake no matter how hard I pinch myself.

More sticky notes on the wall say I live a normal life, despite the amnesia hang-up. I'm seventeen, a junior at Clement High School. My best friend's name is Sam, short for Samantha. My name is Braidan.

"Braidan." The name rolls off my tongue, but it feels wrong. All wrong.

Determination to find answers builds in my chest and beats stronger than the heart beneath my pink nightshirt. A familiar anger rolls over my body, one I've certainly felt before.

How could I know this? I can't even remember my name.

Braidan, I remind myself. Braidan.

Deep down, I know I'm not Braidan. At least, I don't think I'm the Braidan standing in front of the mirror.

"Braidan," a voice calls from behind the door, startling

me. "It's your mom."

My mom?

"Braidan, read the green note on the mirror."

I scan the notes and find a tattered green one attached to the edge. It's written in the same awkward pen as the other twelve-hundred.

Mom's name: Sheila

Appears: 7:30am

Let her in.

"Uh, hold on." My eyes roam over the paper, evaluating its hue.

How do I know this is green and that is a mirror, but I have to be reminded who my mother is?

"Bray, Honey, it'll be okay." Her strained voice travels through the thick panels.

My muscles tense until I can barely make them obey as I twist the handle and step back. I don't know who will emerge, only that the note says it will be my mom. I'm ready for anything, fear etching away at my sanity.

The door opens slowly, and the woman pokes her head through the crack. At the sight of her face, all feelings of alarm melt away. I don't recognize her, but she doesn't appear threatening. A large clip pulls back her medium-length, strawberry-blonde hair, wisps framing her delicate features. Her sorrowful hazel eyes search mine before she swings the door open the rest of the way.

"Are you doing okay? Have you read all your notes yet this morning?"

"I do this every morning?" I manage to squeak out as I blink back the welling tears.

"Yes, but you do fine," she says, heading for the attached bathroom. "You need to get in the shower before Sam comes for you." The hiss of water echoes off the walls in the small room. "You have some more notes in here and in the shower. They usually make you feel better about your day." She places fresh, sage-green towels upon the marble counter, then stands in the doorway, watching me with guarded eyes. She allows a long, frustrated sigh to tumble from her mouth, then heads for the door, giving my arm a gentle pat as she passes.

"What happened? Why don't I remember anything?" I try to suck in the breath before the waves of horror break through my words.

Sheila twists on her heels, wringing her hands in nervous circles, like she's massaging lotion into her dry skin. "They aren't sure. You started with the notes when you realized you were losing your memory. Some days are better than others. Today looks like a good one."

I stare at nothing, the panic in my chest screaming for escape. If this is a good day, what will a bad one look like?

The walls of my world tumble inward around me, crashing at my feet.

I turn to the bathroom, away from her scrutinizing eyes. Tears slip down my cheeks, and I close the door behind me without another word.

The steam in the bathroom masks the mirror as I undress, which is good, since I don't think I can handle looking at the stranger reflecting back.

Notes fill the bathroom like wallpaper, and I look for another shred of assurance that what I'm going through is normal.

This feeling passes by lunch. School is easy. You always remember how to do math.

How is that possible? How come I can't remember my name or even my face? I yank open the shower door, only to find laminated notes papering the inside. The nagging in my stomach says this should all feel very familiar, but my heart bursts into tiny pieces as I step in.

Closing my eyes, I lean against the wall under the steady stream of water, praying that I will wake. That this is a dream.

That everything will be as it once was, however it had been. That this is not my life.

This is not my life. This is not my...

Silent sobs break from my clenched jaw, and I allow myself to drift down the wall to the floor. I hug my knees and rock back and forth, not knowing how long I'll be allowed to hide from the world awaiting me on the other side of the door.

When I convince my eyes to part, the note sticking to the bottom of the wall makes a trickle of hope flutter in my chest.

I know it doesn't feel this way right now, but you will be okay.

I stare at the sticky note, reading it over and over again. I know it means I've been here before and will surely be here again.

Search for answers.

I bite back the painful realization that even if I find any answers, I will forget them the next time I wake. Then I'll sit here and do this all over again.

What type of answer should I look for? Answers to my illness, if that's what it is? Surely, medical teams are working on my memory crisis, right? Or maybe it isn't a crisis. Maybe it's a blessing. Maybe God's sparing me from the awful knowledge of my past.

Out of the shower, I head to the walk-in closet. My clothes are lined in perfect color order, mostly t-shirts and jeans. I grab the first white top my hand finds and examine the front, looking for some recollection. *Switchfoot* is written across the top, with colorful balloons falling from the base of the letters. I wait for some preference to strike me, but it doesn't, so I just pull the shirt on over my tank top. I grab a pair of blue jeans from the tall stack and slip them over my hips. I gaze at the procession of rubber soles and grab the first pair, skipping the socks.

I read every note I come across. I need to feel normal by the time my friend Sam comes to get me.

Normal.

What is normal? This *is* normal, says my mom.

I pinch my eyes shut and shake my head. No. This can't be normal. It can't.

The clues around the mirror tell me about my personality.

*Your nickname
is Bray.*

*Don't let anyone call
you Ray. Especially
not the jerk,
Lucas Tress.*

I say the name Lucas Tress in my head, hoping I'll remember it, since it seems to be important.

A long string of yellow notes line the left wall, listing my supposed likes and dislikes. I glance over them, but nothing sticks out as important.

A small picture book draws what remains of my attention. My fingers outline letters engraved in the brown leather.

"Made with love by Sam." The words sound somehow empty. I will myself to open the book. My hand grasps the edge, and before I can chicken out, the pages flutter open.

Every available space holds pictures of Sam and me on

adventures I can't remember -- running, dancing, making goofy faces, watching movies, and posing for each other with a fast food clown. In every one, both of us grin as if we're truly best friends.

Guilt tugs at my mind. I want to smile at these happy memories, but they're someone else's memories, not mine. How could I forget these things?

My eyes wander to the mirror and stare at perfect red wisps framing the pale skin of my face and the blonde chunk covering half my brow. I see the same girl as in the pictures, no one can deny that. The same blue eyes peer back at me. The same dimpled cheek when I force a smile. The same white teeth.

I set the book down and pull in a deep breath.

How can any of this be okay? Even though my thoughts ravage anything positive, I need to accept that it is. I don't want to spend my day in misery, even though I won't remember it tomorrow.

Another note is stuck to the bottom of the picture frame on my nightstand. My face is here, along with Sheila's and three others. A man with dark hair graying at his temples has his arm around Sheila. The note indicates he's my father, James. With a gentle but firm gaze, he stares through the glass as though trying to hold the family to a high standard. His nose curves at the tip and reminds me of my reflection.

The two boys in the photo are my brothers, ages fourteen and eight. The oldest, Drew, has dark hair and eyes. He crosses his arms in a rebellious, displeased gesture. Tanner, on the other hand, sits on my lap, and his eyes twinkle from inside the pixels of ink. His tousled, blond hair sticks out in every direction at the top of his head, as if someone forgot to tell him to comb it that morning. The note says my nickname for him is Squirt. Seems appropriate.

I gaze at my now familiar face. I'm smiling, and while it doesn't appear authentic, I can't say it looks completely fake either. My eyes are dull and lifeless, as if I realize the photo is being taken solely to remind me who my family is.

"Bray, you're running late!" Sheila's muffled voice echoes down the hall outside my room.

I stare at the picture of my family, trying to burn their faces into my retinas.

The note near the light switch is purple.

> *Don't forget your*
> *black backpack.*
> *Everything you*
> *need is in there.*
> *Including sticky notes.*

I peek into the bag and suppress a laugh. Sticky notes of every color line the bottom, nestled up against a collection of pens and a math book.

My hand rests on the knob for a good minute before I

convince myself to twist it and head toward the voices. Voices I don't recognize. Voices of my family.

I put one foot in front of the other down the narrow hall, rattling the names off in my head. Mom is Sheila. Dad is James. My brothers are Drew and Tanner -- Squirt.

They're sitting in the large eat-in kitchen when I enter, but no one looks up. Sheila stands at the stove, busying herself with a pot of something steaming. Smells like oatmeal, but how do I know that?

"Bray?" James says, startling me. "Are you going to have breakfast?"

Sheila doesn't turn to acknowledge me, but the boys look up briefly from their bowls before they refocus on their breakfast.

"Sure." I clutch the strap of my backpack, hoping it will steel my nerves.

"The oatmeal is ready." Sheila pulls the food from the stove. "Boys, you're going to miss the bus. Hurry up." She nudges Drew, who's not moving. "I'm not taking you if you miss it again."

Drew groans but hops up from the table just as I sit. I watch as Tanner heads for the door, shoulders slumped, defeated in some unseen battle. His eyes connect with mine, and before he can turn away, I see sadness waiting there. Is it for me? Or for him because I don't remember who he is? "Hey, Tanner?" I call, unsure what has made me speak up.

He flips around, and his eyes sparkle as in the

photograph, lit with anticipation.

"Have a good day, Squirt."

I don't even realize he's moving until his arms are around my neck.

Everyone stares, frozen in shock.

"I love you, Bray," he whispers so quietly I can barely hear him.

"I love you too, Squirt," I whisper back.

"Please remember," he says, then lets me go and runs from the house, the screen door slamming behind him.

Drew's mouth hangs open in disbelief, and his eyes pinch together with something more than annoyance.

Sheila and James stare after the boy who's obviously gone outside the normal confines of our daily routine. Or is it me who's done something new? I remind myself I'd nicknamed him Squirt. Surely this isn't the first time I've called him that?

"Drew, go," Sheila says, bumping his arm again.

He watches for another moment before grabbing his backpack, with much more force than necessary, and heading for the door.

Great. So one brother hates me and the other wants me to remember. But what am I supposed to remember? Him? My life? I flop into the chair and stare into my bowl, wondering if oatmeal is even on my list of likes.

14

"Did I do something wrong?" I don't look up for a response, but I can hear Sheila's deep, sorrowful sigh.

"No, Honey, it's just..."

James clears his throat, which draws my head up. My parents are locked in a silent stare for what seems like hours before a knock at the door brings life back to the room.

"That's Sam," Sheila says, trying to hide her voice from cracking. "She's a little early. Bray, why don't you take a granola bar instead." She hands the green metallic package to me when I stand.

"Have a good day, Kiddo." Dad rises and gives me an awkward embrace. "Try to take everything in stride."

I nod, biting back the knot growing in my stomach. As soon as I open the door, the safe haven of this home will be no more. I'll have to deal with life as it comes. Will I be able to handle this? The expression on my parents' faces says I can. They believe in me. Tanner believes in me. I should believe in me, too.

The world moves in slow motion as I head for the door.

The smiling girl behind the pane melts every bit of anxiety built up in my body. Sam stands there, blonde hair up in a ponytail, sunglasses on her head, happy to see me.

"You ready, Bray?" she says, as if she doesn't realize this is the first time I've laid eyes on her.

"As ready as I'll ever be," I reply, then close the door to the safety behind me.

2

Scenery whips by the window as I sit silently in the leather seat of Sam's little lime-green Volkswagen Beetle. The Bug smells of strawberries and vanilla, likely due to the pair of fuzzy red dice hanging from the rearview mirror. The music is low, leaving me free to start any conversation, but I have no idea where to begin. I've got so many questions I'm sure she has answers to.

Sam acts as though she's content not saying a word. Maybe she thinks it's better this way, but the urge to find answers builds in my chest with every block we travel away from the house.

"So," I begin, but I'm not sure which question to ask first.

"Wow, that's a record," Sam says, still looking forward.

I don't hide my frown. "What?"

"Usually, as soon as the door clicks shut, you start grilling me all the way to school."

"How long is our drive?"

"From here, it's only another five minutes or so, enough time to get the important ones answered. Not sure, yes, no, and of course." She flashes a contagious smile.

I grin, wondering if she really knows what question I'll ask first. "So, do you know why I've lost my memory?"

She frowns, eyes still on the road. "No. No one does. Your doctor thinks it's some kind of selective amnesia. One day you were fine and the next, you couldn't remember your own name."

"And I'm really okay with this by lunch?"

"Yeah. Weird, huh?"

I nod, gazing into the field of tall grass outside the window. "And people really don't treat me like I'm a freak or something?"

"Definitely not." Sam pushes her sunglasses over her head. The grin reaches her ears. "People think this whole deal is pretty cool." She snickers and turns left across the busy traffic. "Since you can't remember what happened yesterday, you don't hold grudges... which can be a very good thing." She groans. "Sometimes I wish I had your ability. There are people who really piss me off."

I allow a genuine smile to crawl across my face. "You're jealous I don't remember?"

"Of course!" she says, throwing her hands in the air. "It's totally cool you don't remember the jerks." She touches my arm. "You read the note about Lucas, right? He's truly the only one you want to remember to hold a grudge against."

"Why?"

"I dunno," she says, her eyes back on the road. "Before you lost your memory, you two dated. You didn't tell me what happened, but you wanted me to help you remember to keep him at a football field's distance, if you know what I mean. We've both told him to lay off, but he doesn't seem to get the hint, even when it's screamed in his ear."

My heart flip-flops nervously at the sight of the school in front of us.

"Breathe, Bray. It won't do either of us any good for you to pass out on campus today."

I draw in a breath and plaster a smile back on my face. Today. She said today. Had I passed out before? "How do I know where my classes are?" I can't hide the worry creeping into my words.

"Your locker location, code, schedule, and a map should be in the front of all your books, but you have a great sense of direction, unlike me. One glance and you're usually on track again. By the end of the day you've gotten the whole campus mastered."

"Only to have to do it all over again tomorrow."

She shrugs. "It's not all that bad."

Sam pulls into a free parking spot near the front and turns off the ignition.

I can't help but hesitate after she opens her door. Kids litter the sidewalks and the front of the building, like vultures waiting for their next meal. Glances at the car, and at me, add to the growing uneasiness in my stomach.

"You coming?" Sam pokes her head through the window.

"Yeah." I pull the handle and step into the early morning sun. I watch the faces of those nearby, but no one turns. Maybe I'm overreacting. Maybe everything will be fine, like Sam says. Maybe I really will be okay by lunch.

"Let's go, Bray. Math class waits for no one, not even you." She tucks her arm through mine and escorts me down the hall, stopping at a large orange door with the number A-17 stenciled in black.

"Looks like a prison label."

Sam laughs and frees my arm, "You say that every morning." She leans in. "Between you and me, this class is prison. Lucas is in there with you. Good luck." She turns, but I grab her.

"How do I know which one he is?" I try to keep my voice from wavering.

Sam pulls the door open and peeks in the classroom. "He's not here yet, but when you see him, you'll know who he is." She watches my face for a second before patting my arm. "It's hard to believe, but you always know him. He's hard to forget, even for you." Sam turns. "I've got to get to class. I'll see you in art," she calls back, then disappears around the corner.

The classroom is cold and dim. Half the lights are off, and an overhead projector duplicates equations onto a white screen near the front. The soft hum of the machine mixes with the chatter of the few students already inside.

"Braidan, sit here," the teacher says, pointing to a seat near the back, where he stands. He's in his upper fifties, grey hair barely covering his balding head. His smile welcomes me when I place my things on the desk. "I'm Mr. Harris," he says, extending his hand. He leans down and mumbles, "and you love math." He winks before releasing my hand and returns to his desk to shuffle through papers as the rest of the students filter in.

Each time the door opens, the harsh contrast of light pouring into the dark room silhouettes the bodies coming through. Once my vision returns, I search the faces carefully for something alerting me to Lucas' presence, but no indicators blink red.

The bell rings, and more students rush into the room, but I still sense nothing. Mr. Harris takes roll, checking names off his list. Two seats remain empty, one next to me and another near the front.

The door swings open, and my breath catches as I gaze at the outline. The boy has a sturdy build, and his head tilts to the side, as if he's looking for something... or someone.

I glance around, but no one pays him any attention. The only alarms going off are in my own head. When the door clicks behind him and my eyes adjust, my breath returns in a large gasp. I struggle to deflate my lungs as the boy runs his fingers through his dark, disheveled hair, then saunters to the seat right beside me.

"Mr. Tress, if you're late to my class one more time, don't bother attending."

"Yes, sir." His voice is rich, like caramel on my tongue. He pulls his book from his bag, at the same time casting me a sideways glance. Reaching down, he sets the bag on the floor, leaning as close as he can without touching me. He draws in a deep breath through his nose, clicks his tongue, and sits up, tapping his pencil on his desk.

Every fiber of my being screams at the presence of this boy, either in protest or excitement, I'm not sure. Everything about his blue eyes, perfect eyebrows, pronounced jaw, toned body, even his clothing, draws me forward. I either want to slug him or make out with him right there on the spot.

Nice warning.

I rip open my bag, searching for a sticky note. My blue pen rolls over the orange note in quick strides, and I write in big letters.

LUCAS EVOKES

FEELINGS YOU'LL

WANT TO ACT ON.

DON'T DO IT!

"Act on them, Ray." The voice in my ear makes me jump.

I look up and find Lucas so close I can feel his breath on

22

my cheek. I smell cinnamon on his breath. His eyes look deep into mine, then dart to my lips. My stomach drops and rises with the butterflies lingering there.

"Sam doesn't know what's best for you, Ray. Let me back in. Let me show you what you're missing. Let me help you remember. I know I can." His whispers are soft, and even though I know I shouldn't believe him, something stirs inside, and I do.

"I..." My breath comes in short intervals as he draws closer still. My eyes dart to his lips, and I want to kiss him.

"Is there a problem, Mr. Tress?"

The enchantment breaks, and I turn to Mr. Harris, away from Lucas, who sits up in his seat.

"No sir, just asking Braidan for a piece of paper."

"You come to my class late and unprepared?" He turns back to the projector. "Strike two."

I suck in an uneasy breath, remembering the note at home calling Lucas trouble. Boy, was that one right. A quick side-glance proves he still watches my every move.

The words in front of me mock the very thoughts in my head. I press my lips into a fine line as I pull the paper from the stack and open my book only to freeze. Almost identical reminders paper the inside, barely leaving room for my schedule. I groan and stick it inside the cover anyway.

I stare at the clock, wishing for the class to end. Lucas' eyes poke into me like darts, each releasing a melting pot of emotion.

The bell rings, and I'm not sure if I should wait around or rush for the door. My indecision holds me captive, and Lucas is on his feet in front of me before I can move.

"I'll walk you to your next class if you want." The words ripple from his throat, soaked with remorse. He clasps his hands in front of his body, a silver ring on his right hand drawing what bit of attention I have left. It has a weird Celtic knot etched into the band, and I can't help but stare.

Did the knot just twist?

I blink. I blink again, certain I'm hallucinating.

"Braidan?" he says, waving his hand in front of me.

I see a flash. Then, instead of the boy I watched through class, another stands before me, eyes angry and intent, rushing toward me, reaching for my throat. I recoil and fall from my desk. The vision ends when my butt hits the floor.

"Whoa. Are you okay? Your eyes just glossed over," Lucas says and reaches down to help me to my feet.

A spark of electricity races through my body as he touches my forearm. I pull myself from his grasp and stumble into my desk, almost knocking it over. My arm reddens and throbs, burning like someone has pressed a hot iron to it. The imprint of his fingers fades and is completely gone by the time he looks down.

My heart pulsates, as if the shock has jumpstarted every nerve ending in my body, awakening them from their slumber. The ticking of the classroom clock blares like a horn. The dragging of feet and the creak of the door magnify to screeching decibels. The paper Mr. Harris shuffles assaults my ears like a tornado rushing through the plains.

"I..." I try to think of something to say, unsure what's happening. "No, I don't need help." I rub my forehead where the headache pounds my frontal lobe. "I got it." I push past Lucas and head for the door.

"Bray?" He calls for me, but I refuse to look back.

Something is very wrong. I have to find Sam.

The breeze greets me like a hurricane sweeping across the crowded hall, rattling my eardrums. I frantically search every face that passes, hoping one of them will be Sam's. The buildings open up, and a large, triangle-shaped, cement patio filled with mingling kids stretches across the expanse. I grip my ears as the amplified voices reverberate off every surface.

My feet break into a full run and carry me down a nearby hall, away from the booming voices. The rustle of trees adds to the cacophony, weaving its way into the tremendous pain throbbing through my skull. I turn further into the campus. A piercing sound echoes through my mind, and I grit my teeth, clutching at my ears.

I rip open the nearby door and pull it tight behind me.

Silence. My headache is suddenly gone.

My lungs inflate, and a sigh escapes my parted lips.

"Excuse me?"

I flip around and seize the door handle, ready to bolt.

"Whoa, where's the fire?"

My eyes dart around the room, seeking the source of the question. I'm about to consider it a figment of my imagination when movement at the back of the room draws my attention. A boy sits on the floor, book in hand, leaning against the wall.

"Oh, sorry to interrupt. I was just..." His face comes into view, and something pings in the back of my mind as I take in his features. "Do I know you?"

He stands and strides toward me.

Irregular heartbeats pound my chest as I stare into the pool of his chocolate eyes. His hair is two-tone brown and blond and sticks up in random spikes across the top his head. With broad shoulders and long legs, he crosses the room in mere seconds. When he smiles, my heart picks up speed.

"I'm new here at Clement," he says, drawing the words out in a slight southern drawl. He moves in, until I can smell his musky cologne. "I'm Ian." He stretches his hand in greeting, but I only stare, wondering if I should take it.

I tentatively reach out. "I'm Braidan." I resist the urge to pull away when our palms touch and make no effort to hide the relief that pushes over my lips when no jolts of electricity shoot through my body.

"Hard day?" he asks, releasing his grasp.

"You have no idea," I say, feeling foolish. "What are you doing in here alone?"

"I have a free period while they sort out my schedule. Sort of like study hall, only I have nothing to study, so I thought I'd catch up on some reading." He taps a book on the heel of his hand.

"*To Kill a Mockingbird.* That's a good one." The words come out even before I realize what I've said. I remember this book. Quite clearly. And it rattles me. I feel distress coating my face, and Ian frowns.

I squeeze my eyes shut, wondering how I can recall the details of a book but not my own life. He clears his throat, and my eyes pop open.

"Sorry, headache." I twist my hand around the strap of my backpack. "So, why aren't you outside, meeting all your new classmates?"

He shrugs, unfazed by my momentary lapse of sanity. "I'm not so good at the socializing thing."

I snicker in disbelief. He's cute, very cute, and I have a hard time believing anyone like him would have social problems.

The side of his mouth turns up in a playful grin as if he knows exactly what I'm thinking. He lowers his eyes to the floor, then brings them slowly back up. "When you enter a school midyear, it's hard to find a place among the cliques. Everyone seems to have their group of friends, and I don't feel like competing for status."

"You switch schools a lot?"

He bobs his head from side to side. "More than average, I

guess. My dad moves us a lot to establish new offices around the world, so starting over gets easier. You just adapt and hope some random girl bumps into you and makes your day."

I make no attempt to hide my wide smile. "Well, starting over might be easy for you, but I'm having a time of it." The words pour over my lips before I can take them back.

"Oh? You're new here, too?"

"Well, no. At least, I don't think so anyway." I watch him carefully, trying to decipher his reaction. Do I tell him my issues or just let him figure it out tomorrow when he says hello and I look at him like he's contracted the plague?

When I grunt my frustration, he laughs.

"Sorry, it's complicated."

"How complicated could it be? You either are or you aren't," he says, tapping his leg with the book.

"It feels like I am. I've got some sort of amnesia or something going on right now. I'm told the doctors are working on it, but I don't know that for sure. All I know is what has happened today. Tomorrow, it starts over again." I lean against the door.

His eyebrows furrow. "You're serious?"

"Why would I make up such a freak story?" I rub my forehead and place my hand on the doorknob, my smile gone. "Nice to meet you, Ian. I've got to go."

"That's it, then?" He crosses his arms, studying me.

"Well, it's not like I'll remember I met you tomorrow. Regardless what you say or do, it won't matter. So why waste your time?"

He stuffs one hand in his pocket. "So, if I told you I thought you were the most beautiful girl I've ever laid eyes on and I'd like to have your phone number, you'd forget by tomorrow?"

His words echo in my head, and he closes the small gap between us, searching for a reaction.

"I... uh..."

He pushes a stray hair from my face, gently brushing my chin with his finger. Our eyes lock, and a wave of déjà vu explodes over me. I see him drawing me forward into his world. A world of comfort and understanding. A world not plagued with missing memories. A world I desire.

I stumble backward as the door flies open. Struggling to remain upright, I flip around and almost whack my head on the nearby wall. Regaining my footing, I push myself up, directly into Sam's worried face.

"Thank God I found you. What the heck is going on?" She looks to Ian, mere inches away.

"Sam," I blurt out breathlessly.

"And who are you?" She places one hand on her hip, seeming more like a mother than a best friend.

"Well, nice to meet you too," Ian says, extending his hand. "I'm Ian. Braidan and I were just talking."

She wrinkles her forehead, ignoring his gesture. "Yeah, well, Ian," she says, her voice dripping with annoyance, "we've got to go." Sam yanks me through the open door.

Confusion fills the boy's face as the door shuts behind me, probably the same expression plastered across my own.

Sam quite literally drags me down the hall and into a locker cove.

I rip my arm from her and straighten my clothes. "What the heck are you doing?" I ask, annoyed at being towed away for no good reason.

"Alone anywhere with anyone is bad news. Someone could take advantage of you or..." She pulls on her ponytail, tightening the already taut hairs. "What happened? Lucas grabbed me in the hall and told me you freaked out in math."

I purse my lips. "No offense to you or my former self, but to say I needed to stay away from Lucas was the understatement of the century."

"What do you mean? What did he do?" She crosses her arms and taps her foot in a furious pattern. "I swear, I told him to--"

"No, he didn't really do anything. He just touched me and... I don't know what happened. My arm felt like it was on fire!"

"Shhhh," she says, glancing around the nearby hall. "Don't scream it out for the world. We don't need that kind of freak show today."

"What?"

"Never mind. What were you thinking about?" She folds her hands across her body, suddenly the concerned friend.

The heat rises in my cheeks. "Why does it matter?"

"Look, this is why you have to stay away from Lucas. He brings up things you can't control."

"No freaking kidding," I say to the ground, the embarrassment of the situation registering full in my mind. "It was like one minute I wanted to kiss him and the next rip his head off. And then there was this blink, and I just kind of flipped. I can't explain it. It was just weird. Do I do this a lot?"

"At least once a week. The school just needs to heed the warning and get him out of that class already." She grunts and continues before I can respond. "I think we need to make a better reminder for you until they do. Maybe stick one in my car so you don't take any of it lightly." She lets out a long sigh of frustration and rubs her temples. "This time Lucas is the one to blame. He knows better. He just needs to back off and forget you two were ever anything."

"What does that mean, Sam? What aren't you telling me?"

She snorts. "It just means he's trouble. Period."

"So I've heard." I can't help the sarcasm floating from my mouth.

Her eyes search the crowd filtering through the campus, then glance at her watch. "I've gotta go. You going to be okay? Want me to walk you to your next class?"

"No, I'll be okay. All the prison doors have numbers on them. It takes an idiot to get lost in this school."

The color returns to Sam's face, and she smiles. "There's the Bray I know." She winks and hikes her backpack over her shoulder. "Hey, who was that boy?" she asks, now focusing on my face.

I feel the blush creeping up my neck. "A new kid. I warned him I might not remember him tomorrow." I can't help but smile. "He seems pretty nice. He asked for my phone number." My eyebrows bob up and down with pleasure.

"You didn't give it to him, did you?" she jests, but I can tell she's happy.

"Well, I might have... if I'd known it. He was cute, don't you think?"

Sam laughs and throws her arm around me, leading me from the locker cove. "And good thing, too. You don't give your phone number to a boy the first time he asks. Make him wait for it," she says, looking out of the corner of her eye. "Besides, it means he'll have to introduce himself again tomorrow and make the same impression."

"And what would that be?" I ask, but I know I'm completely transparent. Ian made quite an impression, and I bet she could read it all over my face.

Sam pushes my arm. "Some things never change. You get more boys interested in one day than I've had in my whole life." She throws her arms playfully into the air. "Just once... ONCE, I'd like to be the one with the boy issues." She winks, then turns. "See you in art. It's right before lunch."

I watch her stroll away and can't help feeling a dart of hope shoot through my chest that maybe I will be okay by lunch. With a quick check of my schedule, I find my next class before the bell rings. Settling into my seat, the chatter around me buzzes at a normal level, reminding me of the electric jolt from Lucas and the calm that poured over me when I met Ian.

Ian.

There are definitely no notes warning me to stay away from Ian. How could there be? I just met him a few minutes ago.

I hold in my sigh and wonder how it would work to date a guy I wouldn't recognize each day. Or would I? My subconscious seemed to know Lucas. It knew I wanted to kiss him or punch his lights out. So maybe, just maybe, it could work.

My words come easily as I write myself a note:

Ian is a good guy.

You want to remember him.

I tap the pencil to my lips, watching the English teacher scrawl information on the board.

Ian stirred something in my subconscious when I laid eyes on him. Maybe he will be the key to all this. Maybe he'll be the reason I pull out of this amnesia sickness. Maybe I'll remember him tomorrow. Oh man, I hope so.

~

"My English teacher could have been speaking French for all I know." I settle into my seat next to Sam and pull out my sketchpad. "It was like every time I focused on the board, all I could think about was Ian and those deep brown eyes."

Sam leans toward me. "Don't tell me you've been struck by the stupid fairy," she says, tilting her head to the side.

"What's that supposed to mean?" I sneer.

"How's that going to work, Bray? Think about it."

"Yeah, I've thought about it. But maybe, just maybe--"

"Maybe he's the one that's going to break the spell? Maybe he's going to ride in on his white horse, kiss you, and you're going to magically wake up and remember?"

I stare, trying to hide my shock.

"Really, Bray? I mean really? That's a fairytale, not real world crap. No offense, but those types of things don't happen 'round these parts."

36

I push out the breath I'm holding. "Well okay, so it sounds farfetched, but..." I lower my voice and lean toward her, "something has to work, right? I can't be like this forever."

"You've been this way a while," she says, her sad eyes meeting mine. "It's foolish to think anything else right now. We just... I mean, they're looking for a way out of this, but right now it's like a dead end road." She sits up in her seat when the teacher walks through the room. "It's a nice thought, really it is. But it's just not possible right now."

My eyes search the side of Sam's face. Am I reading into it, or did I really hear what I think I did? I try to push the feelings away. She just messed up, I assure myself, but something in the back of my head nags, telling me to take her words and pick them apart.

They are looking for a way out of this? Who are *they*? And why did she couple herself in there at first? Are *they* the doctors, or someone else entirely different?

The lines at the corners of Sam's eyes wrinkle as she chats with the boy in front of her. I glance to the girl beside me and study her eyes. No lines. Looking back at Sam, I realize she has more sun marks on her face than any other teenager in class. Sam rests her left hand on the table in front of her, and I notice a faint white line is evident on her ring finger.

When she twists toward me, I snap forward, hoping she didn't see my intrusion. My mouth is dry, and the room spins as the new information settles on my consciousness.

Sam isn't who I think she is.

4

Mrs. Harris supervises while everyone in art class works on 3D pencil sketches of an eighteenth-century rocking chair.

One peek over at Sam's drawing, and I realize my artistic talents aren't terrible, but they certainly aren't up to her level. Her pencil lines are distinct and look nothing like my work.

"Sam, you've got talent beyond your years," Mrs. Harris says, passing by. "You see things others miss. Good job."

Sam puts her hand over her sketch. "Thanks, Mrs. Harris." The words spew out as if in response to criticism rather than praise. She glares after the teacher, who's already complimenting the prodigy at the next table.

"You are good, you know." I pick up my own drawing and set it next to hers. "Compared to you, I'm a first grader with a crayon." I turn my head sideways, trying to evaluate what I thought I was drawing.

Sam shuffles her sketchbook into her bag and throws in the pencil. "I just don't like the attention she gives me. I..." She pauses mid-sentence and frowns. "I've asked her to stop calling me out like that. It makes me uncomfortable." Resting her chin on one hand, she flicks the eraser remnants littering the area with the other.

"Sam?" I lower my voice, trying to hold it steady as I speak. "How long have we been friends?" I hope it's a question I've asked before.

She stares at the paper as she flicks another piece of rubber. "A long time. Maybe since like fifth grade?" She brushes the table clean and sits up. "Yeah, I think it was fifth grade. Why?" Her focus settles on my face.

"I just... I'm wondering how come none of my other friends are as close as you are." I shift my eyes back to my depiction of the rocking chair. "Did they really all just bail when my issues hit?"

Sam lets out a long, irritated breath. "You know, Bray, I..." She leans toward me. "Yeah. They couldn't deal with it."

"How come you do?" My eyes trace the lines of my drawing. "I mean, how come you didn't ditch me, too?"

"There was no way I could leave you," she says, a hint of bitterness at the end. "You need me, and I can't walk away from that, even if I wanted to." She rubs her face, worry lines evident in her brow. "You have me. Isn't that enough?"

"Oh no, that isn't what I meant. I'm sorry, Sam." I finger the corner of my paper. "I'm just trying to figure it all out."

"It's a useless ploy. Even if you figure anything out, you'll forget tomorrow."

My eyes meet hers, and instead of understanding, I see

exasperation and the same bitterness as in her voice. I bite my lip and stuff the drawing pad into my bag. If it's not my imagination, Sam sees our friendship as a job. My mind roams over the fact she said there is something to figure out that I could forget tomorrow. Something she knows. But it is something.

The bell rings, jostling me from my chair. Sam tugs my arm like a toddler and heads for the door before I can even fully rise. She releases me, expecting me to follow, but my stubbornness roots me to the spot.

"Braidan?" Mrs. Harris calls before I can detach myself from the linoleum floor. "How's your day been?"

I shrug. "I guess it's going as well as can be expected. And since it's lunch now, the rest of the day just gets better." I try to smile, but the questions about Sam plague my mind.

"You sure? You aren't exactly acting normal." She stops in front of me, hands on her hips.

I try not to laugh in her face, but the sounds come from my chest anyway. "I wouldn't know what normal is at this point. I'm just getting by."

She presses her lips into a fine line and considers me.

"Bray? Are you coming?" Sam's annoyance carries through the room from the door.

My eyes dart between the two. "I should go."

"Have a good day, Braidan."

"Thanks." I shoulder my backpack and head for the door.

"What was that all about?" Sam hooks her arm through mine. She's back to being my parole officer.

"She just asked how my day was going."

Sam tows me through the lunch line, sticking food on my tray when I don't take any. I sit quietly at the table, unable to articulate the thoughts holding my tongue captive. Sam eats in silence, the anger and resentment I'd tasted in art class still lingering around her edges. One piece of me wants to suck it up and blurt out my thoughts and fears, but another says to keep quiet and make a note of her behavior later.

"Well, hello there." Ian's voice pierces the silence. "Mind if I have a seat?" He carries his tray in one hand and his backpack in the other.

"Sure." I feel no need to ask my guardian's permission before I scoot sideways. The oddest sensation crawls over me as Ian's arm touches mine, like waves of warmth radiating from his body. Not the heat I felt when Lucas touched me, but rather pure pleasure.

Sam snarls toward Ian when I venture a peek at her.

"You came out of hiding," I say, ignoring Sam's silent, desperate attempts at communication.

"You convinced me the scenery's better out here." His eyes remain fixed on me.

"How are you faring as the new kid?" I twist away and try to hide my grin by sticking a fry in my mouth.

"Probably as well as you are," he says, nudging my arm.

"You know, getting lost every turn. The curious looks."

"Ha!" I nudge him back. "I haven't gotten lost once." I let out a soft giggle and smile even wider, if that's even possible.

Sam clears her throat, begging for attention. Her curt grin and the way she's dangling the fry from her fingertips says her displeasure has risen to an all-time high.

"Sam, right?" Ian says, offering his hand.

"Ian, right?" she replies, her words dripping with much more hatred then necessary. Instead of taking his hand, Sam wipes her fingers on the nearby napkin. "So what do you want, Ian? Any guy okay with Bray's issues is up to something."

I stare at Sam in shock.

Ian does the same.

"Really... out with it," she says, jamming a fry into her mouth.

"Wait, wait, wait." I hold up my hand to stop Ian from uttering a single syllable. "Just because a guy chooses to befriend me means he's up to no good?"

Sam tilts her head to the side and raises her eyebrows, keeping her focus on Ian.

"That's crap, Sam." I throw my napkin to the tray and stand.

This takes her completely off guard, and she stumbles from the bench to her feet.

"I don't know who you think you are, but I don't think I like you right now."

"Bray, get over yourself, and sit back down." She reaches over the table and grasps my arm.

I shake loose and grab for my backpack. "You know, Sam, if you're truly my best friend, you wouldn't be jealous that a guy pays a little attention to me."

"Jealous? JEALOUS!? What. Ever." Sam grabs her tray and pitches it in the nearby trash. "You don't even have a clue." She flings her hands in the air. "Fine. Let him take advantage of you. What do I care?" She glares at Ian, then storms off, plucking her cell phone from her pocket as she rounds the corner.

Numb, I sit back at the table, unable to understand what has just transpired.

"Whoa," Ian says, fingering the edges of his tray.

I rest my elbows on the table and put my head in my hands. "I'm sorry," I say, unsure why.

"No. No, it should be me who's apologizing. I could have sat somewhere else."

"Are you kidding? I'm glad you came over. I've been... well, let's just say the blow-up has been building since last period when..." I look up and find him intent on me. He watches me with a mixture of victory and pleasure.

At the sight of his face, I realize Sam could be right. And I hate her for it.

Ian's eyes linger on mine, making me think he might just have ulterior motives. But how could he? I'm the one that intruded on his space, not vice versa.

That's it. I'm a head case.

I push my tray away. "Can I just get through this day and start over again? Forget the doubts and questions in my brain?" I shake my head and suppress the sarcastic laugh threatening to bubble out. "I get it now when she told me she was jealous of my ability to forget. Tomorrow I'll treat her like the best friend I believe her to be, and she'll still have the memories of me yelling and accusing her of being jealous."

I can tell Ian contemplates something as he watches. No doubt my sanity.

"So, what if tomorrow you wake up and you've got all your memories back? Or at least the memories from today? Would you wish for them to be gone again?"

I stare into his face, weighing the words that fall heavy on my heart. "No. No, I guess I wouldn't."

"Which means...?" He lifts his eyebrows, urging me to come to the same conclusion he has.

My jaw tightens. I don't want to say it, but I know I must. "Which probably means I need to apologize to her." I toss aside the soggy fry that had fallen on my tray. "Cuz... regardless what I remember tomorrow, she'll remember everything." I let out a long, aggravated sigh through only slightly parted lips. "I'll go find her." I push to my feet but freeze when I realize Ian's hand covers mine.

"I want you to remember me tomorrow." He squeezes gently but allows my hand to lift from the table.

A grin creeps across my face. "Hold up there, Sport. Today isn't over yet."

His smile is so wide. Dimples I didn't seen before now show clearly, adding to his already irresistible personality. "Go find Sam. I'll be here a little longer, then I have to get lost finding chemistry. Maybe we will bump into each other again in the hall. It'll give me something to look forward to."

I reach in my bag and offer Ian a beige stack of sticky notes. "You can write me a couple reminders for tomorrow." He clasps his hand over mine, and I don't pull away.

Movement in the fringe of my vision snaps me to attention, and I turn to see Lucas standing five feet away, staring us down.

"I'll find you after school and give you these," Ian says, shaking the pad in the air.

"You'd better." I smile, knowing Lucas watches.

"Now, go find Sam. You'll thank me later."

"Maybe I should thank you now, in case I forget," I tease. I then turn, glancing at Lucas, who looks downright furious.

"I'm banking that you won't." His words echo around me in a cocoon of hope. No, I don't believe in fairytales, but I can dream. Dream that someday, someone will make the difference and I'll be able to remember again.

I follow the path Sam disappeared down moments earlier.

She shouldn't be far. An eeriness creeps over me as I round the next corner and almost run into her back. I'm about to call out, but she's on her cell phone. Then I hear my name. I dart back around the corner before she realizes I'm there.

"No, you don't understand... Yes, she's fine, physically. Lucas set something off earlier, and she's..." She pauses while the other person comments. "She's acting weird, and there's this new guy. Has anyone done a background check? He just started today. Ian... No, I don't have a last name. I didn't exactly want to buddy up to him, not knowing who he was." She lets out a long groan. "Fine. Text me the details. We just had a blow-up, and I'm not sure how the rest of the school day will play out." More chatter on the other line. "Yeah, well you know, McCready, this isn't what I signed up for... Yes, I'll make sure her parents know." She snaps the phone shut, and I sprint away before she can catch me.

I hurry back to Ian and flop down on the bench beside him.

"That was--" He interrupts himself, and his eyes grow wide. "You look like you've seen a ghost. What happened?"

"I don't know, but I can't talk about it right now. Sam's coming back, and I need to get my mind on something else."

"Okay. Uh..." He wipes his hands together over his tray.

Sam appears from around the corner on the warpath, heading straight for us.

"Here she comes." I twist toward Ian and plead with him. "I need something from you."

Ian's look of confusion raises the panic in my blood. "What?"

"I don't know. A distraction? Something?" I whisper, franticness bursting in my chest. "Anything," I push over my lips, afraid I'm going to come apart.

Before I can register what's happening, his hand is behind my neck, and his warm mouth is on mine, pressing tenderly. I think I should pull away, but instead I grasp his sweatshirt and pull him closer, welcoming his spicy, sweet taste. The weight on my lips releases, and he backs up with his hand still on my face, his thumb stroking my jaw line. My hands remain lost in the tangle of his sweatshirt, while he searches for evidence of my approval.

"What the heck was that?" Lucas' voice startles me. He's standing at the other end of the table, crossing his arms. The veins in his neck bulge like he's about to come unglued. Sam is beside him, her face also wrought with anger and disbelief.

Ian releases me and clears his throat as I flick my teeth with my tongue, trying hard not to smile, figuring it would only make matters worse. Though, what do I care?

Diversion successful.

I grab my bag and stand. "Ian, I'll see you later." I turn without saying a word to the two gawkers. Apologies can wait until I've had the chance to cool down, but right now I'm not willing to cool anything. Ian's kiss stirred something within me so profound I want to dwell in it... at least for a little while.

5

I'm in the bathroom, splashing water on my face, when Sam finds me. She stands silent at the end of the counter, arms crossed, foot tapping. The conversation I overheard pokes at my mind, but the taste of Ian's lips still blushes my cheeks.

The paper towels are behind Sam, but I grab at them anyway, refusing to make eye contact, fearing she will see right through me. Slowly, I wipe my face, wondering if I should just play dumb and get through the day, but that isn't a possibility. I still need a ride home, seeing as how I have no idea where I live or who to ask.

"Look." I toss the used towel into the bin, "I'm sorry I blew up at you. It's been a rough day and... I'm... just sorry." I pick up my bag, but my shoulders still slump in apology.

"It's fine. It happens. You're going through a lot... every day." She holds the bridge of her nose, as if fighting a migraine. "Tell me, what was that back there? You just met that guy this morning, and you're already kissing him?" She throws her hand in the air, but continues before I can squeeze in a word. "I know you don't believe it, but people

49

will take advantage of you. Jerks like Ian know if they screw around with you today, it won't matter tomorrow, and they can try it all over again."

"Is that what happened with Lucas?"

"What? No. I mean..." She lets out a perturbed growl.

"What do you mean, Sam? What you tell me is that you have no idea what happened between Lucas and me, but twice today you've made mention that you know more. Which is it?" I cross my arms and wait for her to dig herself out of this one.

"Fine. I know a little more, but seriously, it's not worth it right now. It won't matter tomorrow."

"But what if it matters today? If you didn't notice, I just kissed a guy right in front of him."

"Yeah, I think the whole school saw that one," she says, rubbing her forehead. "Look, I don't know specifics. I do know Lucas loved you... but you guys had to break it off."

Her words echo in the small bathroom, and I feel I'm going to be sick. "I loved him too, didn't I?" I ask, already knowing the answer. I look down at my arm, willing the red marks to appear again, and remember his touch.

"Yes. You did. Which is why you have to stay away. It's better for you both. I know it doesn't make sense, but the feelings he stirs up are dangerous."

I turn to hide the tear streaking down my face. I nod despite my lack of understanding. How can our love have put

50

anyone in danger? At the moment, I'm only in danger of bursting into uncontrollable tears.

"So what was that with you and Ian? You don't kiss a guy the first time you meet him."

I wipe my hand across my face and spin on my heels. "I don't know. It just kind of happened. One minute I'm asking him for a distraction, the next he's kissing me."

"It looked like you were kissing him back," she says, leaning against the counter in a more relaxed pose.

"I was. It just felt right. I... I don't know."

Sam shakes her head. "It might have felt right, but he's bad news. All boys, not just Ian. It'll only end in heartbreak."

"How can it? I won't remember tomorrow."

"Not for you... for them."

Her words crush me like a ton of bricks.

She's right. I grind my teeth together and push the breath through my nostrils, refusing to let on that I'm this upset. It doesn't work.

Sam embraces me for a long moment, then steps back. She pushes the hair from my face and smooths my cheek. "You're stronger than this, Braidan O'Donnell. Don't let boys ruin what remains of your day. Just tread with caution."

I gather myself, peering into the face of the girl who calls me friend, and wonder if she truly does care or if it's just a job. I nod to appease her.

"You want me to walk you to class?" she asks, bringing her hand down to my own.

"No. I need to pee," I lie. "I can make it there. It's just around the corner."

"I don't know. Maybe I should, just in case," she says, scanning my face.

"No really, Sam. I get it now. I'll be more careful. I'm fine. Really."

She considers my words, apparently reading my body language, and shrugs when she finds whatever it is she's looking for. "You sure?"

"Yes, really. I'm fine." I allow a smile as I let out a small, aggravated sigh.

"Okay, whatever. Just be careful. Let's get through this day without any more episodes. I'll meet you after school by your locker. You good with that?" She squeezes my hand as she stares into my eyes.

"Of course. I'll be fine. I just need to give myself some better notes."

She hikes her bag over her shoulder and chuckles. "We keep trying..." she trails off as she heads from the bathroom, the door thumping behind her.

I stare at myself in the mirror, craving for some recollection of love, pain, happiness, despair, anything to bring truth to Sam's words. But nothing comes.

I splash my face one last time, then head to class, pain

throbbing in my heart every step of the way.

The next two periods pass with ease as I concentrate on making good notes for myself, thankful no one shares either class with me.

There's no doubt I have strong feelings for Lucas. Even though I can't remember his face, I feel he holds an unrelinquished piece of my heart. My mind flashes to the jolt that shot through me at his touch. Could this be the danger Sam referred to? It was probably static electricity accidentally discharging itself. However, I can't explain why my senses were overloaded.

*You were in love
with Lucas once.*

My heart twists in my chest as I press the note into place. You loved him, Braidan. Past tense. Whatever happened before, it's obviously over, and you have moved on.

I pull in a deep breath and amend the note with:

But it's over.

Ian's face pops into my memory, and I smile, remembering the warmth he radiated. I shake my head as my pen hovers over the note. How can I have feelings for a boy I only met a few hours ago? Yet I have no doubt something is there. Otherwise, why on earth would I allow him to kiss me? My cheeks flush at the thought of his mouth on mine. I certainly didn't have any jolts jumping through my body when he kissed me, at least not the dangerous kind, so that must be a good thing... right?

My hand shakes in anticipation of seeing him again, and I can't stop grinning as I write the next note.

You kissed the new kid, Ian.

And you liked it.

I press it next to the note about Lucas as Sam's face enters my rim of consciousness. I groan. My parents trust her, which means I should trust her. Regardless of my suspicions or what I've heard, she's in my life for a purpose, I try to convince myself, even as I write.

Sam is just trying to help. She means well.

Peeling the note from the stack, I recall the conversation I overhead, and it grates on my nerves. It sounded like I was a job, not a best friend. And what about that background check thing? I tap the paper between my fingers, then wad it up and begin another.

Question everything Sam does. She's hiding something.

My last class could not have come a moment too soon. The weariness hits as I fall into a seat near the back. I've been through a gamut of emotions today, and while a few of them were fun and I may want to experience them again, I'm exhausted.

As soon as the thought exits my head, Ian plops himself in the desk beside mine, and I can't help but smile. I'll take this one again.

"So, we share a class? Score," he says, lacing his fingers over the backpack on his desk.

"Get lost anymore?"

"Nope. Funny thing, all the doors have letters and numbers, kind of like a prison."

I grin and release a chuckle.

"How about you? You talk to Sam yet?"

"Yeah, I think we're cool."

"What about that guy who was practically shooting darts through my skull? Who was he?"

My chest constricts, and I gaze at my hands. "Well, he was a little upset a total stranger was kissing his ex-girlfriend."

Ian tries to hide his surprised laugh. "Yeah, I'd have probably been upset to see someone else kissing you."

The flush creeps up my neck at his words.

"About that," he says, leaning closer and lowering his voice to a whisper. "I'm sorry that happened. I don't know what came over me. I just... did the first thing that came to mind."

"It's okay. It wasn't like I didn't enjoy it." The heat rises to my cheeks, but the pang of guilt in my chest overrides the flattery. "It's just... nothing good can come of this, especially if I don't remember you tomorrow." I turn toward his stone-cold stare, hurt already evident in his face.

"You mean, I don't even get a chance?"

I look away before his eyes bore holes in my resolve. "It's not a good idea."

"Braidan, can't I at least try to get to know you? Help you through this time in your life?"

"We just met, Ian. I…"

"Just a chance. I just want a chance."

The teacher calls the class to attention, but Ian's focus is still on me. He wants me to answer, but how can I? How can I say I'll even entertain this possibility when I may not remember?

"Okay." The words leave my lips before I realize I've spoken.

He exhales, and without looking, I know he's smiling.

"No history for you today," the teacher starts, and the class erupts in cheers. He pulls the standalone television cart to the front of the room. "Your assignment is to watch the news for the next forty-four minutes and pull out a current event you think might become history for future generations. Take good notes, and feel free to discuss quietly among yourselves. Your paper is due Monday as soon as you walk into my room."

Groans bounce off the narrow walls as the teacher flaps his hands like a hatchling attempting its first flight. "Your moans are in vain. At least I didn't tell you the paper was due tomorrow. You have some research time this weekend to make the paper excellent. Use the internet, library, your parents, or some other reliable resource." He clicks on the television, and the news comes to life. "I'll be in the back observing and grading midterms."

Most of the class sits in silence for the first couple of minutes, watching the newscast and trying to catch the words in the red bar scrolling across the bottom. Kids get up and stand closer to the television, writing down specific items from the banner. I watch from my seat, trying to gather my idea.

I wonder how it's going to work for me to do a research paper when I won't remember it's due. Maybe I'll need to complete it today. I suppose worse things have happened, like say... my whole situation. I laugh at the irony of me writing a paper on an event future generations will remember but possibly not me.

"What are you laughing about over there?" Ian whispers just loud enough for me to hear.

"I was just wondering how often I'm let off homework because of my... condition." I twirl my pencil in the air and bat my eyelashes.

"Are you sure you've even got a condition?"

"Like I said, that's what I've been told, and I tend to believe it when I can't remember what I ate for breakfast yesterday."

"Well, neither can I, but that doesn't mean much."

"Come to think of it, I probably had oatmeal or a granola bar."

The anchor's voice cuts through my thoughts. I immediately tune into his words and swivel toward the television.

"Police officials are baffled this week after a rash of

break-ins at top secret facilities across the country. In a press conference this morning, a representative from Saber Corp states that although the break-ins have caused a significant amount of property damage, nothing seems to have been stolen."

The name Saber Corp flaps around in my mind, seeking a place to settle, but as it tries to poke its tentacles into my memory, each tether is zapped, moments before it can connect with my brain.

The screen flashes to a man in a white lab coat. The ticker at the bottom gives his name as Dr. Morgan Graham. "It's an inconvenience, and I can assure you Saber Corp is doing everything in their power to find and stop those responsible for these villainous acts." The man's eyes dart in every direction, then bore through the screen directly into mine. My eyes fall to the logo on his breast. The emblem looks similar to the NASA insignia, only instead of a red swoop around the universe, a silver sword jabs through the words SABER over what appears to be a depiction of Earth.

Ian tries to speak, but I hold my hand up as my mind scrambles for anything. I scratch the word Saber across my page and stare at it. The temperature in the room shifts, and beads of sweat erupt from my brow. Something in the recesses of my memory rattles me, screaming for me to find it, to pluck it out and bring it to life. But no matter how hard I concentrate, I can pull nothing forward.

The room is silent, which doesn't make sense. The television is still on, and students' mouths still move.

My eyes track toward Ian. He's speaking, but no sound

penetrates my ears. When my head hits the desk, blackness takes over my mind.

~

"Braidan?"

My mind flickers awake, and I open my eyes, my head pounding with pain.

"Are you okay?" Ian whispers, and I realize I can hear the television again.

"Yeah, I just... blacked out for a second." I sit up, rub my forehead, and scan the room, worried the whole class witnessed my blackout, but everyone seems to be off in their own worlds, eyes still fixed on the television. "I'll be okay," I assure him when he continues to stare at me. "I'm just tired. Maybe I fell asleep listening." I wonder if he believes me.

I remain silent the rest of the class, hoping not to pass out again. Ian seems to get the hint and keeps to himself, writing notes from the television like everyone else. I jot down some details about Saber Corp. I realize this isn't what the teacher had in mind, yet I can't bring myself to stop, as if I know the information is vital and I shouldn't forget it.

Pictures of recent earthquakes fill my vision when I glance at the television. With quick strokes, I fill another sheet of paper with the information scrolling across the screen. The locations. The magnitude. The devastation. I'm certain this will be an event generations will remember. I can do my paper on this.

When the final bell rings, I can't help but release a thankful sigh. My daily prison sentence is over.

Ian hovers around my desk waiting for me to gather my backpack. "So you're really willing to give me a chance?" he says, once we are alone, outside the door.

"My brain says you're nuts, but my heart spoke first."

"Remind me to thank your heart next time I see it." His eyes twinkle as he speaks. He pulls me from the wave of kids heading toward the buses and into a small locker cove.

I lean against a cold metal locker, Ian's hand resting beside my head. His breathing is irregular, and he stares at the ground.

"Thank you for giving me a chance, Braidan." Ian fights back emotion, which puzzles me. He searches the faces of the nearby kids, then switches his focus back, and my heart skips a beat. "Can I kiss you again?"

My breath catches when his eyes dart to my mouth. Without waiting for my reply, his lips are on mine, searching for a passion he knows is there. He reaches behind my head and draws me in. I wrap my arms around his torso, welcoming the intensity he is pressing toward me. Lost in his embrace, I whimper when he pulls away, and his kiss moves to my forehead, to my cheek, and finally to my ear, where he whispers with ragged breath.

"Oh Bray, I've missed this."

The vise-grip around my heart yanks shut, and I can't breathe.

He kisses my forehead once more and backs up, handing me the beige stack of sticky notes I'd given him earlier.

"See you tomorrow," he says, then disappears in the sea of kids in the open hallway.

I look down at the top note in my hand, my breath still struggling for release.

Ian wants you to
remember him.

I hide the notes in my backpack before approaching my
locker to find Sam. Questions swarm my head about...
everything -- me, my life, my memory, my parents, Sam,
Lucas, and now Ian.

What did he mean when he said, "I missed this"? Did we
know each other before? And if so, why didn't Sam know
him? And who was she talking to about a background check?
And for that matter, why would anyone need to do a
background check on a teenager?

The hysteria gurgles in my chest, but I push it down,
afraid what will happen if I show my fear in front of Sam.

"How was history?" she says, watching me twist the
combination on my locker.

Fourteen, pass thirty-two, stop at thirty-two, then to
seven. The locker clicks open, and I freeze. How did I know
that?

"Bray? How'd you do that?" Sam's eyes are round as a full
moon.

I unzip my bag and open the cover of my history book, hoping the combo is inside. To my relief, it's there, along with the location and number. I tap the page and stuff the book into the locker, careful to avert my eyes. "I read it in class before the bell rang." I hope she believes me. "It's not that hard of a combo to remember." My heart races. Could I be remembering?

"Okay, well, don't freak me out like that," she says, then backtracks. "I mean, you've never done it without looking before. It was just weird."

Sam doesn't want me to remember.

My heart rate picks up as the shock hits me square in the chest. The knowledge that my parents may have something to do with it slams into my resolve, shaking me. I take a step forward and fall into Sam.

"Whoa, what's wrong?" Her voice shows genuine concern as she helps me upright.

"I… I must have tripped." I look for the invisible item on the ground that caused me to fall. "I'm fine. Let's go." I head for the parking lot before she can respond.

The ride home is quiet as I lean against the window, peering at the landscape that smears past my vision. Sam pulls to the curb but doesn't get out. My mom opens the front door and waves. Sam's duty for the day is complete. She's delivered me safely back home into… what? I'm not sure anymore.

My mom grills me on the day's events, and the way she

speaks, I know she has been told something happened. The tug-of-war on my heart between Ian and Lucas is still too fresh in my mind to offer any details without bursting into tears. None of it makes any sense. Notes plaster everything, telling me to stay away from Lucas, so I should. Right? But even as I think it, my heart screams this is not how it should be. This is not what I want. Yet, on every wall is some note telling me to keep away.

Then there is Ian. Maybe he will replace the crushed and broken heart beating erratically in my chest. Thinking about Ian's lips on mine feels like a betrayal, but I can't help it. His touch made me feel alive. Made me believe I can confide in him. Maybe my next sea of notes will be about him. About the fact that I want to trust him. I need to trust him. That he is the reason I'm getting better.

Hope flickers but is snuffed out before the idea can truly catch fire. Even though I try to ignore the intense feeling of deception, it's there, staring me down like an elephant in the room, ripping my heart into pieces.

I excuse myself from Sheila's presence and race to the solace of my room. The door lock slides into place with a click, and I toss my bag onto the bed, trying desperately to ignore every note in the room, wishing I could escape the reality that is my life. I head to the bathroom and sit, fully clothed, behind the closed door. Maybe if I go to bed early, if this does start over tomorrow, I won't feel like this. Maybe I'll forget I kissed a total stranger right in front of the boy that seems to hold my heart. It's likely. And that stings.

Tears trickle from my eyes, and I look up, hoping to calm

them before they become a torrent. The notes around the bathroom crawl under my skin, and I want to rip them all down, but I know I may need them tomorrow. I can't stop the emotions flooding through my body. My limbs shake, the sorrow mixing with rage that seeps into every muscle. I want to lash out. I want someone to pay for this feeling. I clench my fists and hit the floor once... twice... three times, until the throbbing in my knuckles becomes a balm, slowly soothing the pain in my heart.

My eyes are swollen by the time I emerge from the bathroom, and not even splashing water on them can hide the fact I've been crying. My knuckles are red from the repeated beating on the tile floor, but it's a good reminder that whatever this is, I'm ready for it to be over. And soon.

"Bray?" Sheila calls through the door. "Dinner's in twenty minutes."

Her footsteps echo down the hall as I plop down next to my backpack and pull it across the bed. The blankets bunch up at the bottom with the weight of the tug, and with one quick yank, I'm staring at a stack of notes in Ian's handwriting. I peel off the one I've already read and stick it to my nightstand. The next one makes my heart wiggle.

> Ian Bailey wants to
> kiss you again and
> you want to kiss
> him back.

I press my tongue against my teeth while I debate what to do. I can't very well stick the note to the bathroom mirror. What if someone finds it? The heat returns to my face at the thought of his lips on mine. Everything screams of how wrong these thoughts are, but I don't care. The very idea of having Ian in my life brings me comfort. I tap my chin, then stick the note in the shoes by the closet door. This morning I went for those, which means tomorrow I might do the same, and while it won't make sense when I wake, it will when I see Ian again.

Ian's digits
797-4485
He does want you
to call tonight.

Will my mom allow me to use the phone? Of course she will. I'm not two years old. I grab the handset off the desk and check the lock on the door, knowing I only have about fifteen minutes until they expect me to appear at the dinner table.

I dial the number and wait to hit *Send*. I have so many questions I want to ask him, but how do I start? Maybe with the obvious and flat out ask if we've met before. It couldn't hurt.

I push *Send*.

It rings only once before he picks up. "Hello?"

"Uh, hi Ian." The nervous tension is not easy to disguise. I run my fingers through my hair and stare at the notepad in front of me. "It's Braidan."

"Hey, hold on a sec... Okay?" Before I can respond, the line goes silent.

The corners of my nail beds pay the price for my nervosa as I wait for him to come back on the line.

"Braidan." His voice is low and breathless. "I'm so glad you called."

"Well... I read your first couple notes, and I got to the one that says to call you. So I did."

"Aren't you the obedient one?" He chuckles, and I hear the depth of his smile through the phone. "Did you read them all?"

"No, not yet. I figured I could read them while I'm on the phone, to give you a hard time." I lean against the headboard and draw my feet onto the bed.

"What did you think about that second one?" he asks, still barely above a whisper.

"I liked that one. I put it in my shoes so I would make sure to catch it tomorrow."

He sighs with happiness, shooting a tingle from my toes all the way up my spine. "Oh Braidan, you don't know how happy that would make me... but I need you to read the rest of the notes before you decide it's what you want to do." The smile in his voice drops, and worry creeps in.

The questions start firing in my mind again, and before I can close my mouth the first pops out. "Ian, tell me the truth. Have we met before?"

Silence.

"Ian?"

"Braidan..." I hear him struggle for words and imagine him running his fingers through his hair. "Yes."

My mouth goes dry as I register his reply.

"It's hard to explain over the phone, but I need you to do something for me. Then, I promise tomorrow I'll tell you everything I know."

My breaths come quick, and I can barely formulate the next word. "What?"

"Don't let them give you any meds tonight."

"What? How do you know they give me meds?" My words find the air quickly, insistent on answers.

"I don't know for sure, but it could be the reason you can't remember. They're repressing your memories."

"Why would they do that?" I whisper, my eyes darting around the room. I no longer feel safe.

"I could make some guesses, but--"

"Ian, who are you?"

"A boy who's hopelessly in love with a dream and wants to keep that dream alive."

A tear slips down my cheek. "I don't understand."

He lets out a long, cumbersome groan. "All I can tell you right now is the enemy is close, and they know where you are."

The word enemy echoes, skipping back and forth in my mind, laughing at me.

"Should I warn my parents? I mean they must know something."

"It's no good. We've been trying to warn them, and they aren't listening to reason. It's up to you now to come off the meds and remember. It will be much easier if you can."

I nod, tears streaming down my face.

"Braidan?"

"Yeah, I'm here."

"You can do this, Bray. Flip to the last one in the stack."

I flip to the last note and finger the little blue pill taped to the back.

"You need to take that tonight when your body goes through withdrawal. You're going to feel like you're dying, but that'll help you through it."

"I'm scared, Ian. I don't want to do this alone."

I hear him grimace. "Oh Braidan, I don't want you to go

through this alone either, but we have to get you out of this walking coma... tonight."

"Braidan?" Mom rattles the door. "Braidan? Dinner's ready."

"I've got to go." I throw the pad back into my backpack and run to the bathroom.

"If you need me any time tonight, call. Okay?"

"I'm so scared," I manage through trembling lips.

"It'll all be okay tomorrow. You'll be back to your old self in no time."

I push *End* on the receiver without saying good-bye. My brain is on information overload, and it's time for dinner. I rip open the bathroom drawers and find some cover up, blotting it to hide the bags under my blue eyes. They peer back at me from the mirror, and I stand taller, wondering if what he says is true.

Could someone be after me, and are my parents ignoring it? I'm just a kid. What could they want with me? Uneasiness settles in the bottom of my stomach, and I can't decipher if it's because I feel Ian is lying or that he is dead right.

I twist my doorknob and head toward the kitchen, determined to find out one way or another.

7

At the dinner table, Mom and Dad speak to each other about their day and what awaits them tomorrow. No one speaks to me, and the cold chill in their voices tells me they're happy about starting over again tomorrow.

Not if I can help it.

When we are done, Dad and the boys rise from the table without a word, then disappear into the living room. Mom instructs me to clear the remaining dishes. A minute later I'm heading back to my room.

I stand in the door, searching the walls for something I might have missed. Something that will help me decide what to do next. What if Ian's right and they'll be giving me meds within the next few hours? If that's true, I need to have a plan.

"Hey, Bray?" Tanner's timid voice calls down the hall, and I turn.

"What's up, Squirt?"

His little feet carry him to my open arms. "Will you play a

game with me?"

"Sure. What game do you want to play?" I ruffle his hair and stare into his big blues.

"Can we play cards?" His eyes sparkle with hope.

I squint, pretending to be intimidated. "Hmm, you going to go easy on me?"

He grins from ear to ear and races out of sight, aiming for what I can only assume are the cards. I head into my room to grab a hoodie, but before I can exit, he dives onto my bed and spreads the cards.

"We can play in here," he says, attempting to shuffle the large deck of multi-colored cards.

I pull the sweatshirt over my head, then sit on the bed and move my backpack, grabbing my math book for a playing board.

His pudgy fingers grasp the chaotic stack in his hands as he fumbles with the cards for another thirty seconds. His tongue sticks out from the side of his mouth as he concentrates on the number of cards he deals, stopping for a moment to calculate with his fingers.

"Do you remember if we need seven or ten?" he asks, peering sideways though his blond bangs in need of a trim.

"Seven." The number sounds right, but I'm not sure. "Ten is rummy or something, right?" I pick up the cards and mentally count them.

His eyes peek out, and he considers my response. "Yeah,

you're right. It's weird how you remember stuff like that but not..." He trails off, and his eyes flutter back to the cards.

"Tanner," I practically whisper, "what can't I remember?"

He continues staring down at his cards, fingering the deck into a smart stack on the book between us. "I dunno. Nothing important, I guess." He flings his hair back and tries to spread the cards to view them.

"Tanner, you mentioned something this morning."

"Well, I didn't mean anything by it," he quips. The way he twitches tells me he's lying.

I flip the top card over and cringe. The card telling me to draw four stares me down.

"You first." His twisted smile mocks me.

"Isn't there a rule that you have to draw another start card?" I playfully rip my cards from the stack.

Tanner giggles.

We play in silence, apart from the appropriate *Ha!* or *Dangit!*, until I catch him with one card before he can call out his sanctuary.

He draws two cards as his punishment and grunts. "You always beat me."

"Do we play this a lot?" I say, hoping he'll spill something unintended.

"Sometimes. But sometimes you're too *stressed*," he says,

throwing up air quotes.

"What could I have to be stressed about?" I draw a card from the stockpile.

"You know, just stuff. When you have flashbacks you can get pretty weird."

Nerves prickle up my neck. "What kind of flashbacks?"

"Ones from before. You know. Bad stuff." He keeps staring down at the pile as he draws a card. I remain silent, hoping to coax him forward. "You haven't had any recently." He looks up and shrugs. "I guess it really doesn't matter, because it was before they fixed it."

I draw a card, moving as slowly as possible, so the spell doesn't dissolve.

"Sometimes I'm glad you're fixed, but sometimes I miss the old Bray," he says, playing a *red seven*. "Mom says it's better like this. Dad isn't so sure."

The air in my lungs burns for release, but I don't dare. Instead, I play a *red two* and hope he continues.

"Are you glad you're fixed?" His eyes meet mine, and I'm unsure what my response should be.

I glance at the stack of cards, letting out my breath slowly. "I don't really know, Tan. I don't think I was given a choice."

He picks a card and stares at it. "Maybe not. But you're home more, and you play games with me." He places the card on the stack. A *draw four*. "Blue."

I draw my cards, my subconscious warning me to keep silent but my mind hungry for more. I place a card on the pile and squint.

"You didn't do anything with me before. No one did. Everyone was too busy with…" He stops.

"What?" My heart pounds inside my chest.

He slaps a card down and screams his single card sanctuary. "Ha!"

I look at the *blue five* and let out a slow, steady sigh of disappointment.

"Don't have any blues?" He wags his eyebrows.

I push my handful of blues together and tuck them under my leg. "Yup." I flip the top card and show him it's a yellow reverse.

He squeals with delight and lays down his last card.

"Best outta three?" I ask as he gathers the cards to shuffle.

He's giggling furiously. "Okay." He watches me stuff the liars hand into the middle of his pile.

"I thought you said you would go easy on me?" I punch his arm playfully.

He continues to fill the room with his laughter and deals again. He spreads his cards, and we're thrust into silence. His eyes dart up to mine, and he considers me. "Bray, do you like taking your medicine?"

I swallow, willing myself to be calm. "I dunno." I take my cards from the bed. "I don't think I'm given a choice. And I guess if it helps me, it can't be that bad."

"Dad thinks it's not good for you." He presses the stack together on the book and flips over the top card. "He also thinks it's been long enough that you'd be fine remembering."

"Remembering what, Tanner?" I'm frozen in time, watching his face. I see him pulling back into his shell when he realizes he's said too much. "Please, Tanner," I quietly beg, reaching across our playing area for his hand. "If I don't remember tomorrow, why does it matter what you tell me today?" My skin has gone ice cold and goose bumps erupt over every inch of my body.

His head twists toward my open door, then slowly back. "I'm not supposed to say anything. To anyone. Ever." His eyes pulsate with fear.

"But certainly it doesn't matter with me, right?" I'm hoping the reasoning works on an eight-year-old. "I mean, regardless what you tell me, I won't remember. So..." I falter, and his eyes find the door again. "Please, Tanner? Surely you've shared with me before?"

He shakes his head, terror still evident in his eyes when they find mine.

"It's okay, Squirt. You don't have to." I tap the cards on the book. "You're first."

His eyebrows almost touch in the middle when he frowns. The cards curl from his tight grip, and his eyes dart around the room. "You can't tell Mom. Or Dad. Or anyone."

The temperature in the room rises to smoldering as I wait for his admission. Beads of sweat press through my skin, each drop a painful prick to my senses. Tanner's breathing echoes in my ears, and his lips move in slow motion. The thunk of the cards under his finger strums like a bass on my eardrums.

"You died."

"Hey, Tanner, bath time!" Sheila's voice slices through the air and lands on my ears, silencing the war in my head.

Tanner jumps up, strewing the cards over the bed and floor. He runs from the room, knocking into her as he pushes through the opening. "Sorry, Mom," he says, but continues down the hall to the bathroom. He slams the door shut, and the water is on within seconds.

Sheila leans against the doorjamb. "Did you beat him that badly?" She crosses her arms over her body and grins.

My insides feel like they're in a blender as I gather the cards, willing the tremor in my hands to stop matching the pace of my heart. "Yeah, I guess so."

"What's wrong, Bray?" she asks when I rise from the bed.

"It's just been a long day." I turn away to set the cards on my desk.

"Do you have any homework?"

My mind flips over my classes and lands on Saber Corp.

"Yeah, I need to do a paper for history."

"You can use your laptop there to type it out," she says, pointing at the machine on my desk. I hadn't realized it was a laptop until this moment.

"Oh." I pivot toward her, steady in my resolution. "Do I have to do anything to get on the internet?"

"What type of assignment is it?" She's searching my face for an answer.

"We have to research a current event from the news that we think will be taught to our children's children or something." I twist the cord on my hoodie.

"Did he give you examples?"

"We watched the news, and the recent earthquakes struck me as something all generations might remember."

She nods, her eyes glazing over as she looks off into space. "It has been a pretty devastating set of events." Her focus comes back to me. "I think that's a good one. I'll have Dad unlock the firewall for the next hour. That should be long enough," she says and heads for the living room.

I suck in my breath, blackness swarming the room. I'm going to pass out again. I sit on the bed and throw my head between my legs, pretending to dig for something underneath. The ink smudging my vision recedes, pulling back the veil threatening to consume me.

My feet push against the floor, propelling me to the connected bathroom. I brace myself against the closed door, twisting the lock at the sound of my mom entering my bedroom.

"Dad said you're all clear. I'll be back in an hour to check on you."

"Okay, Mom. Thanks," I call through the panels, hoping she can't hear my voice waver. I press my face against the cold wood of the door, the cadence of her steps ricocheting off the walls of my heart.

I can't decide what's worse, knowing I'm being drugged or finding out I'd died. I heave into the toilet, unable to fathom the circumstances I'm forced to believe.

My hands fumble through the cabinet under the sink, searching. Cotton balls, alcohol pads, bandages, earplugs, saline, and other odds and ends in a basket. I reach over the stack of tissue, and my hand thumps into something hard. I pull it out and freeze when a box of used needles hits the light. My body trembles as I draw out the pharmaceutical box with *Not for Resale* labels covering most of the drug information. Prying up the edge of a sticker, I uncover the name of the drug inside.

Midazolam-amalgam.

I slip my fingers under the cardboard and pop open the top. My eyes land on the orange-labeled syringes filled with clear liquid.

Ian's words assault my mind, reminding me of the need to deny my medication tonight.

I grab the top five needles and press the plungers down

into the sink, watching the liquid swirl down the drain. The potential consequences hover around my mind's edge, but I don't have time to weigh them. I zero in on the saline solution under the counter, and an idea hits me like an arctic breeze. I squeeze the liquid into a disposable cup from the dispenser, using more force than necessary. Backwash from the spray shoots in every direction.

My jaw clenches as I thrust the first empty syringe into the cup, drawing the liquid into the barrel. I turn it upright with trembling hands and tap the syringe several times, dislodging the bubbles. I force the unwelcome air from the needle and check the fluid level inside. Perfect match. I also do this for the others, carefully wiping each for any residue and replacing the protective caps.

I drop to the floor, needles in my grasp, and lay them carefully on top of the others, figuring whoever comes in to give me my medicine will blindly reach for them. I position one sideways and leave the box lid slightly unhooked, so they won't be jostled. I only have one shot at this. I snort at the irony. Technically, I have five.

Positive the cupboard appears untouched, I close the door softly. Sweat pours from my brow, seeping into my eyes, a stinging, painful reminder that all of this, whatever it is… is real. I splash my face with cool water, blotting the droplets with a white towel. Smudges of dirt tarnish the towel's purity. I stare at the marks, wondering if this is how my life will be -- one minute unsoiled and pure, the next, stained and in need of cleansing.

My heart presses against my chest as I sit at the desk and

open the silver laptop. For the next hour I search every available resource I can find about Midazolam-amalgam. Each entry I read further solidifies my earlier actions by identifying the drug for its memory repressing qualities, but they say nothing about keeping someone alive, after or near death.

Ten minutes before I think my time will run out, I scan the recent earthquake news. My hands brush across a button, and a side bar pops onto the screen showing the history of my recent activity. My eyes focus on the word Midazolam-amalgam listed down the screen.

The room closes in on me, and panic flushes my veins. I click on the links, wondering how to remove the evidence. On a whim, I right-click, and a menu pops up over each set of words. I click the *delete from history* option over every one, sending any proof into oblivion.

Footsteps echo down the hall, but three more links remain. My fingers quiver on the mouse, clicking frantically until only the news network remains. I click the "x" in the corner of the small sidebar, and the page returns to full size just as the handle to my door twists.

"You about done?"

"Yeah, I guess," I say, without looking at her. "I didn't type it out yet, but at least I have more information." The pencil hovers over the pad of paper. I watch the lead tip vibrate in my death grip. "It should only take me a few minutes since it's still fresh in my mind." I avoid any eye contact, hoping she doesn't realize the page is blank.

"Okay, but it's getting late. You need to get ready for bed soon." She crosses the small expanse and rubs my arm. "You okay, honey?" She places the back of her hand on my forehead. "Are you feeling alright? You're not getting a fever are you?"

"I don't think so. I'm just tired." I look into her eyes, attempting to hide my deceit.

"When's the paper due?"

"Monday. So I guess I have all weekend to write it. I just..." My heart beats out of control as I speak. "I'm not sure how I'll remember to do it..." As my voice trails off, I glance at the computer.

She pushes a lock of hair behind my ear. "I can remind you. We can work on it this weekend."

"Thanks." I look up and meet her glance.

Her eyes light with her smile, and she pats my arm. "Why don't you wrap up? I'll be back in a bit." Without even waiting for my response, she leaves.

My eyes dart around the notes in my room, and I will myself not to rip each one to shreds. It is a lie. All a lie.

My life.

My family.

My lost memories.

My friends.

The words of Tanner slosh around in my head, drowning in a sea of questions. He said I'd died.

Died.

What does that mean? Did I really die? Was I in some kind of accident?

In front of the mirror, I yank off my hoodie, then shirt, inspecting the pale skin beneath.

No scars on my torso. None on my arms or neck. I turn to check the reflection of my back. A long, pink line zigzags across my skin, about five inches below the band of my white bra. My fingers find the thick ridge, but it's not tender, indicating an old injury. I check the rest of my body and find nothing. No sign of scrapes, even on my kneecaps. Nothing but a perfect complexion covers the remainder of my skin.

My eyes peer over my shoulder at the reflection again, shock now registering full force in every cell. Ian said my enemy was close. Maybe the very enemy who dealt me this scar. Maybe the same one who was behind my death. I'm doing the right thing by not accepting the meds. I won't go into this blind.... I won't be put back under and risk getting hurt again. Or worse.

I pull my shirt back over my body and collapse on the bed, wrapping the pillow around my head, tears slipping down onto the cotton. I feel like a child, crying into my pillow like this, but I can't help it. The whole situation is overwhelming, and I don't understand.

But Ian does. And he will tell me tomorrow.

My hands reach for the backpack and pluck out what I hope will be my redemption, written by Ian's pen. I tear the last note from the back, finger the blue pill, and stuff it into the underside of my pillowcase.

Ian's number finds a home in the pocket of my jeans. I flip over the stack and tear the next note from the top.

> The next 24 hours
> will reshape your
> life.
>
> Go with it.

It doesn't take me long to wad up this one and uncover the next.

> Really, call me at
> any point tonight.
>
> I will help you
> through this.

I touch the pen strokes and allow myself a sad smile. I will be alone tonight in my possible misery, but the hope of calling Ian during the storm twinkles in my heart.

Act "normal".
Don't panic. Repeat
today and you will
be with me in no time.

I crumble this one in my palm, revealing the next that simply reads:

Remember to
breathe.

This one goes on my wall next to a few other useless facts I'd stuck there who knows when. I doubt I'll really need a reminder to breathe, but something about the words calms my building frazzled nerves.

The next is blank, along with the following. I thumb through the remainder of the pad and am about to chuck it into the bottom of my backpack when a crinkled edge near the middle catches my eye. I pry the pad open and discover my last note tucked into the middle.

Hoping to find
something more?
See you tomorrow.
Good Luck!

Footsteps in the hall cause me to jump from the bed and click the laptop closed. I throw the notepad and paper I'd been pretending to take notes on into my backpack, sealing it with a zip as Sheila enters the room.

"All done?"

"Yeah." I cross the room to the small walk-in closet.

"Okay. I'll get your medicine ready."

Out of sight, I pause, hand on the pajamas I'd discarded on the small dresser. I make little noise while my ears strain to hear the sounds twelve feet away. The cupboard in the bathroom bumps, and I hear her sigh.

When I exit, she's sitting in the small papasan chair next to my bed. The now familiar needle sits next to the picture frame, along with an alcohol wipe, cotton ball, and bandage. I avert my eyes and walk into the bathroom to brush my teeth. Knowing my mom watches me, I linger over the sink, hoping nothing is out of place.

Her eyes meet mine when I exit, and I can see the emotion she's pressing back. I wonder if she isn't as sure about her decision as I am. It won't matter tomorrow. Life will change tomorrow.

"Lie on your side facing the wall." She tugs the back of my pants down just a bit. I hear a rip, then feel her wipe the cold alcohol across my exposed skin. "Are you ready?" she asks.

My lip quivers, and I'm terribly close to breaking down, so I just nod.

With a sharp pinch, she plunges the needle into my skin. The cold liquid enters my body, and I pray she's grabbed the imposter.

"You'll get tired pretty quickly, Braidan, so don't try to get up again tonight. You may fall." She presses the cotton ball to the puncture and places the bandage over it. She replaces my waistband and kisses my head. "Sleep well," she says, heading for the door, but she stops. Waiting. Watching. I'm almost sure she's probing for a missed step.

"I love you, Mom." My words come out in a forced dreamy voice.

Happy relief breaks through her silence. "Love you too, Bray. Very much."

She pulls the door shut behind her, and with a soft click, I'm alone to battle demons.

Shadows creep in from under the door, and in a blink the darkness surrounds me. My body desires sleep, but I can still rise, and my thoughts remain lucid.

The door creaks, piercing the silence, and footsteps echo through the small space, bouncing off the walls, mocking me. I tense when whoever it is stops next to my head. I lie perfectly still, forcing the choking breath evenly from my lungs.

A hand brushes hair from my temple, and I resist the urge to jump and grasp it. I hear my mom's now familiar sigh. She tugs the covers from my shoulder, then gently moves my waistband, removing the bandage from my skin. She runs her hand over my hair again, seals her love with a kiss, and slips from the room like a ghost.

My eyes grow heavy, and the world spins on its axis. I fight to stay awake, the panic of the situation causing my body to tremble, but my efforts are in vain as I feel exhaustion overtake my mind.

Pain sears my senses, bolting me upright in bed. Sweat covers my body, and the sheets stick like cellophane. My heart races, pounding against the walls of my chest with no regard for blood flow. The intense stabbing in my skull sends my neurons scrambling for cover. I'm going to puke.

I dart to the bathroom just in time. Cramps assault my muscles as I gag again. I feel the ground shudder, but it's only me quivering. It takes every ounce of energy I have to lift and pull myself across the bathroom floor and crawl back to the bed, toward the pill Ian claimed will be my savior.

My fingers fumble at the covers and pillow. Relief bursts over my lips when it's finally in my hand. I throw it down my throat but choke when I discover it's stuck in a dry cocoon. I grab at the plastic bottle on the nightstand and pour it across my lips. Water spills onto the floor, the nearby bed, and me, but the pill thankfully slides down. I hug the bottle to my chest, willing Ian's pill to do its magic.

Sweat still pours from my temples when the chills hit. I pull my sweatshirt out from under me, struggling with the coordination it takes to accomplish the task. I shove my arms into the sleeves and tug the warmth over my head, leaving the hood up to fight the intense shaking taking over my muscles. I grasp the bed and heave myself onto the mattress, then burrow into the covers.

My eyes droop into half slits until I see movement through the open bathroom door. A bright flash illuminates the scene, casting an eerie haze onto the glowering eyes before me.

My mind jumps.

Get up!

Run!

I'm immobilized with fear, unable to move my limbs even an inch. I try in vain to call for help, but my throat closes.

The figure moves closer.

Another flash bursts through the room, silhouetting a huge knife. In slow motion, the shadow lunges, but I can't see the face in the dim light. I brace for pain and squeeze my lids together.

Nothing.

Silence.

Cold.

I open my eyes and see the doorway, empty as it had been before. Tears spill down my face as I wrap the pillow around my head, my arms freely able to move again. Doubts batter my sanity, and the room shifts beneath me in waves.

What did I see? Was it real? Did I do the right thing? Did Ian know what he was talking about? Is my lack of meds or this pill going to kill me tonight?

My eyes close as a deep serenity passes over me like a mist. The haze becomes murky. Then inky. Then everything goes black.

The hollow buzz of the alarm clock pulls me from my turbulent slumber, and I smack the snooze button without uncovering my head. I'm lying motionless, wishing for five more minutes of sleep, when Ian's face dances through my memory.

I shoot up from the bed and glance around the room, the familiar setting of the night before unmistakably recalled in my mind. I jump from the covers and suppress everything that makes me want to dance and scream joyfully. I don't remember anything before yesterday, but yesterday I remember.

Touching my lips, I consider Ian's kiss and that he wants another today. I jump, kicking my feet in the air like a cheerleader.

The knock breaks my reverie. "Braidan?"

I leap up but pause with my hand on the knob, remembering I was reeling when I awoke yesterday, and hesitate behind the door.

Memories of the night hammer my senses, and I dart to

the bathroom to flush the evidence that anything unusual happened.

"Braidan, there's a pink note on the mirror. Can you read it?"

As I pass the mirror, I catch my reflection and rip the hoodie over my head and toss it out of sight. I go for the door, hesitating only long enough to make her believe my apprehension. When her sorrowful smile appears through the crack, I'm confident she suspects nothing.

The rest of the morning plays like déjà vu. Everyone takes their turns, moving about like chess pieces played in the same manner as the day before, only with different clothing. I manage to arrive at the breakfast table much earlier. Drew all but ignores me, and Tanner attempts conversation, asking me how I'm feeling.

Mom serves me oatmeal, and I'm able to enjoy the hot breakfast. I drench the oats in milk and sprinkle generously with brown sugar, knowing for certain this is the way I like it.

"You seem happy today," Drew spits across the table, as if it bothers him immensely.

I pause, spoon halfway to my lips. My eyebrows push together as I consider him, trying to keep my smile at bay. "I read my notes." I stick the bite in my mouth and gaze down at my bowl, pretending to be embarrassed.

Drew shoves himself away from the table, his chair scraping the linoleum. Mom tries to reprimand him, but he's out the side door before she's said two words.

I glance at Tanner, who grins as he brings his juice glass to his mouth. I wink, and his face goes stone-cold. His mouth falls open, and he stares at me with wild eyes. With Dad engrossed in his paper, I shake my head ever so slightly, pleading with him to remain quiet.

Tanner pushes his glass toward the table, knocking over the open milk container. The liquid sloshes across the surface before anyone can grab it and spills into Dad's suited lap.

"Tanner!" He jumps to his feet, milk streaming down his leg, and tries to wipe the mess, but the damage has been done. "Sheila, do I have another pair of clean, grey suit pants?"

"You might be in luck," she says, mopping the milk off the table and floor. She glares sideways at Tanner, who sits withdrawn in his chair. "Finish your breakfast and get going," she says admonishing him. "Braidan, if the doorbell rings, that's Sam."

I nod, willing Tanner to look at me.

Mom and Dad head down the hall to take care of the soiled suit, leaving the kitchen in awkward silence.

The oats in my bowl glob onto my spoon. "What's wrong, Tanner?"

His eyes dart to mine, and he shrugs, but I can tell he wants to speak, so I wait. He hesitates another thirty seconds, then leans forward. "Do you remember playing cards with me yesterday?"

I don't even have to answer. His expression changes from

99

shock to complete fear.

"Tanner, don't tell, okay?" I look at my bowl again. "Maybe I'm getting better." I raise my eyebrows, hoping he notices my happiness. "I'm going to tell Mom and Dad. I just want to make sure it's not a fluke." I'm only half-lying. "Ask me again tomorrow, and if I still remember, I promise I'll tell them."

He offers me an uncertain nod.

"Besides, didn't you say yesterday you wanted me to remember?"

He shrugs, pushing his spoon around in his bowl. "I guess. I just miss you."

"I miss you too, Squirt." This time I'm not lying. I do miss him. My heart longs to go back to my room and kick his butt in cards.

"Do you really think things can go back to the way they were before?" he whispers.

"I dunno, Tan. I don't even know how it was before or if it's okay for me to go back." I shrug, wishing I was with Ian receiving answers instead of here.

"It has to be okay, Bray. I think people need you." He stands and grabs his backpack.

"What did you just say?" My heart leaps into my throat.

"It's true." He pulls the straps over his shoulders.

I'm on my feet before I realize I've moved. "Tanner, what

does that mean?" I cross the small kitchen and grasp his arm, frantic for answers.

Tanner shakes free, his eyebrows dipping in the middle. "I've gotta go." He vanishes from the kitchen, leaving me stunned.

Sam's car smells like strawberries and vanilla when I enter, and I'm almost giddy that I remember this. I have to hide my grin with a cough when I see the note stuck to her dashboard about Lucas. I ask her the same sequence of questions, and she answers almost verbatim to the day before. When I'm done, she mentions Ian. I can't help but suck in a breath.

"You okay?" she asks, pushing her sunglasses over her head.

"Yeah, I'm fine. Just a lot to take in, I guess. Go ahead. Finish what you were saying." I turn toward the window, hiding the smile that wants to break out.

"So right, there's this new guy, Ian. I think it's a good idea to avoid him, too. You can make yourself a note if you want."

"I'll do that when I get to school," I lie.

"He... uh." She hesitates, choosing her words wisely. "He's just bad news."

I grab my cheek, preventing myself from turning to glare. The realization that this might be the same reason I've been warned to stay away from Lucas hits me in the chest, piercing my heart. I can't deny the feelings he radiated yesterday, and I certainly can't forget the anger and hurt in his face when he saw me kissing Ian.

Pulling into the school parking lot, I can't hold the sigh.

"Your schedule and a map are at the front of your books, so if you get lost, it's all there."

My eyes search the campus as I push my way out of the Bug and head to class. I want to find Ian and figure out a time to talk without Sam breathing down my neck.

She deposits me in class and wishes me luck, pointing out Lucas, who scowls at her. My heart beats in an irregular rhythm when I sit in the seat beside him.

"You're choosing to sit here even after the warnings?"

Oh crap. "Uh, I can move." I glance around the room and realize I could have chosen at least twelve other seats.

"No, no," he says, reaching out for me.

Panic screams through my mind as his hand touches my arm, but I only feel skin on skin.

"No, it's fine. I was just being an idiot. Please stay."

I stare down at his fingers as he releases me, noticing the ring he wore yesterday is no longer on his hand. "What happened to your ring?" I ask, before I can think better of it.

"What? You remember my ring?"

Aw, shoot. I bite my lip and turn away. "I guess."

"What else do you remember, Bray?" He sounds hopeful, so I look at him.

"Nothing, Lucas. I don't remember anything." It's easy for me to meet his eyes when I say this. I don't remember anything before yesterday.

He shifts uneasily in his seat. "Are you sure?"

Twisting my head forward, I let my eyes roam over the words on the board for a distraction. "Why would it matter anyway? My notes say you're bad news."

"That's B.S., and you know it." He leans back in his chair, thumping his pencil on the book in front of him. "You've always known it. I don't care how…"

My head snaps around, knowing he is about to reveal something. "What, Lucas?"

"Nothing," he says, and turns away. "Nothing at all."

All through class, Lucas shows his irritation by overreacting to everything. When I glance at him, his eyes darken, but he attempts to smile.

The bell rings, and Lucas is up from his seat before I can close my bag. "Stay away from Ian today," he says, leaning in practically nose-to-nose with me.

"What?" I spit out, outrage growing in my chest.

"Stay away from Ian. He's the one who's bad news."

"How would you know?" I retort, standing and shoving my book into the bag.

"Just trust me, Braidan," he says, standing erect again. "Wait, do you even remember Ian?"

I glare and push past.

"No, no. Wait, Braidan." He grabs my arm and flips me around. "Do you?"

"Screw you, Lucas. Leave me alone." I rip my arm from his grasp and make for the door. I don't know why I'm so agitated, but if I don't leave Lucas' presence, I'll spill something I don't intend to.

"Braidan, stop," he says, catching me in the open hall. "What's going on?" His anger has turned to confusion as he searches for answers.

"What do you mean?" I cross my arms over my body, hoping to hide the tremors.

"I mean this." He motions at me. "What's going on?"

"Nothing." I push past him again, but he grabs my arm and forces me to face him. "Would you get your hands off me?" I scream, rage surging through my veins. "I don't know what we used to be, but we aren't any more, Lucas." I press my index finger on his chest, unable to contain myself. I thrust him against the wall using minimal force. "Unless you want to see what I'm capable of, I suggest you back off." The words spill from my lips, and I'm unsure what they even mean. What am I capable of? And why am I so angry? I shove Lucas one more time, my eyes hard on his perplexed face. "Leave. Me. Alone."

Before he can respond, I'm out of sight, rounding the corner and rushing into the bathroom. My whole body is on fire.

I wait for the bell before emerging from the bathroom. I scan the halls for any sign of Sam. No doubt, Lucas did his duty and reported my outburst to my babysitter. I curse under my breath. With a quick check of my schedule and map, I sprint to my next class. When I enter, the teacher doesn't say a word, probably considering it normal for me to get lost around campus. That's mostly true. I feel like I'm losing my mind.

The hands on the clock cannot move fast enough as I stew in silence.

Why am I so angry? Am I right to direct it at Lucas? Or is he just the first person I can safely release it on?

My mind jumbles through the thoughts fighting for placement in my head. Anger boils under my skin, and nothing I do calms it. Then it hits me. Ian's behind all this. If he'd never come into my life, I'd be going about my day, none the wiser to these surging emotions.

The bell rings, and I'm up from my seat before anyone can move. I thrust my way from the room, determined to give Ian a piece of my mind and find out what he knows. I hope it's nothing. I hope he's just an ignorant boy who has a crush, but a small voice inside says I couldn't be more wrong.

"Hello, beautiful," the sultry accent echoes around me. My steps falter.

I twist to find Ian sitting on the stone wall only a few feet away. The fire in his eyes says he knows his plan has worked, and I know who he is. My nerves suddenly fail, so I pretend not to recognize him. Tears spring to the surface as I hurry through the halls, hoping to get away before he can see them.

"Hey. Hey, Braidan?" he calls, and my determination melts like a candle under a fiery white flame.

I stop and allow him to catch up.

"Braidan, may I talk with you?" The waver in his voice suggests he's just as uncertain about this as I am.

Setting my jaw, I wipe my cheek and face him. My lip quivers when my eyes meet his, and emotions rip through me like floodwaters through a dam fracture. They lap the sides of my head and body, pushing me toward insanity. I'm drowning in misery, suddenly sorry I listened to this stranger.

I don't want this.

I rear around, ready to run, but a hand on my arm stops me and pulls me face to face with Ian, pain evident in his grimace.

"I'm sorry," he says, like I'm supposed to believe he means it. "It has to be this way. You have to come out of it."

He grasps the sides of my face, and I squeeze my eyes shut and shake my head.

"No. No. Please let me go." The words come out in sobs, but he doesn't release me.

"Braidan, look at me. Look. At. Me."

I pry open my eyes and peer through a blurry haze. He seems sincere, but my heart screams in alarm. What have I done?

"What are you doing?" Lucas' voice ruptures the air. Before I can move, he's thrown himself between Ian and me, one hand on my shoulder, and the other on Ian's chest.

"Back off, man," Lucas threatens, curling his arm protectively around me.

With my head down, the tears come even harder.

Ian doesn't say a word as Lucas escorts me from the scene, kids parting like the Red Sea to allow us through. Lucas pushes his way into the girls' bathroom, and freshmen scatter from our presence.

My breaths come in ragged pants, and blackness fills my vision.

Lucas leans me over the sink and splashes water on my face. He runs his hand over my neck, sprinkling droplets, cooling the fire coursing through my body.

"Take some deep breaths, Bray. Deep breaths." He breathes in deep, coaxing me to do the same.

The blackness ebbs, and I stand, tears still falling down my cheeks. Lucas' body language says he's unsure what to do, which makes me furious. I lunge, pushing him back against the wall. I want to scream. I want to lose control. I want to make him pay for this pain I feel.

His hands rise in surrender, and fear floods his face.

A visceral shriek looses from my throat followed by tears that fall afresh. I turn from him, ashamed of my behavior, sobs overtaking my body. He grips my shoulders, and I melt into his arms, my body shaking with moans. I bury my head in his shirt and inhale his scent, attempting to control myself. My consciousness blinks, and I'm outside my body.

I see myself in his arms, standing in the middle of a street, rain pouring down in sheets upon us. I step away from his embrace and see his grief. I turn, unwilling to watch the pain seep from every fiber of his being. I've never seen him defeated like this. It hurts.

"I can't do it, Braidan. I'm not strong enough."

The words I want to say are, "I'm not strong enough either." But I can't. I have to be steady in my resolve. "It's not your choice, Luke." I push the soaking blonde chunk of hair from my face. My voice cracks with uncertainty. "I've got to disappear, and you can't come."

"Why not?" he pleads, grabbing for my hand.

My heart breaks into millions of shards. I can't put him in any more danger than he's already in just by being with me. I can't. I won't. I shake my hand free and take another step away. "You... just can't. It has to end here." I take a few more steps away and freeze. Do I have the strength to do this? "It's not like two sixteen-year-olds really know what they want in life anyway." I bite back the sob threatening to escape. "You'll be okay." But I don't know if *I* will.

"Braidan," I hear him whisper through the pounding rain. "Please."

Something fractures, and I twist, my arms finding his and our lips meeting with what I know is our final good-bye. Tears flood my vision as I pull away, shredding our hearts into pieces. "Goodbye, Lucas." I don't wait for a response before I sprint away from the scene and vanish into the shadows.

Another blink and I'm back in the bathroom, sobs calmed, clutching the boy I once loved. My body is limp, and I realize Lucas is holding me up. He silently brushes my hair with his hand, content to hold me. Does he know what I've seen?

"Why am I like this? What happened to me?" I manage in a strangled whisper.

Lucas says nothing but tightens his grip around my shoulders. He knows something.

I struggle from his grasp, pushing him to arm's length. I recognize the confusion in his face but continue on, rooting myself to the floor. "Why am I like this, Lucas?"

His eyes flutter to his feet and back to my face. "I can't tell you, Bray."

"Why not?" I squeak out. "Why can't I know? What if Ian is right? What if they've found me?"

Lucas glares and moves toward me, causing me to step back. "What the hell did Ian say?" Fear is now clearly visible in his face.

I blink away the angry tears. "You know, a total stranger is willing to tell me what I need to know. In fact, Ian's helping me get out of this walking coma everyone thinks is right for me." I grab my bag from the floor, now furious with him for keeping me in the dark. "You've lied to me, Lucas."

My words pierce him, and he leans on the counter, hiding his face from view. "Only because they told me to," his voice struggles to remain calm.

"Who, Lucas? Who?!" I scream, willing him to tell me the truth.

When he looks up, his eyes are wet, and his lip quivers. "I can't, Bray." He takes another step toward me, and I hold out my hand, stopping him in his tracks.

"Then we are done... forever." Before I can think twice, I'm out the door, storming down the hall. Anger, hurt, resentment, fear, and uncertainty rumble through my body at every step. I don't know where I'm going, but I'm not staying at school.

I retrace my morning and stomp through the aisles of cars in the parking lot. A car revs to life, and I spin around to see Ian in the seat of a Mustang convertible.

"Going somewhere?"

I stare, wondering how he knew I'd take to the streets.

"It's okay to be mad at me, but you have to hear the truth," he says, glancing back toward the school. "And by the looks of it, you've got about two minutes before you'll be dragged back onto campus." He flicks his head back the way I'd come.

People dart from every angle, running toward me and the idling vehicle.

Ian pulls his car from the parking spot, moving the passenger door within my grasp. "Your choice, Bray. You can wait for them to catch you and drug you back up... or you can find out the truth and have a fighting chance. The ball is in your court now."

My head screams contradictions as I glance between the safety of Ian's car and the uncertainty galloping toward me.

I'm buckling my seatbelt before I can listen to another reason why I shouldn't. Ian peels from the parking lot in seconds, and the panic subsides in my chest. Maybe this was the right decision.

Ian chuckles when he catches me checking behind us yet again to make sure no one is following.

"I feel like I'm in a police drama or something." I twist my eyes to the road.

"You might be before the day is out." His eyebrows lift as the words leave his mouth.

I stare. What is that supposed to mean?

Trees flank the sides of the road as we wind down and under the highway, following signs toward a lake. We stop at the guard shack for a day pass and head to the mesa where the land opens up, overlooking the crystal blue water. The park is mostly abandoned, with only two or three cars parked on the other side of the roundabout.

"What are we doing here?" I ask as he opens his door.

"We need to talk without being overhead," he says, flipping his keys in one hand and motioning for me to follow with his other.

The weathered, wooden bench creaks under me as I settle next to him. We watch a boat meander through the canal and motor out into the glassy lake, but neither of us utters a word.

I look between him and the surrounding scene, wondering if I'm ready to hear what he has to say. Tanner says I died, Ian says someone is after me, Lucas is hiding something, and I have a parole officer for a best friend.

The breeze shifts, and strands of red hair tumble across my face. I tug the mass into my collar and pull my feet up on the bench, twisting toward Ian and grasping my legs.

Ian watches as my need for information bubbles. The desperate urge to know everything starts as a small rolling in my belly and increases like someone stirring the water as it rises. Ready or not, I need to get this over with. I need to know who I am. I need to know how I died. I need to know the danger. I rest my chin on my knees and inhale.

"Have a rough night?" he says, maintaining eye contact.

I nod once and bite the inside of my lips.

"You're still upright, which means the pill worked, but, you're going to need another soon. The withdrawal lasts for a few days, but it's not so bad if you counteract it."

"Why are they drugging me, Ian?"

His eyes flicker to sorrow as he averts my gaze and twists the gold ring on his finger. "He thought it would help keep you safe."

"He? Safe from what?"

Ian rubs the back of his neck, still unwilling to make eye contact. "There are people who shouldn't have found out where you were." He gives me a fleeting glance before continuing. "We aren't sure how, but news leaked, and when the rumors escalated that they knew where you were, your parents weren't willing to believe it." He presses his fingertips together until they turn white. The veins in his neck compress to a tight line, and his lips purse.

"Who are they, Ian? Why does it matter if they find me?" My heart slams against my chest. "Do they have something to do with my death?"

Ian's eyes fix upon mine. "What? Who told you that?"

"Tanner spilled last night. I kind of tricked him into telling."

Ian crinkles his forehead but grins. "You're good at that."

"And you'd know because we've met before." I say it as a statement not a question.

The breath he holds ripples over his lips, and his smile fades, "Yes. Yes, we've met before. Right after..." His eyes search mine, and he looks back into the water. "We got pretty close, and it killed me that they took you away, but it was for your safety. I couldn't protest. All I could do was watch as your life crumbled around you and everyone you loved."

"What happened?" My voice is barely audible over the hum of the wind.

Blink.

Instead of sitting on the bench, I'm in a grey polyester airplane seat. The loud vibrato in the air masks every noise, save the beating of my heart echoing in my ears. My pulse races, and sweat seeps through my cotton shirt. The bindings on my arms and legs dig into my skin as I twist and thrash against them.

Panic stirs my insides when the forward cabin door opens and a tall man lumbers toward me. His dark brown hair hangs in locks over the pale skin of a ghost. When he reaches for me, I writhe from his touch.

The man flicks open a silver blade and wags his eyebrows. He runs the knife across my arm and I shriek, red blood oozing down my skin. He laughs as he collects the sample.

I spit in his face, and he backhands me. I taste copper on my tongue as fury surges through me.

He drops the blood into a machine in the corner and waits for it to print the information he requires. He reads the small slip of paper, then yells something in a language I can't understand.

A woman appears in my periphery. She's carrying a large syringe and has a wicked gleam in her eyes. She's wearing a white smock with a familiar logo on it. Saber Corp.

They discuss the results my blood has given them, eyeing me as they talk.

Panic reverberates in my chest when the woman nods. Without another word, they both descend. The man holds my head and the woman plunges the needle into my artery. The liquid breeds fire in its wake.

My body shakes violently, having nothing to do with turbulence. There's lava in my veins, and it wants out. The warmth tracks down my arms into every cell of my body. My eyes roll back in my head as I succumb to the pain coursing through me.

Though the man's accent is thick, I now understand him. "Any moment now we'll know if it has worked," he says to the woman. "This will either be the best thing we've ever done or our worst mistake." He wipes something over the wound on my arm, and his voice drifts away from me. "I'll check the progress."

I let my head loll to the side with the toss of the plane as I take in the conversation.

"She only has another minute or so to live if we're wrong," the woman comments in a thick Swedish accent.

"But, if we're right..."

"Mmm, we'll see."

White-hot rage presses on my mind, and the shaking of my limbs ceases. Every cell in my body awakens and shifts, yet I don't dare twitch. I feel my DNA rearranging and morphing into new strands, knowing it has everything to do with the concoction they've thrust into my neck.

The man's breathing pulsates in my ears. The woman's picking at her fingernails. Someone's stomach churns. The click of teeth. Everything is amplified, but I search for one sound.

Clink.

Without looking up, I can see the scene playing out in the small fuselage, as if it were an animated dot matrix printout consisting of thousands of shifting dots.

Clink.

It's to my left, resting in the case attached to the man's belt.

Clink.

It whispers to me as it gently taps the leather of the case when he moves.

Clink.

Without wasting another moment, I pull the knife's molecules toward me. In one motion, I catch it in my upturned hand and slice my bonds. The man doesn't even blink before I'm thrusting the knife into his stomach. I swivel on my heels and slam my foot into the woman, propelling her to the back of the plane. She crashes against the metal and crumples motionless to the floor.

I twist toward the cabin door near the cockpit and see a man reaching for his gun. I focus on the particles in the gun, but the silver bullet rockets from the chamber. The projectile races toward me in slow motion, and I raise my hand and coax the life from the bullet. Like drops of water, the metal explodes before it can reach its intended target. Me.

The man jumps from the plane controls and slams the door shut. I hear multiple locks close and the seat squeak under the weight of his girth. The plane shudders, and the altitude changes, throwing me to the roof like a ragdoll. My body crashes to the floor of the plane, but oddly, I feel nothing.

A growl tumbles from my lips, and I push myself up, racing for the rear door. Just before I reach it, my mind clicks, much like a computer pulling up analytics. At first, I'm confused, but as it ticks off possible escape plans, I watch in silent awe, taking in everything passing my cornea. An alarm sounds in the cabin as it loses pressure, and masks fall from the ceiling all over the small cabin.

The idea rocks around my head, but I refuse to debate another second. My mind coils and pries the pins from the locked door, forcing it open. I brace myself against the wind and prepare to jump from the plane.

The reflection in the nearby steel panel causes me to hesitate. A thick blonde streak has appeared in my hair, as if the color has been stripped. I inspect the rest of my head and see only red. My mind lands on only one probability.

A symptom of another change.

I curse at the evidence, slam my fist into the metal, bending it like plastic, then leap from the plane.

My mind takes over my body, knowing exactly what needs to happen. My hands pull at the air, calling metal fragments I can mold into anything to help me survive the jump. The silver rubble shoots through the sky and joins together, first wrapping my feet, then my calves. I push toward the ground at an alarming speed, but I'm not frightened.

The tall field of yellow grass below me grows larger as I posture myself to land. A boom resonates through the pasture, scattering the hidden birds. My feet plant firmly on the ground, my knees bent, eyes searching.

12

My chest collapses as the landscape blinks again. Ian sits in front of me, his arms on mine, face so close I can smell the spice of his breath.

"Braidan? Braidan?" He shakes me.

"I'm... okay," I choke out, trying to pry his hands off. Sweat pours from my forehead, and my body trembles.

"No, you're not." He thrusts his hand into his pocket and produces another magic pill. "Can you dry-swallow this?"

I'm so cold I just stare, unable to convince my mouth to move over the chatter of my teeth. I part my lips, and he shoves the pill as far back as he can. I gag, but it goes down.

He removes his coat and wraps it around my shoulders, rubbing my arms furiously, like it's negative twenty outside, not seventy-five. He jumps from the bench and scoops me up, rushing to the car. He sets me in the backseat and starts the car with the heat on high. He climbs into the back and wraps his arms around my shuddering body.

My mind replays my flashback on a continuous loop.

No. I shake my head. No, this can't be a flashback. This can't be real. These are delusions of withdrawal. But my mind skips back again to assure me this is reality.

"What am I?" I manage, through half-parted lips.

"Don't worry about it right now. Just relax and focus on your breathing," he says, pulling me toward him.

My head lies on his chest, and he strokes my arms.

Blink.

I see myself as an awkward red-headed fifteen year old, standing in a line of others about my age. The adults around us wear white Saber Corp smocks and talk as if we are going to an amusement park. The lady at the head of the line holds a clipboard and asks each kid questions, marking their answers on the paper in her grasp. She struggles to keep her smile as tears well at the corners of her eyes.

This will be no amusement park.

. I debate whether to scream for help, but we've been warned against acting out. Ever since we started this program at age eight we were told not to question what was best for us. Saber Corp had our best interests at heart. Somehow, I know this is all a lie.

My parents stand behind the cement barrier. They wave excitedly at my departure, as if boarding this blue Saber Corp bus is some kind of incentive.

I swallow the bile rising in my throat and count the kids in the bus and the ones still in line. Ten. Only ten of us are

120

left. They told us a few had left, but with the whispered accusations of foul play, I didn't believe anyone could opt out of this program and remain alive.

My consciousness wavers.

Blink.

I'm standing in an observation room with one door and ten two-way windows. All ten of us stand gawking over the television that has been rolled in on our behalf.

Flames engulf the familiar bus sitting at the bottom of a steep embankment. No one understands what has happened until the ticker at the bottom of the screen pronounces all ten teens and chaperones... dead.

It hits everyone at once. The world believes we are dead. Our friends. Our teachers. Our siblings. Our parents.

The single door slides open, and a tall, pale-skinned man comes through. His expression tells me he's pleased with our reactions, but when he laughs I want to hurt him.

Blink.

I'm back in Ian's arms, my body no longer plagued with convulsions. I'm resting in the safety of his grasp. My emotions feel as out of control as my body, and my tears are unstoppable.

Ian brushes his hands over my hair but remains silent. I'm lost in his comfort, unwilling to move, but I must. I need answers.

"I need to know." The words come out in a whisper, but

I'm certain he's heard me when his body tenses. "Is it all true?" My voice comes out in panicked pleas. "What I'm seeing. Is it true?"

A long, sorrowful sigh escapes his lips, but he nods. "They're all repressed memories coming back. It happens when you're coming off the amalgam."

I shudder and gulp hard, trying to press the saliva past the lump in my throat. "So... my parents thought I died?"

"Yeah, probably." The irritation in his voice bounces around me.

The car has gone from comfortable to sweltering in seconds. "I'm going to puke." I push from the backseat just in time to lose it on the ground. I'm steadying myself against the side of the car when Ian joins me, hand resting on my back for support.

"Let's sit." He nudges me toward the bench again.

The cool wind teases every drop of sweat still clinging to my neck and forehead. A chill scurries up my spine and settles on the same spot Ian's hand still rests.

I shove aside the welling emotions and brush him away. "What am I, Ian?"

He rubs his face and laces his fingers in front of him. "You're... You're a hybrid."

"A what?

"A hybrid. Like the real thing, only better." A grin crawls across his lips, as he's seemingly proud of this admission.

"How?" I squeak out. The woman with the syringe blinks in my mind. "The people on the plane. They made me this way?"

He bobs his head from right to left. "Well, sort of. You were already a hybrid since your first injections, before they tried to alter your DNA again. They were hoping they could enhance what was already there with a new serum."

My mouth goes dry.

"It's still up for debate if they got what they desired. I think it's safe to say they weren't ready for how your body reacted."

Feeling the bile rise again, I suck in a breath. Pictures of the man lying on the floor with a knife in his gut flash through my mind. "I think I killed them." I retch again, and Ian pats my back.

"They deserve whatever they got," he says, trying to justify my cold-blooded murder. "But, I have it on good authority that they lived, so don't let that one bother your conscience."

I twist my head and squint, trying to figure him out. "That one?" I pull in another labored breath.

He shook his head. "Unfortunately, it'll all come back. But you can't allow yourself to feel any guilt. It wasn't your fault. You couldn't always control..."

"You mean..." I feel my head lift as if filled with helium, and I shake it away. I swallow and try again. "I've done other things like this?"

He shrugs but nods. "I met you a year ago, and you were pretty private about that stuff. I only know a little."

"And how did we meet?"

His eyebrows wag as his smile widens. "We were in training together."

He watches my face, but I have no idea what type of training he might be referring to.

"I'm a hybrid too, Braidan."

Once the words register, I know they're true. I'm not sure how I know, but I know. "Does that mean you can...?" I lift my hands and copy what I saw in my vision, somewhat resembling kung fu. But instead of fighting off bad guys, my hands mimic pulling fragments of metal for my needs.

Ian frowns and averts his eyes, releasing a soft ironic laugh. "That requires extra genetic mutations. Mutations I don't have. Mutations that happened on the plane." He lifts his eyes to mine, and I can tell he's wrestling with his words. He tilts his head as though he's thought better of what he was going to say. "No one else has them, that we know of. As far as they know, your genes are an anomaly."

"How do they know that?"

He clears his throat and sits straight up. "They tried it in other hosts, and it... it didn't have the same effect. They think maybe it mutates inside the hybrid with specific DNA strands. Yours."

I grab Ian's sleeve and pull him around to face me. "Saber

Corp is doing this?"

He looks down at the hand grasping his sleeve. "Yeah. Adrian Saber is the one responsible. He claims it's just a vaccine side effect, but when he created you, it blew that theory out of the water."

"My flashback. I saw my parents wishing me well when they took me. How can they be okay with this?"

"Let's get one thing straight. None of the parents knew what was going on. In the beginning, they were just told the hybrid serum was created as a vaccine. The test audience was from a small community north of San Francisco. At first, the kids had no reaction to the injections, or none they could track. But as the days wore on, the vaccine mutated or maybe it just needed time to enhance the chemicals in their brains. Either way, when several of the children exhibited new talents and abilities, they realized these side effects were worth researching. One day of music or martial arts training, and the host had it mastered." He leans in. "Then, when they injected the second serum into the right person, the mutation went beyond learning skills to telekinetic enhancements."

"Plural?" I gulp, wondering what else my freak show of a body can do.

He chuckles as he watches me. "It's not as bad as you think. It's kinda cool," he says and nudges my elbow. "Sure you had to learn how to control all these new emotions and abilities that were cropping up, because when you go from just another hybrid to a mutant-hybrid of heroic magnitudes, things get a little tricky."

The blood drains from my face, and the cold creeps over my body, sending shivers racing through my limbs. "So none of the other nine hybrids were given the second serum?" My eyes flicker to his.

His face hardens as he considers me. "Nope, none of the other ten received the second serum. Mostly because they knew from the trial runs it wouldn't do anything."

I search his face for understanding while he rubs his hand over his jaw line. "I only saw ten of us in my flashback."

"I was the first hybrid Saber created. My dad, Michael Bailey, worked for Saber, and allowed them test me for the genetic alternations. When things started to go awry..." He twists toward me and presses his lips together.

"He faked your death, didn't he?"

He nods. "It was the only way out of the program."

"But what about the others? What about me? He just left us there to be tested like lab rats?" I hold back the tear that wants to escape.

His hands run through his hair. "Braidan, you're free because my father helped you escape. He lined up a special security company to watch over every one of you and made sure Saber Corp couldn't get within a hundred miles."

The fire in my chest simmers, and I gulp back the saliva that has collected in my mouth. "But they found me?"

He grunts. "Yeah. They found you, and that's when they injected the new serum, turning you into what you are now."

When he glances sideways, his cheek twitches into a partial smile. "You gave them a run for their money, that's for sure. It didn't take you long to bust out of their facility, and luckily, you found your way back to your parents before Saber could."

I shake my head, unable to believe the story I was being told. But I had proof of it all running through my memories and my veins. "So when did I train with you then?" My head swells with all the information being shoved at me.

"When you escaped Saber, your parents thought it was a good idea that you learn what your body could do to protect you, and..." He considers me an extra moment before continuing. "You were also having some side effects they didn't know how to control."

I gulp back my breath. "Like what?"

"Untamed rage. Night and day dreams so violent you'd wake screaming in cold sweats or lunging at whomever snapped you out of it."

"That's why they were drugging me. Wasn't it?" The sound comes out in barely a squeak.

He nods. "They were only looking out for you. You can't blame them for that. My dad was working on a long-term fix for you, but we ran out of time. Somehow they discovered you might be in his care. You had to leave, and I had to go underground again," he says, flicking a piece of fuzz from his jeans.

"Did you love me?" I'm staring at the side of his face

when I say it, but he doesn't look up.

He pulls in a deep, shaky breath and looks at his fingers, pressed together in a triangle. "Yeah. Yeah, I did." He twists toward me. His eyes glisten as he prepares the next words. "And you loved--"

The chirp of a cell phone interrupts him, and he grabs for his front pocket. "Yeah?" His eyes dart to the park entrance. "What? Are you sure?" He curses and waves at me as he rushes to the car. "Thanks."

"Who was that? What's going on?" My hands fumble with the door handle to his Mustang before he can end his call.

"That was my father," he says as we get into the car. "They've broken into your house."

My heart drops into the depths of my stomach, and I feel I'm going to puke again. My hands tremble as I latch the seatbelt. "Let's go. We can't let them..."

Ian grabs my arm, making me look up. "Braidan, we can't."

"What!?" I screech. "We have to. Ian, my parents. My brothers."

He peels out of the parking lot. "Sam will take care of them." Eyes intent, he speeds down the windy road to the highway.

My body flies forward when he slams on the brakes. In the road in front of us is a blue SUV with a Saber Corp logo plastered on the door.

Ian throws the Mustang into reverse and flips around, his tires squealing against the pavement. The scent of burnt rubber hangs in the air as the car speeds through the visitor's gate in the oncoming lane. He flies down the two-lane road, his hands gripping the steering wheel so tightly his knuckles turn white.

Two blue Saber Corp SUVs tail us, matching our speed but maintaining their distance.

"What do they want?"

Ian scoffs. "You."

He's telling the truth, but I wish he weren't. My stomach churns in uneasy motions having nothing to do with the car's movement. I jump when the cell phone rings in the console between us.

He glances at the caller ID and picks up the phone. "They found us," he growls. "What do you think I did? I'm certainly not going to hand her over." His eyes dart to me, then back to the road. "Yeah, I'm working on it." He jams the *off* button, then tosses the phone into the backseat.

"Who was that?" I clutch the door handle, watching the speedometer click higher and higher.

"My dad. Look, I'm going to need you to manipulate some things here in a bit. There's no way we're going to make it out of this park unscathed unless you can slow them down." His eyes swing to mine as the engine continues maxing out.

"What? How do I do that?"

He glances in the rearview mirror and smacks the steering wheel. "I don't know, Braidan. You didn't exactly share that with anyone. It can't be that hard. Just concentrate on whatever and feel it."

My heart leaps into my throat, and sweat bursts over my brow. I've no idea what he wants me to do.

He glares sideways. "See if you can down some trees or something." I know he's not directing his anger at me but at the situation.

I can't help but grimace. How am I supposed to do this? I press my fingers to my temples, massaging them like I think maybe I should. My eyes find a tree and concentrate, but nothing happens.

The blue vehicles rev closer, like they realize I'm trying to stop them somehow. Visions of the day I was injected pop into my head and the landscape around me transforms into pixels. Everything in my vision seems color-coded, but I don't know the cipher. I dig through my foggy flashback. How did I command those metals to do my bidding?

"Anytime, Braidan, we're running out of road."

I glower at the side of Ian's face and twist toward the back window again. The gears of the Mustang grind together and pops of color bounce around my vision, seemingly attached to the sound waves ricocheting through the air.

The sound waves tug at my mind, and I realize what I need to do. I stare at another tree, focusing on the dots making up each of its fibers. I imagine them ripping, breaking, tearing, collapsing. The cacophony of sound envelops me, and the tree shudders before tumbling from its stand, crashing just behind the blue SUVs.

Ian laughs, his face lit with anticipation. "That was awesome, Braidan. I knew you could do it."

"I just need to time it and have it fall in front of them." I meet Ian's smile with one of my own, the power of my actions coursing through my body in tremors of pleasure.

I search the road ahead, and with quick calculation I decide how long it will take to bring the tree down right behind us. I focus on one a few hundred feet ahead, hoping it will tumble at the same speed as the last. I hear the pop within seconds, and the tree falls to the earth.

Ian curses and whips to the right, narrowly scooting out of the way.

One of the SUVs clears the branches before the tree comes to rest, but the other collides with the heavy plank, sending flames and sparks shooting in every direction.

"That was close," Ian says, checking the mirror. "You got

one. Can you get the other?"

I focus on the next tree.

CRACK!

My body lunges forward, my head barely missing the dash. The remaining Saber Corp vehicle slams into the back of us and revs to do it again.

Ian swerves to the right, throwing me against the window. "Quick! Do it!" he screams.

I select another tree and hear the reverberations around me. The brittle wood snaps in half and falls toward us in slow motion. My breath catches in my throat as the tree collapses even faster than the last.

"Ian!" I shriek, but it's too late.

The tree slams to the ground in front of us. We crash into the branches and flip end over end, tossed down the road like a skipping rock. Glass shatters in every direction. Shards bounce off my skin. The Mustang comes to rest on its side, leaving me suspended in the air above Ian, who lies sprawled motionless against the door. Blood dapples his forehead and face. He's unconscious.

Unclipping my seatbelt, I'm careful not to fall on him, bracing myself against the seat and dashboard. I snatch the cell phone near his head and shove it in my pocket. I yank his belt off and pull him up out of the seat. Within seconds of the car coming to rest we're safely through the missing front window.

The crunch of glass underfoot echoes around me, but I can't see who's walking our way. Anger builds in my chest, and the heat radiates off me in waves. I blink, but instead of smoke, I see the dot matrix of colored pixels again, including some shades my human eyes can't see. A bright red hue catches my attention, and my ears tune to the gentle slosh of liquid. My eyes focus.

Gasoline.

My mind wraps around the energy of the liquid teasing my senses. I feel the friction building in the tank. I crouch and toss Ian over my shoulder like a rag doll, then return my focus to the gas tank. I see the molecules in the liquid expanding, and I hear the click of flint. My feet carry us toward the nearby embankment, and I'm out of sight when a fireball engulfs the car. I scramble away from the heat and freeze when a voice tugs at my senses.

"Braidan."

Someone has called my name. Someone whom I recognize. Most of me wants to dash away and ignore the call, but the small part that desires to listen wins. I lay Ian on the terrace and climb through the brush to peek at the face.

A man ambles around the blazing car, and I have to hold back my gasp when I recognize him from the plane.

"Braidan? I know you can hear me, so I need you to listen." His thick accent sends resentment coursing through my veins. "Saber Corp just wants to help. We aren't the bad guys." The man runs a hand through his hair, and I can tell he's beyond exasperated. "The guy who's taken you under his wing, he isn't the good guy. In fact, he may be the very thing he's claiming to run from."

My head swivels toward Ian. Blood still flows from the gash in his forehead, but he's completely unconscious. The nagging in the pit of my stomach tells me not to believe this man from Saber Corp -- the people ultimately responsible for my situation and death.

"Braidan? I know you have many questions, and I can answer them all for you, but I need you to come with me. We will make sure your family is safe. We only want to talk with you."

My heart picks up speed, but I shake away the lies. I can't believe him. He wants to put me in the dark again... or worse.

"Braidan, we can help you with the withdrawals."

Regardless what this Saber Corp moron says, I'm not willing to go back into the dark. The panic of yesterday is still too fresh to even assume it's a possibility I wish to explore. And even though he claims he'll help, I know as soon as I'm within reach, I'll be drugged again. They don't want me remembering, which is all the more reason I must.

I run as fast as my hybrid legs will carry me and Ian, whose unconscious body drapes over my shoulders. I've no idea where I'm going, but I know I have to get as far away from the smoke and flames as I can. Saber Corp helicopters stalk overhead, but I'm careful to stay within the shadows. I double back, hoping to throw them off the trail, and when the ugly blue birds head the opposite way, I know my plan has worked. My feet pound tirelessly over the terrain, and instead of fatigue, strength pumps through my veins.

Once I'm sure I've traveled far enough, I enter a thicket and set Ian gently on the ground. His wounds have clotted, but he's still breathing heavily, as if he's been the one running. I lift his bloodied shirt from his abdomen to reveal a puncture still oozing something other than blood.

"Oh no!" I press my hand over the wound and retract at the heat. I fumble for the phone in my pocket and call the last person Ian talked with. His father, Michael.

"Ian, where are you?" Michael's worried voice sounds over the line.

"It's not Ian, it's Braidan," I say, through the tears tumbling down my cheeks. "Ian's hurt. I think he broke a rib, and it's punctured his lung."

The man draws in a single, long breath. "Put Ian on the line."

"I can't! He's been unconscious since the accident. I don't know what to do." Panic pushes over my quivering lips.

"Where are you?" he questions, emotionless.

"I don't know. We were at a lake, and I had to run. Saber Corp people are crawling all over the place. They have helicopters and..." I feel myself helplessly losing control.

The landscape blinks around me.

A voice bounces off the walls, and I see not one, but two well-built men standing guard in front of a door. I flail my body against them, but they're immovable.

"Really now, Braidan," a voice mocks from the small speaker above the door.

"You can't keep me here," I scream at the two-sided glass to my left. My head whips around, and I assess my surroundings. The walls and ceiling of the small room are light green and seamless. When my eyes focus into the dot matrix, I realize the walls are made of some sort of rubber compound, which I can't do a thing with. When did they discover rubber of all things was incredibly hard for me to manipulate?

I throw myself on the cot in the corner. The wool threads of the blanket squeak in my ears. My mind races through ideas as I tick them off one by one. When I reach the end of the list I realize not a single idea will work. Maybe they've really got me this time.

The men standing by the door stare at the back wall as I scan them for any metal they may have missed. I find nothing but cotton from head to toe. Their pants don't even have snaps.

"It's no use, Braidan," the invisible voice booms. "We've removed all temptations. If you cooperate, life will be that much easier for you."

My eyes flicker to the man on the left as his nostrils flare and his cheek twitches. He's hiding something. I rescan his body, almost missing the waver of energy from his mouth. He has an alloy filling. I probe harder and hear his tongue flicking his tooth. Bingo.

Everything in the room explodes into dots, and I pinpoint the mercury in his tooth, siphoning it out in slow, deliberate motions with my mind. I don't want to kill the man, but putting just enough poison into his blood stream to knock him out will send the other man into chaos. I know enough about mercury to know that once heated, the vapors could send the man's nervous system into shock.

He starts to gag as the taste fills his mouth. His eyes flash to mine, but I refuse to move a muscle. I lock his jaw with one swift thought, so he can't spit the toxin out, and begin to heat the liquid silver. He grabs at his throat and then the shoulder of the man next to him, who refuses to move.

"Braidan, what are you doing?" the panicked voice in the speaker shouts.

I ignore him as the energy continues releasing the deadly fumes. As they concentrate, the man begins to twitch. He's trying everything to remain steady, but the vile taste of the metal accompanied with the vapor is too much for him to handle. He flips around and beats on the handle-less door, grunting. He falls to the ground when the toxins hit his central nervous system.

The second man is sweating now but moves only his jaw, which tightens every few seconds as he listens to his buddy writhe in pain.

My feet find the floor, and I stand in front of the nervous guard.

"Hold your ground," he's advised, and I laugh.

"Yeah, stand your ground, clone. You really think you're a match for me?" I dart forward, and he jumps back, smacking his head against the low ceiling entry. He falls unconscious to the ground, atop the first.

The man in the speaker barks commands as I pull the threads from the blanket into long cords. When the door swings open, I force the cords forward, binding the men moments before I jump over everyone.

Outside the door, the metal in the hallway makes me giddy. I tug at everything I can, which flies to me like I've pulled a string, and wraps my body in armor. Something ricochets off my back, and I grin at the tranquilizers hitting the floor.

I pivot and dash for the small window vent as my mind pulls it apart. I form the steps faster than I can scale them and dive from the window, mere seconds since my cell door opened. I laugh as the glowing Saber Corp logo vanishes behind me over the horizon.

Blink.

I'm clutching a phone, flat on my back, lying next to Ian. My body convulses. I need to take another of those magic pills, but I can't get my limbs to move.

A vortex of thumping surrounds me, alerting me to the presence of a helicopter nearby. I need to get up. I need to get Ian out of here. Desperation fills my veins, but the withdrawal symptoms immobilize me. Any moment they'll find and capture us. I have to move, but my body won't cooperate. The rustle of leaves close by tells me it's too late.

14

"Braidan?" Lucas' voice slices the air, and I want to cry.

Can it be? Or is this a trap? Is he with Saber Corp?

I want to scream for him, tell him to hide, but my vocal chords won't utter a sound.

Lucas rushes to my side, grasping my head in his hands. Worry consumes his face as he checks my body. "Where are the pills?" His eyes plead with mine.

Fear courses through my veins. I don't want to tell him, even if I could. He wants to put me back under, into my coma of unawareness, and I can't let that happen. But my body just shakes.

He lays me down gently in the leaves and searches Ian's pockets. I can do nothing to stop him. He's going to trash the pills and all this, maybe even Ian's life, will be lost. I can't let him. I can't. Lucas grunts and comes back into view. He sits me up and stuffs a pill through my clenched, chattering jaws.

He doesn't want to drug me... He wants to help.

"Come on, Bray, swallow it. Swallow it!" he demands.

Tears rush down my face as I try desperately to push the pill past my swollen tongue. The bitterness of sanity wreaks havoc on my senses, and I feel another flashback rushing to the surface.

Blink.

I'm with Lucas on a bench near the oceanfront. One of his hands is lost in my pure red hair, the other wraps my hands in love and safety. His eyes sparkle when he looks at me, and I feel the energy bursting from his touch.

"I want to marry you, Braidan O'Donnell," he says, his eyes never leaving mine.

"Lucas, we're only fifteen. Don't you think we are a little too young for that?" That's what I say, but I feel what he says with all my heart. I love this boy. He's my everything.

"I didn't say now. Maybe not even when we graduate. But I will marry you, Ray."

I twist my fingers into his and glance down at the ring on his finger that morphs and bends with the same pleasure I feel. "My parents always told me after college they would pay for a wedding. Do you think you can wait that long?"

He groans and rests his forehead on my shoulder. "If I have to, I will. But that doesn't mean I want to wait." He chuckles and lifts his face even with mine.

I feel the excitement in me simmer and nervousness creep in. "Do you think the rumors are true? You know, about

Saber Corp?"

His eyes grow dark. "I don't really know, Bray. We just have to take it day by day."

"I hate them," I say through clenched teeth.

"I don't." His reply catches me off guard, and I shrink from his touch.

"What?!"

He pushes down bits of laughter. "They brought you to me. How could I hate them for that?"

"Okay, Romeo. Besides that, I hate them."

He bobbed his head. "I admit, they're not my favorite people right now."

"But what if it's all true? What if those kids didn't leave the program? What if their vaccine killed them, or worse?"

He shakes his head at me to stop my foolish talk.

"And what if they really did know what they were doing by giving us the vaccine, and it wasn't just a side effect of a routine one?"

"It's so hard to believe, Bray. People have side effects from vaccines all the time."

"But have you ever heard of people having one of our side effects?" I lift my eyebrows. "You can't deny that we're different from the others. And why would they want to study only ten of us if it was just some random side effect?"

He shrugs. "Maybe they were curious. It is science after all. It's not every day they accidently create a hybrid-human. My parents think it's awesome that I want to have my nose stuck in a book all the time. They don't see a thing wrong with a vaccine that will help me be a four-point-oh student." He stares at me with a lopsided grin. "Besides, they claim it was in everyone's vaccine, and we're the only ones having these side effects. We're the hybrid valedictorians. Speaking of which," he says, stretching his arms back over the bench. "I hope you don't mind I'm going to bump you out of first place this week with my paper."

I jab him in the side, making him double over. "In your dreams, pretty boy. You haven't seen mine yet."

We laugh for a moment as we poke each other, then rest in each other's arms.

"So, are you really going to marry me?" He's so close his breath tickles the hairs on my cheek.

"You've already got me until death do us part," I say, then lean up to kiss him.

Blink.

The scene dissolves, and I see Lucas' worried face staring down at me. I'm gasping for air, but my body no longer shudders from the withdrawal.

"Lucas," I manage, grabbing onto his neck. "Lucas, I didn't know." My silent sobs break through my chest as I cling to him, frantic for understanding.

"Bray, it's okay. I'm here. But I have to get you guys to

safety. What happened to Ian?"

I push up from the ground, trying to gain my bearings. "The car. We crashed into a tree, and he's been unconscious since. I think he has some broken ribs and maybe a punctured lung."

Lucas helps steady me on my feet. "Well, did you fix it?"

My eyes flash to his. He's dead serious. "What do you mean? Did I fix it?"

"You don't know yet. Uh, okay," he says and kneels next to Ian, pressing his hand against the hot wound. "You can move things with your mind, seen or unseen, using telekinesis. Only yours is a bit more advanced. You can pull out one element, or several, from a mass, and make it do what you want."

"Oh. I've done that today. It's the reason Ian is injured. The tree fell too soon. It was supposed to hit the Saber Corp vehicle, not us." I study Lucas' face, and it occurs to me he's waiting for me to have some revelation of how I can help Ian, using this ability. But I can only shake my head.

"Braidan, you can fix his rib and inflate his lung."

"What? No, I can't." I lean away from Ian as if he has some sort of contagious, incurable disease.

"Bray, you can. I've seen you set broken bones before..." He turns back to Ian. "You just have to focus on the bone and pull it into place."

"But what if I hurt him more than he already is?"

143

Lucas tries to stifle his exasperated laugh. "I don't think you could make it any worse."

I take in Ian's face, red and bloated, sweat pouring from his temples. His breaths remain uneven at best, and he looks much worse than just minutes ago.

"So, do you know how I'm supposed to do this?" My voice shakes as I lay my hands on the distorted area of his torso. "I've seen a couple flashbacks, but I don't really get it. I mean, I toppled a couple trees, but he's a human."

Lucas gives me a doubtful expression, and I continue before he can reply.

"I didn't tell you how I did it either? Of course not. I didn't tell anyone. Why would I?" Aggravation pushes through my words. Air fills my lungs as I close my eyes, imagining the dot display that accompanies my abilities. The dots blink for a second, then dissipate.

What sound does blood make? My mind pushes away the thump of the nearby helicopter, and I press every bit of my energy into Ian. A gentle *whoosh, whoosh, whoosh*, penetrates my ears. My answer. I focus on the thrum of blood pulsing through his heart, which brings me into the right frame of mind.

As I gaze at Ian, I see everything clearly. Three ribs are broken, and as I suspected, one has pierced his lung. The pale color of bone is easy for my mind to grasp, and when I tug on the first rib, it clicks into place, causing Ian to quiver.

"Good job, Bray. Keep it up."

The next rib jerks up with a slight flick, but this time Ian remains still. The last rib is a bit trickier since it's engulfed in the small mass of his collapsed lung. I know the lung is a major organ and don't want to injure it any more than it is, so I draw the bone up slowly, allowing the lung to release it. When it's clear of the grey tissue, I snap it back into place, and Ian moans. My eyes roam over the three ribs, checking their closure. I see the cracks, but the ribs are back together.

"His lung has a hole in it. Do you think I can pull it back together?" I say without breaking my gaze.

"Try it."

The weak hiss of air calls to me as my mind takes hold of the soft tissue on each side of the hole. I stretch the membrane until they touch, holding it there while I pull every last dangling piece. Once they've all extended to a line, Ian's body takes over and does the rest.

Like little fingers, his cells reach out and bond to each other, over and over until a small clot of cells covers each patch. After the fourth clot, I'm confident I can release my hold. I do so slowly, watching for signs of distress. When my mind has completely backed off, the tissues hold fast. Ian's chest settles down, and he takes a deep, easy breath.

"I think I did it." Relief tumbles from my mouth as I lay my hand on Lucas'.

"I knew you could." His eyes lock on my touch, and I feel the hesitation as he slips his hand out from under mine. He checks Ian's pulse and frowns. "His heart rate is pretty irregular. We need to get him to a doctor."

I grab Lucas' sleeve. "Do you know Ian?"

He shakes his head. "No. I've got no idea who he is."

"But he said he was the first hybrid."

Lucas freezes. "He what?" Lucas turns Ian's face toward him.

Ice crawls through my veins as I watch him inspect the face of the unconscious boy. Could the Saber Corp guy have been right? Could Ian be the very thing I'm running from?

Lucas grimaces. "I don't think so. He wasn't part of our hybrid program, are you sure you heard him right?"

"He knew everything about the program and about me."

Lucas' eyes flash to mine. "How do you know he told you the truth?" He shakes his head. "You know what, never mind. I need to get you both out of here. Those choppers are still circling. It won't be long before they deploy footmen, if they haven't already." He heaves the unconscious boy onto his shoulder as carefully as he can.

"If he's lying, why are you helping him?"

"That's an excellent question." He glares sideways. "Not one I want to get into right now. I know they're after you, but because he's running, it's my duty to save him too."

"Your duty?" I follow him through the trees as he shifts the weight of his load.

"Yeah. You can't fall into the hands of Saber Corp." His voice changes from concern to annoyance. "For that reason alone I'm helping you both."

"Why? What does Saber Corp want with me?" I stumble over the rocky landscape after him, now yearning for answers.

He stops and pivots on his heels, his eyes boring holes into mine. "You mean your boyfriend hasn't told you yet?"

My eyes narrow. "He's not my boyfriend."

He flips back around and scoffs. "Could have fooled me with your lips attached to his yesterday at lunch."

Heat rushes into my cheeks. "For your information, I needed a diversion, and he provided it. And yes, I wanted to kiss him. Sue me. I'm a bit at a loss as to whom I'm supposed to be trusting... or kissing. And it seems you know a whole lot more about it than you let on."

He growls, pushing his way through the underbrush. "Braidan, people do things all the time for selfless reasons. Letting you go was one of them. It killed me, but there was nothing I could do about it. People change, especially..." He halts and twists his head toward me. "What do you know? What has this clown told you?"

"Don't be a jerk, Lucas. At least he was willing to bring me out of the fog and try to save me from Saber Corp."

"Oh really, then what am I doing?" His hateful tone sends me reeling backward.

"We were doing fine before you happened upon us." My stubborn spirit oozes from my mouth as I throw my hands in the air.

He flips around and takes a step toward me. "Really?"

I cross my arms over my chest. "Really."

Our stare down lasts a few moments before he swings around and continues through the trees.

"You're so hardheaded, Braidan. Some things never change."

"Well, according to my flashback, you liked me that way."

The words echo around us as he freezes. "You've had a flashback about... us?"

"Obviously, it doesn't matter. Let's get out of here."

~

I'm not sure how far we walk before the rushing waters of the river ahead drown out the echo of the choppers in the valley. Lucas bristles at every accidental touch, making the blood rage in my veins. If the flashbacks are true, he shouldn't feel like this, should he? Though even as I think it, I know my actions with Ian, heck, the very presence of Ian, probably cut him more deeply than I can fathom.

We follow the river to what I can best judge as north. Climbing over the terrain, I watch Lucas carefully as he picks his way through the rocky embankment. He's sure-footed, as if he has walked this way many times before. Meanwhile, I struggle, stumbling over the jagged surfaces, even tumbling to my butt on more than one occasion.

I release a primal screech when my foot catches between two rocks. Without another thought, the scene bursts into pixels, and I toss the offending boulder into the nearby rapids.

"You've really got to work on taming that temper of yours," Lucas says, not even bothering to turn around.

"And you've really got to work on that not-being-a-jerk thing." Resentment boils in me like molten lava, and my body tingles all over. The emotion rolls through my chest, settling on the tips of my fingers. They want me to react. They want me to cause him physical pain. But I refuse to hurt Ian.

"So if you're not working for those Saber freaks and you don't know Ian, who are you working for?" I freeze in my tracks, my foot landing hard on the rock in front of me. "Sam! You and Sam work for the same people, don't you?" My finger points accusations at his back, but he doesn't even slow his pace.

"Nope. I'm a hybrid, Braidan. I don't work for anyone. I just work for me." He hikes up a small boulder and hops down again. "You see, once upon a time I was in love with a girl. I promised her I'd do anything to keep her safe, and I meant it." Irritation seeps through his words. "Even when she treats me like sh--"

A helicopter drops through the surrounding trees, its blades cutting at the branches as it descends like a spider ambushing its prey. The whooshing of the rotors resonates in my ears, and the backwash presses hard on my chest, making me stumble and fall.

"Run!" The hurricane winds around us make Lucas' voice barely audible.

I push to my feet and dash toward the trees, where Lucas has disappeared. The clunk of metal on the rock bed reverberates in my ears, and I flip around.

What am I doing? I can stop them!

I turn and brace myself. The landscape bursts into a map of color. I focus on the pale-green dots making up the helicopter. I yank and tug with my mind, but nothing moves. My eyes dart around the scene and notice everything is this color, even the bodies jumping from the craft.

"Braidan, run!"

Before I can respond, I feel a sharp jab in my leg. Then another. Tranquilizers. A dart burrows into my arm, and I wince in pain as I snatch it. I twist on my heels and head for the trees. The sedative travels through my veins like a dry wick catching fire.

Another dart tags my back, and I hear the men yelling to each other and racing toward me. My feet falter, and I tumble toward the earth. Blackness fills my vision, and before I touch the ground, the world has gone silent.

15

Thick straps secure my feet and hands when my consciousness returns. I'm lying on a cold, bare cot inside a familiar light-green room. I know Saber Corp has captured me, even before the voice clicks over the speaker.

"Good morning, Braidan. I trust you've slept well?"

My head throbs as I struggle to call forth my abilities, but nothing happens. I yank against the straps, but my body feels beaten and every muscle aches.

"I can assure you we've taken every precaution to ensure you don't escape this time. However, none of this would be necessary if you would just cooperate with us."

My jaws clamp down hard, and I continue to writhe, ignoring the pain in my limbs.

"Have it your way. But I dare say you'll change your mind shortly." The speaker clicks off, thrusting the room into uncomfortable silence.

The pale-green dots my eyes bring to life cause a roar of panic flushing through my body in waves of despair. I'm in the same room from my flashback, but there are no guards this time. I have no idea how to escape. One glance at the same color on my cuffs, and I know they've been working on materials to detain me.

I release a laugh of aggravation. The irony is that I don't even know why they want to confine me. The fact that they've gone through all this trouble sends rivulets of fear pumping through my body. I twist my hands back and forth in the tight bindings and feel the material slicing into my skin.

"Braidan?" A scared voice echoes through the small space and stops my heart. Tanner!

I yank against my straps and unleash the scream building in my chest. "No!"

"Oh yes, Braidan. They're all here."

His sweet, saucy voice raises venom in my veins. Tanner's muffled cry in the background tears me into pieces, smoldering my anger.

"Stop! Please stop!"

Tears stream down my face, and I pull against my restraints as hard as possible. They cut deeper into my skin as the scent of metal permeates my senses. Dots burst through the room, fueling my anger, and I see small black flecks of metal seeping from my cuts.

Blood has iron in it.

I continue to fight against the straps, and they cut painfully into my flesh, but I endure. Pain is better than insanity.

"Now Braidan, no harm will come to your family if you'll just agree to cooperate."

The ties around my feet slice painfully into my tissue, releasing more fresh blood, and I relax against the bed, hoping it appears I've given up. I grit my teeth. I have to go along with it, at least for a little while.

"Please don't hurt them," I say with a fake sob. "I'll do whatever you want."

"That's my girl," he says, his voice dripping with triumph. "I'll send someone in to clean you up."

The speaker clicks off, and I envelop the room with my mind, pulling every bit of iron seeping from my body into the palm of my hand. I tuck it alongside my body in slow repetition, hoping whoever watches will not see the tiny flecks. It's barely enough to fashion a thumbtack, but I'm sure it will be my savior.

I'm placing the last of the iron into my balled fist when the door slides open. I assume it's a man that enters. He's covered from head to toe in what appears to be a white hazmat suit. One quick survey tells me the suit is made with the same material the room and my bindings are.

The odor of antiseptic fills my nostrils when he hastily wipes the blood from my ankles and wrists. The cloth is made of the same stupid material as everything else.

Rubber-covered shackles dangle over his arm, and once my wounds are clean, he wastes no time cuffing the first pair around my ankles. He's wise not to release the straps yet, because my first thought is to kick the crap out of him. Instead, he binds my right hand, and before I can register what he's doing, he yanks me forward and clips the ring to my legs. I'm bent in half, and the strap cuts into my flesh again with the awkward angle. I wince, but really don't care. He clips the final shackle into place and snaps it to the loop at my waist.

They're hobbling me like an animal.

I grunt. With the emotions raging through my body and what I've seen in my flashbacks, they have every right to be afraid of me. My own thoughts take me by surprise, but I welcome them, pushing away the fear and grasping the hatred. If they want me to become their worst nightmare, so be it. Ian was right about that one.

"Get up." The warden's muffled voice carries through his thick rubber mask.

When I don't move fast enough, he shoves my legs and whirls me around. My head smacks into the wall, and I almost slip from the bench.

"Get up!" he commands.

"Keep your shorts on!" The room spins from the impact, but as I sit up it stabilizes, and I'm able to stand.

He shoves me in the back with his arm, pushing me toward the door. I can't even stand straight, shackled as I am, but I hold my head up anyway, ready to face whatever this is.

"All clear," he calls, presumably to the speaker listening.

I hold my breath as I wait for the door to open. If I could remember who I was before, my mind might ping with every possible use for the small metal finding in my hand to help my escape. Instead, the fear I've been fighting to keep at bay courses through me, twisting around the hope of knowledge.

The door slides open, and three more suited blobs stand there with tranquilizer guns aimed right at my chest.

"Don't even attempt it. One false move and we'll shoot and ask questions later," says one of the marshmallows.

One quick scan of my surroundings tells me they've even made the guns out of this synthesized material.

My first sentinel nudges me forward. The three others walk backwards down the narrow rubber hall.

I release a pent-up chuckle, freezing everyone. "Sorry, I just can't imagine why four grown men are so afraid of a seventeen-year-old girl." They turn their heads slightly toward each other but set their sights back on me. "Or maybe you're women, they way you're cowering and all."

The freak behind me rams my back, and I crash to the ground. A dart whizzes past my ear and thuds into the rubber floor right next to my head. I watch the clear liquid leach into the mat before strong arms jerk me to my feet.

"No more talking. Move!"

I obey because I have no other choice. Even if I could use anything in this narrow hall in combination with the metal clutched in my hand, I still have no way out of the cuffs.

The door at the end glides open, and light filters through the hall between long plastic sheets of material hanging over the door, like decontamination panels. The suits back into the room, sights still set on me as I step through and nudge the plastic panels aside with my head.

I'm not surprised to find another noncompliant room. There are three doors with blinking red lights beside their keycard pads, all covered in the same rubber. Even the furniture is covered in this artificial material. I'm thrust into a chair on the opposite side of a table as the men set up around the room, still pointing their guns at me.

The click of expensive shoes echoes through the room behind me, and I know, even before I look, who is coming. His gait alone sends strings of disgust pulsating through me.

"Braidan." The trill of his accent says he's happy to see me.

I don't want to look up as he seats himself across the table. I don't want to see the face of the man I believe is ultimately responsible for everything I'm going through.

"What, no hello for an old friend?" From the corner of my eyes, I see him stretch back in his chair and cross his legs, far too relaxed for my liking.

"What do you want?" I growl.

"You mean you don't know? Surely they haven't been drugging you that much, have they?"

I maintain my downward gaze, and he laughs, full and rich. It bounces around the room, mocking me.

My senses erupt into dots, and I gasp at the thick scar tissue across his midsection. Evidence of a wound I had inflicted.

"Braidan, what I'm about to tell you may come as a shock, but I'm not the bad guy. You and I used to work together."

My eyes flash to his. "Was this before or after you had me injected with that crap?" I stare into the face of the man from my flashback.

He narrows his focus, his hand drumming on the tattered folders he entered with. "You welcomed that injection."

I scoff. "I've witnessed the scene in my flashbacks. It didn't look like I welcomed anything."

"Okay, so you needed a little persuasion, but certainly you see the benefits now. I mean, look at you." He motions, in awe of this thing he's created. "You're one of a kind." His well-manicured eyebrows bob up and down above his grey eyes as he speaks, and he runs a hand through his wavy blond locks. His shirt tugs on his bulging biceps when he rests his hands on the table between us. "It may be difficult to believe, but you thanked me for this transformation."

I shake my head, unwilling to accept. "Yeah, between my violent flashbacks I'm sure I thanked you."

"Tsk-tsk. You weren't having those when you were under my care. I'm not sure what happened to you when you left. Maybe someone else induced them, but I can fix it, Braidan. I'm certain I can." His eyes narrow, and his lip curls in a mischievous grin. "Unfortunately, that does mean I need some samples from you, in order to help--"

"I don't need your help. I'm fine the way I am."

He considers me a moment before his forehead crinkles in the middle. "Really? You enjoy feeling so volatile at the drop of a hat?" He reads the indecision in my eyes and smiles. "I can fix that. All I ask in return is a few vials of blood, then you're free to go."

He's lying.

"However, I have to be able to trust you. And right now..." He motions at the cuffs. "This is the best I can do. You've been nearly impossible to contain in the past."

"Why would you need to contain me if we were working together?" My lips form a hard line as I stare forward.

His left eye twitches, and he looks away. "We didn't always see eye to eye. This is the truth."

"No offense, but I have a hard time believing you are telling me any sort of truth here."

"Fair enough. But I trust when your memory fully returns, you will know I speak truth." He wiggles his hands, fingertips still pressed together.

I watch his face jerk with either pleasure or indecision. I can't decide.

"Do you want coffee?" He snaps his fingers as if calling a maître d'.

"No. I want to know what happened to me... Adrien." I spit his name from my throat. "From the beginning." I need to know if what Ian said is truth.

The sigh that escapes is one of boiling annoyance, like he's wasting his time even having this conversation.

"Braidan, you were born with a gift," he says, leaning on the table. "One not many know about. It's an anomaly in your DNA. Unnoticed, this irregularity is wasted, but when caught, it can be combined with other strings of code to awaken something..." He taps the table as if it were a piano. "Something amazing." His eyes float back to mine, and his agitation level simmers.

"How did you find this error in my DNA?"

The plastic flaps smack together as someone brings in a rubber tea tray and paper cups.

Adrien continues while the hazmat suit pours steaming coffee. "Saber Corp owns nearly every blood lab across the country. Each test that comes through our facility undergoes the genetic code search."

"Why were you even looking for these DNA codes?"

"We were searching for ways to enhance natural abilities through gene manipulation." He leans forward. "I worked closely with some top secret agencies to find candidates that fit our study."

"What happened? You aren't anymore?"

Adrien's cheek twitches as he considers me. "No. The

program was cut short due to unfortunate circumstances."

The way he lingers on the last words makes chills race up my spine.

"You see, Braidan. When you first became a super-hybrid, we weren't prepared for how your body would react. Every cell in your body rebelled against each other. It was like world war three inside your skin. Your emotions were out of control, which sent you on a rampage."

I suck back a breath as his words hit me square in the chest. Ian mentioned my killing others. Had I done it in a fitful rage? I watch Adrien's face carefully for confirmation and find it in his sorrowful eyes.

"If we'd had any idea you'd respond like that, we would have been more careful."

"I'm certain you would have." I lean back in the chair and attempt to cross my arms, but the cuffs won't allow it. "Why are you creating hybrids, Adrien?"

He runs a hand through his hair. His mouth opens halfway, and his tongue clicks against his perfect teeth. The tension in his chin makes me uneasy. "Braidan, the genetics in you can change the way the world looks at war."

The temperature in the room elevates to sweltering as the blood pumps through my veins with uncomfortable pressure. Another dose of withdrawal picks at my senses.

"War?" My mind reels at the word and snakes forward at an alarming pace. He wants to use the hybrids for war?

He stares silently, seemingly knowing what my body threatens to do.

The room spins on its axis, and I see two men sitting in front of me, instead of one. I shake away the flashback, willing myself back into the room.

"Yes, Braidan, war." He laughs. "It's not every day you create the ultimate warrior."

I push the breaths from my nose in slow intervals, struggling to remain coherent amidst the incredible pains shooting through me. His voice echoes in my head, but I can barely see his lips moving through my blurry vision.

"Who do you work for? Who pays you?" I'm not sure why I ask, but something in my hazy mind clings to the answer like dew to a blade of grass.

Just before my mind blinks out I hear his words, and they paralyze me.

"The highest bidder."

16

Convulsions take over my body and throw me to the ground, my muscles tugging against the restraints. I barely understand the chaos around me. Men in suits race around the room, one with a gurney. Adrien Saber grips my head as I shake uncontrollably. Everyone is yelling, but their words muffle in my ears.

Blink.

I'm in the lab. The body of my thirteen-year-old self is strapped to a table, and two men in white smocks walk toward me. One of them carries a clipboard, while the other rolls a machine behind him. My heart pounds against my chest when I recognize what they're wheeling closer. *Alyx*, the blood collection machine. I can't stop the sobs that break free as I plead with them, but they ignore me.

People stand on each side of me, one with a stethoscope to my chest and others prepping my arm for the needle. Someone wipes my skin clear of bacteria, then waits for a cue. The straps are so tight around my torso, arms, and chest, that even though I'm thrashing around, I can barely move a fraction of a centimeter.

"Let me go. Let me go. Let me go," I chant through my breaths, but the men don't even bat an eyelash at my pleas.

A sting in my arm tells me they've inserted the needle and are beginning the blood draw, just as they have every other Monday I've been in the program here. They will drain another thirteen percent of the blood volume from my veins. They're harvesting it for the other hybrids, hoping it will force a genetic mutation like mine.

My fight leaves with the evacuation of blood, and my body lies limp, exhausted from the expenditure. The exhaustion only lasts twenty minutes, as my body works feverishly to replace the blood I've lost. In a mere two days my blood volume will be back at 100%. I know from overhearing the scientists that this, in and of itself, makes my DNA priceless.

The man with the clipboard, who's on the left, taps my cheek, but I'm too tired to acknowledge him. He clears his throat, and his thick drawl encompasses me. "Why are we doing this again? Our tests show it's not working."

"Her genes are still mutating," says the man running *Alyx*. "The only way to check for the right combo is to transfuse her blood into the other hybrids."

"The last hybrid didn't fare so well after the transfusion," the first man says with a disgusted sigh. "How many more children will this man sacrifice for his money?"

There's an awkward silence, and I realize I've moved my head toward the man who touched my cheek. I lie motionless another couple seconds before they continue their conversation. Did they just imply someone died from my blood?

"Besides, you're paid plenty for your time, what do you care?"

I open my left eye to a half-slit and resist the urge to gasp at the face staring down at me. His features are distinct, and sorrow clouds his chocolate brown eyes. A soft smile tugs at the corner of his lips, but with a quick glance at his partner, it vanishes. My eyes flutter to his name tag. Dr. Michael Bailey.

"Isn't that enough?" he says, shifting the clipboard in his grasp and placing the stethoscope on my chest again. "Her heart is slowing too much. That's enough."

The man at the machine grumbles. "If we haven't collected as much as we need, I'll blame you." He pulls the needle from my arm and applies pressure to the puncture. I hear the rip of tape and feel the cotton ball he presses to my skin before he tapes it in place.

The squeak of wheels indicates the machine's retreat. I know the first man has left with it when I hear the heavy door slam and the soft sigh of the man still holding the stethoscope to my chest. My eyes flutter open and land on the face above me.

"Thank you," I manage to whisper through barely parted lips.

His face fills with grief. He releases a heavy sigh and moves a few strands of hair from my face, staring like he wants me to read his mind. Like he has something important to tell me. I gaze back, struggling to understand.

Blink.

I'm back in Saber Corp again, stretched out on a gurney with medical staff around me. Straps hold me stable, much like in my flashback, and panic resonates through my body.

"Stop," I say through parched lips. "Please."

"Back away." Adrien's voice carries through the room. "Are you okay?" he says with genuine concern, which confuses me.

I flip my head from side to side. "Why am I having these flashbacks? Why is my body reacting like this?"

"The drugs your parents were giving you held your memories at bay, but unfortunately the side effect to coming off such a powerful drug is unpleasant. However, the tremors seem to be connected to the flashbacks, so I'm forced to assume they're fighting for a place to settle in your subconscious, like your cells are trying to come to grips with something."

Dread floods my body when a man steps in beside Adrien pushing *Alyx*, the machine from my flashback. They're going to harvest again.

My eyes plead with the man and then flash to Adrien. "Please. Please don't."

"Oh, but surely you realize we must?"

"NO!" The scream comes from my throat before I've opened my mouth. I yank against the restraints, causing

Adrien to back away, fear pulsating in his eyes. "Yeah, you should be afraid of me!" I shriek, tears rushing to the surface. I struggle for a good minute before Adrien clears his throat.

"I don't mean to sound callous, but you need to stop acting like a child and suck it up. There's nothing that can reverse this, and with your blood, many will live more prosperous lives."

"You mean *you* will live a more prosperous life?" I spit at him and instantly regret I've said anything.

Adrien snaps his fingers, and another man steps up with a large needle in his grasp.

I can't hide the fear that seeps through my words. "Please, I just want to be normal."

Adrien scoffs and nods at the man approaching me. "You, dear Braidan, will never be normal."

The man plunges the needle into my thigh and injects fire into my body. My consciousness wavers as Adrien steps closer, the folder from earlier in his hand.

"It will only be a little blood," he says, stroking my hair like I'm a prize.

I try to remain cogent, but I can already tell they've given me another tranquilizer to knock me out. I need to hang on long enough for someone to find me. The piece of metal bounces around in my thoughts, and I realize it's still clutched in my hand.

My body trembles as the concoction hits my heart, and I

frantically fight the restraints, sending everyone a step back. This keeps their attention long enough for me to shove the shard of metal through the fibers of my jumpsuit. The chill of the alloy calms my fears only the slightest bit, but I'm able to stop my limbs from fighting. I clench my jaw and writhe against the heat flowing from my heart into my arteries. A fuzzy haze encroaches on my thoughts as my mind roams over the flashback.

Michael Bailey is the reason I'm alive. Ian's father. The same man who just helped me escape. Ian was telling the truth. My heart flutters with anticipation. Michael has gotten me out before. Maybe he will come for me again.

The drug causes everything around me to go dim. There's nothing I can do about it... yet.

I wake in the same room I was in before my conversation with Adrien. The bandage on my arm assures me it was no flashback and no dream.

My feet find the floor, and I realize the restraints have been removed. Maybe he's collected enough and will allow me to leave.

"Welcome back, Braidan." Adrien's triumphant voice carries through the room from the speaker. "I'm so sorry we had to resort to putting you back into confinement. You gave my scientists quite a fright this afternoon. I hope you understand, but we can't be too careful yet."

"You said you would let me go when you had what you needed."

"I did. But I'm not certain I have everything I need. Sure, the data coming back on your cells is off the charts. I want to make certain we can replicate before we... release you." The way he pauses tells me he doesn't plan to release me. Ever. "Braidan, your blood can change the world."

"Yeah, the world of the highest bidder." I practically yell.

He's silent for long enough that I know he's searching for a response.

My bones shift in my skin when I realize regardless of my actions from this point, Saber Corp might have all they need to sell the hybrid serum and technology to the highest bidder. Possibly terrorists.

The heave comes from nowhere, and I'm on the floor gasping for breath. I need to get out of here and destroy all the data he's collected. Along with my blood.

Dots cover every inch of the room, and hopelessness seeps into my heart. A click in my mind brings my thoughts racing forward.

"Can I see my mom?" The tears fall from my face to the floor.

"Hmm. I suppose that won't hurt anything. Give us a few minutes to ready her for entry."

The door slides open, and I'm on my feet, rushing for the arms of Sheila, who's only wearing a pale green hospital gown. Distress coats her face like war paint when she backs away, tears welling at the corners of her eyes.

"Mom." The words come out through my sobs. "I'm sorry. I'm so sorry."

"Oh, Honey." She grasps my cheeks, forcing me to look at her. "This is not your fault. These are powerful people. There is nothing any of us can do. We tried, Braidan. We tried to keep you away from them," she says as her voice cracks. "We tried. He told us if we didn't put you in the program he would..." She covers her mouth and tears flood her eyes.

"It's okay, Mom. I know they threatened you." I grasp her shoulders, willing this all to be a wild dream. Willing myself to be normal. "After we escaped, how did they find us?"

More distress enters her face as she averts her gaze. "It was an accident. I'm sure of it... He wouldn't." She meets my probing eyes. "Drew."

"What? Why would he?" My mind roams over everything I know about Drew. What would cause him to betray the whole family?

"We don't know. He's missing. If we would have just paid more attention. We knew he was unhappy he had to leave his friends, but we didn't realize he was capable of this." She wrings her hands together between us.

"How did this happen?"

"It seemed like a good decision at the time, Braidan. When we thought you'd died, everything around us died with you. It was all I could do to rise every morning and make myself breathe in and out. It was like the whole world crumbled when you left us." Tears glisten down her face. "When you were given back, it was a miracle. But we had to hide. If they knew where you were..." She pushes some hair from my face. "We tried to help you deal with the emotions, but we couldn't do it. It was just too much. I'm so sorry."

"Do you know they want to sell my DNA to terrorists?"

Waves of emotion course through her, and she covers her mouth to suppress the sobs breaking through her fingers. "I hope you believe we had no choice, Braidan. That he wouldn't let you leave the program once he found out your code was a match."

"I believe you, Mom."

"Time's up," says the voice over the speaker.

I grab Sheila, pulling her toward me, burying my face in her hair. "No. No. No!" I cry loud enough for anyone listening to hear. I suck in a deep breath as I prepare my next question. I hope I'm right. "Michael will come for us."

She gasps and pulls back, her eyes bulging. "How would you know that name?"

The door slides open, and before they can grab her, I tug her toward me in another embrace, burying my lips in her hair. "Mom, he knows we're here. He'll get us out."

With a final yank, they pull her through the opening before it slams shut, sealing me in my prison.

~

The afternoon drags on with no sound from the speaker and no movement of the door. I'm unnerved at being left alone, as if they have everything they need and are merely deciding how to eliminate the security risk sitting in the green room. There's no way they're going to let me leave, but with my abilities, I should at least be able to find a way out if Michael doesn't come for us. But he has to come.

My heart thuds in my chest at the thought of Ian's broken body and of Lucas helping him. My mind swarms with questions I can't answer. How did Lucas find us? Why did he help Ian even though he had no idea who he was?

I stretch and tug the metal shard from my waistband, then lie back on the hard rubber cot, faced away from the peeping eyes behind the two-sided glass. The cold metal in my fingers is my security blanket. All would be lost without it.

Laughter tumbles from my chest. Saber Corp can't take away the air molecules in the room. By bending the air around the metal, it will take perfect shape. Then I can propel it as if fired from a gun. I have no desire to end anyone's life, but I have no problem causing some pain.

Determination burns through my body, painful and real. It reminds me that Saber Corp has to be stopped regardless of the cost.

I've fashioned my bullet outside the eyes of Big Brother before dinner arrives. The slug is small, merely the size of a pea, but it will cause someone serious pain. Testing the pressure of the wind against a piece of lint from my shirt, I'm able to hurl it at the wall with such force it wedges itself in the rubber molecules.

Now all I need is an opportunity to use the bullet. I'll only have one chance unless I make myself bleed again, but that doesn't seem to be possible without Saber noticing. There is nothing in the room besides myself and the cot, which appears to be fashioned out of the wall.

I eat the meager meal slid in to me, barely tasting the turkey and Swiss on a Kaiser roll. Resting on my back, staring up at the blank wall, I wander over the subject poking at my mind. When did I fall for Ian, and why, if Lucas was ready to go to the end of the earth for me? I delve into the unknown recesses of my brain, searching for anything I can pluck out. The knowledge must be in my subconscious, hiding from reality.

Reality.

This is reality, and I must accept it. I'm a hybrid capable of almost anything. A threat to Saber Corp. My family and I are in serious danger. They will no sooner let them leave than me. I have to stop Saber Corp.

The shiver in my limbs catches me off guard, and I want to curse. I know another withdrawal is lurking on the horizon. I've fought against it every time thus far, but something tells me I should relax and accept it this time. As if this meditative state will help me through the tremor and afford more insight to my situation.

As hard as it is, I focus on relaxing every muscle in my small frame when the tugs of pain rocket through my body. My mind screams from every direction. One side says to fight, deny, writhe. The other reminds me to relax and let what will be... be.

Blink.

It's dark. I almost believe I've been rendered unconscious until I hear the steady drip of water.

"Braidan? Wake up." Ian's voice echoes through my mind. "Michael needs to talk to you."

I jump from the bed and tug on a sweatshirt. The apprehension in my veins puzzles me, but I stumble down the hall to the family room, under Ian's pull.

The room is ice cold when we come through the door. Michael sits on the edge of the recliner, hands pressed together, unwilling to look up.

"Please sit, both of you," he says, clearing his throat.

Before our rears hit the couch cushions, he rises and starts to pace the floor in front of the mantel. In my four months with Ian and Michael, I've never seen him quite this worried, and that frightens me. I feel my pulse elevate, and beads of sweat pierce my forehead.

"Braidan, I think you're in danger being in my care," he says, frankly. "Some data leaked out through my office, and I believe Saber Corp might have caught a lead."

Ian grips my hand, assuring me everything will be alright, but I know it's not. I know beyond a shadow of a doubt that if Saber Corp knows I'm alive, my life, as well as Ian's and Michael's, are in danger.

"I've spoken with your parents and arranged for a private organization to protect and hide you, but... we have to cut all ties with you immediately." His bloodshot eyes turn to Ian, who seems to be just registering the situation.

He leaps to his feet. "What? No!"

Michael pats down the air between him and his son, "It's got to be this way, Ian. If they find out I'm involved..." He shifts to me. "We will all die."

His eyes communicate tremendous volumes of sympathy, anger, and solace. They flicker between the mashed emotions as swiftly as the beats of my heart.

"I'll go." I find my feet immediately, but I'm rooted to the spot, unable to fathom what this means for my newly emerging relationship with Ian.

He grabs my hand and holds it to his chest. His heart

pounds in irregular thumps against my fingers. "We will find a way to shut down Saber Corp. I swear it."

My opposite hand rests on Ian's face as he leans forward. Our foreheads meet, and his eyes pool with tears. He grips the side of my neck, pulling me toward him, pressing his lips upon mine, first tentatively, then eagerly until I have to draw back. The relationship between us has blossomed quickly, but I could never quite give him my whole heart, despite trying.

I turn and head for my room. "I'll pack." I glance back only once and see Ian covering his face.

Clothes fly around the room toward the black duffel bag as I hastily throw them. Michael and Ian argue in the hall about the best route to take. I hate that I've put them in danger. I know I have a hard time dealing with the emotional turmoil in my veins, but believing someone else will die because of it is heart wrenching.

With a quick pull, I'm zipping my bag and tossing it over my shoulder. I step into the hall and see Ian leaning against the wall outside the room. I'm not sure what I should say or do. Anything will just prolong the inevitable. I know this means I can't have contact with him. I know it means losing what we have. But I can't put his life in any more danger than it already is. I can't. I won't.

My resolution disintegrates when I see his tear-stained cheeks, and I drop my bag and fall into his arms, wishing the moment would never end. The flash in my cornea throws me off guard, and my body jumps from the fright.

Another memory piggybacks the first. I'm seated on a

long, sterile bench clutching a book, while a handful of other thirteen-year-olds mingle off in the distance. Resentment burrows deeper as my eyes flutter over their faces. No one talks to me or even looks my way, and it's all Saber's fault.

Whatever side effects this vaccine has on us, it clearly reacts differently on me, and they know it. Everyone knows it. If that isn't bad enough, I'm pulled aside for separate tests and given specific privileges, which makes the other kids hate me. I just want it to stop. I want things to go back to the way they were, before these stupid vaccines started giving us these lame side effects.

My vision bursts into color, and the book flies from my grasp, thudding against the wall. I twist my face away from the uncomfortable glances, trying to hide the tears streaking down my face. I've no idea what just happened. I certainly didn't throw the book, yet it slipped from my hands and flew across the room just the same.

"That's a pretty neat trick." The boy's voice startles me, and I repress the scream bursting in my chest.

I grip my body and try to twist away from the voice as I feel his energy slide closer. If he teases me, it's going to take more than a little restraint to keep me from decking him. The thoughts racing through my head make me cringe. I've no idea when this emotional turmoil settled in me, but it's becoming harder and harder to still the rage. Saber seems to think it's just fine, but the other kids keep away from me like I have the plague.

"So..." He clicks his tongue.

I swivel, throwing darts of displeasure at him. "What do you want...?" I pause when I can't recall his name. He's relatively new to the program, as are a few others.

"Lucas," he says, sticking out his hand.

I squint at his gesture.

"You're supposed to take it and tell me your name. But since I already know your name, maybe you can just give me a high five." He twists his palm up and grins, certainly pleased with his wit. "You're going to leave me hanging?" he says, eyes dancing around the room. "Ouch."

I follow his glance to the girls ogling us. I quickly smack his hand as hard as I possibly can without sending him flying backward off the bench. The girls laugh, and a smile tugs at my lips.

Lucas shakes his hand in pain but chuckles. "See, now that wasn't so hard. I'm just glad I didn't ask for a fist bump."

"What do you want, Lucas?" The smile falls from my lips as I sit straight up and stare.

"Nothing. I just wanted to see how you're doing."

I tilt my head sideways and squint, showing my disbelief.

"I'm serious." His eyes flutter to the floor in front of us. "Things have been tough on everyone and... by the look of things..." He lifts his eyes toward mine. "It's been a lot tougher on you."

I watch for any sign of a ruse. Perhaps the others put him up to teasing me, but I find only a sincere boy staring back.

"Why do you care?" My lips say this, but my mind tells me to shut up. I know it would be good to have someone on the inside I can rely on who knows what I'm going through. Someone who understands the frenzy surging through my veins.

"I don't know. Call me stupid, but you're different, and I like that. You aren't just playing the game like these other clones. You're fighting against the vaccine's effects. No one should have to go through this alone." The twinkle in his eye says he's stubborn and will wait until I arrive at the same conclusion.

I need him, maybe as much as he needs me.

My heart flutters.

What is that?

Hope. Hope that maybe, just maybe, I won't feel like this anymore if I have someone to talk with about it.

The grin fills his face, and he turns away. "I know I don't want to do this alone, and if I've read you right, neither do you." His tongue rolls over his lips, wetting the surface. Then his eyes find mine again.

A tingle races from the tips of my toes and rests on my heart. Maybe this will be okay.

Blink.

I'm back in my cell, staring at the rubber green walls.

My heart breaks in two at remembering I had to leave Lucas behind when we escaped Saber Corp. I probably believed I'd never see him again, but when I did, he not only released my intense desire, but also brought forth my anger. No wonder I was warned to stay away. It was for both of our good. I could have killed him.

Curses push over my lips. I hate who I've become, but like Adrien said, there is no way I can go back to normal. I have to find a way to tame these feelings before they all rush to the surface again. That is, if I live to see outside these walls again. I need to find a way out of here.

Glancing around the cell, everything in my being tells me I need to figure out how to manipulate this rubbery material, and fast. Once Adrien knows how to completely duplicate the process my DNA has taken, he won't hesitate in disposing of those who know too much.

The dot matrix pops into my vision, and I stare at the pale-green of the walls. There must be a way to pull something out of these molecules. It seems unlikely I can control everything but them.

Images of splitting molecules flood my thoughts, as if they were search engine results. They scroll so rapidly I can barely comprehend what I'm seeing, but yet, I do. I absorb all the information streaming by my vision, but nothing seems to fit. The images then shift to calculations of the force needed to pry open the material with my bare hands, using telekinetic energy to blast air at the molecules and shove them enough to add my own strength.

Brilliant.

The calculations show I can stretch the material enough

to do almost anything. However, with Big Brother watching through the window, there is no way I can try it out... until tonight.

I sit in the silence of my prison for what seems like hours, planning my escape using the flashbacks and knowledge I procured from the CPU I call my brain. The cold sides of the bullet between my fingers give me an idea. After the next person comes through the door, I will shove the bullet into the door's sliding mechanism. It won't prevent the door from shutting, but it will give me enough space to push air into it and shove the rubber aside. It's a much better plan than injuring someone, which I can't completely wrap my head around yet, regardless of what I've done in the past.

When the door slides open, I jump to my feet, but freeze. It's Adrien, carrying his trusty folder. I carefully run my fingers through my hair and tuck the bullet under the collar of the Saber Corp jumpsuit they've adorned me with.

"What do you want?" I try to keep my voice smooth and even, hiding the anger, distrust, and fear that vibrates my heart. I may be able to do superhuman acts, but this man scares me.

"Now, now, Braidan. Must I have a motive to come see my favorite hybrid?" He holds his arms out in a submissive position, but I can tell he needs something more from me.

I set myself on the cot and twist away from him, fearing my face will give away my resolve.

"I am sorry I have to keep you detained like this, but soon enough you'll be on your way... with your family."

At this, I flip my head around and study his face. His eyes betray him.

"Things are going smoothly in the lab. However, we've hit a little snag." He sits on the cot beside me, and I scoot away. "It seems there are inconsistencies with pieces of your code. While we realize it must still be mutating, they don't match up to any of the old ones we have on file for you." He taps his fingers on his chin. "And, when we test your current samples against what we know, your DNA becomes unstable and collapses." He speaks like I'm a lab rat, not a human. "Do you have any idea why this might be?" His eyes search my face, but I've no idea why he believes I'd know.

"I've got no idea. I'm not the scientist."

He runs his hand over his five o'clock shadow and speaks to the empty air. "See, I don't believe you. Earlier, when I allowed your mom in here, you guys were whispering to each other, and while my microphones didn't pick up everything you said, they did hear a name."

I hold my breath.

"I need to know where he is, Braidan."

"Why would I know where he is?"

Adrien's eyes grow wide briefly before he seems to consider I might be lying. "You don't expect me to believe you've no idea, especially after your little crush on his son."

I can't hold in my gasp as my eyes find his.

"Oh, you didn't think I knew? I know much more than

you can ever imagine. Dr. Bailey was under my payroll."

I clench my jaw, fighting back the surging anger. "No. He was helping me stay away from you."

"Oh, is that what he told you? Hmmm, that's curious. And I'm sure you believe he will bust you out again." A sadistic smile wanders across his face.

Shock registers in my mind, for which I can tell he is pleased. He gives me puppy dog eyes and reaches over to pat my arm, but I swipe it from his touch. "You know the only reason you escaped the first time was so we could see what you'd do in the outside world." He raises his eyebrows as he watches me for understanding.

No. No, it can't be. He's lying. I shake my head, willing him to stop talking, but not trusting my voice to speak.

"Yes, Braidan. It was all part of the arrangement."

My world collapses around me, and I suck in long, strangled breaths as Adrien Saber laughs maniacally.

He rises from the bench as I gasp for air. The exit slides open, and he vanishes.

I don't even have the presence of mind to carry out my plan before the door slams shut, leaving me in my shock.

My mind scrambles to grasp the details spinning out of control. All my thoughts say Saber is lying. I was with Ian when he was running away from Saber, not to them. If he had been a part of them, why did he help me escape? And why then was Michael helping us already?

The room wavers, signaling another flashback. The tremors take over my body, and I'm thrown to the floor, but I don't care. I fight the flashback with everything in me as it rips my heart and soul in two.

Blink.

My steps falter as I draw near an unfamiliar house. The door opens, revealing my parents standing at the opening. I rush toward them, and they take me in their arms.

Michael stands below us on the stoop, wringing his hands. "It's best I be on my way, immediately. I trust McCready has gotten ahold of you?"

"Yes, he's sending someone over today to meet with us and get the situation worked out."

"Very well." He hesitates, glancing at the pavement near his feet. "I hope for your sake, Braidan, that they can hide you better than I could." His eyes flicker with indecision.

James curls his arm around me as he glares at Michael. I'm not sure what happens in the quiet moments, but I feel Dad's pulse rage out of control.

"Thanks for all you've done. I hope we never meet again."

My eyes snap to my dad's face in disbelief. Hasn't Michael done us a favor? Michael nods his understanding and disappears down the walk.

Blink.

My heart skips a beat. Did my dad know Michael was working for Saber?

18

I'm lying on the ground in my cell, roving over the flashback, when a suited man enters.

"Bathroom break." He points his dart gun at my face. I want to shove it down his throat, but it's no use. Three more are waiting behind him.

"I don't need to go." I lie because I don't have the energy to rise. Speculations of what my dad meant flash through my mind and gallop to places I don't want to go.

"Too bad. It's your last chance for the night."

I press my hands against the cold floor and kneel next to my cot. My limbs quiver at the small bit of weight they hold, but I push through the discomfort and straighten myself. He slaps the handcuffs on me and shoves me out the door as soon as I'm stable. Silently and under close guard, we travel down the hall.

He snatches what I realize is a rubber-covered electronic keycard out from under a flap on his suit. The door flings open to reveal a rubberized bathroom, complete with pale-green toilet. They are serious about keeping me here.

He slips off the cuffs and pushes me forward. "Go." Before I can even respond, he slams the door shut.

Scanning the room, I realize they've thought of everything to keep them safe. My eyes wander to the divider near the commode. "Hey!" I turn and whack the door with my palm. "There's no tissue in here!" My voice bounces off the walls in the small bathroom, and I hear the man snicker.

"Drip dry."

"Oh, that's classy."

I growl and reluctantly take care of business, but before I can even attempt to drip dry, the door flings open, and I jump to my feet, yanking my jumpsuit back over my chest.

"Time's up."

I glare and twist away, stretching the stupid suit over one shoulder, then try to get it over the other. Not only did they not intend these for style, but comfort and accessibility definitely went out the design window as well.

"So are you heading to Bill's after shift?" One of the guards' muffled voices carries to my ears.

"Yeah, I think so. Is Trevor going?"

"No, he's got the night watch."

"Who's on post with him?"

"It was supposed to be Felix, but his wife went into labor."

My ears perk up at the conclusion they're drawing for me, and I hesitate, pretending to struggle with the arm of my jumpsuit a little longer.

"Anyone taking over the shift?"

"Nah, nothing happens on night shift. He'll be fine."

The wheels in my head click forward at an alarming pace and settle firmly on a plan.

"Come on. We don't have all night." My babysitter's impatient voice snaps me back to life.

The journey down the hall holds new meaning as I inspect every element of every crevice. Three doors, around seventeen steps between each, and a fourth, being the bathroom. I rub my chin on my shoulder, pretending to itch. The flaps still hang over the cross-examination door at the opposite end of the hall. There were at least three doors in that room, and one of them had been Adrien Saber's entry point, which means a possible exit.

Every minute drags by like a lifetime while I wait for my opportunity, lying as still as I can, pretending to sleep. At some point tonight I will only be guarded by one, rather than four, the reason they made me use the bathroom.

～

It's been at least five hours since I've been back in my cell. If the last meal I ate was around six, the time now must be nearly three in the morning. Time for me to move. Rolling to my back, I flop around, hoping to call attention to my discomfort. Another second or two and I whip around with my feet on the floor and double over as if in pain.

"Excuse me? I need to use the restroom." Standing in front of the window, I cross my legs and bounce slightly.

"I'm sorry. No one is available to take you right now," says the voice over the speaker.

I blow out a long, frustrated, and uncomfortable breath. "How long will I have to wait?" I put my hands on my hips and bend over slightly, feigning distress.

"At least two hours." I hear remorse in his tone.

I groan and flip around, feet thumping against the floor as I pace back and forth across the room, hands still on my hips, making noises expressing serious need. After two minutes, I approach the glass again.

"I really can't hold it any longer. I think it's something I ate."

"It's only been a few minutes. Surely you can hold it longer than that?" There's hope in his voice now, but I can tell he feels sorry for me.

I cross my legs and screech in pain. "I don't think so!" I pull in a strangling breath through my teeth and rush to the back wall. "If you aren't going to let me go, I'll just relieve myself here."

I tug my jumpsuit and barely get it over my shoulder before the voice is back.

"What are you doing?" he gasps. "Don't do that!"

I continue, not caring that my bare skin is being broadcast. "I have to go!" I yell, squatting in the corner.

"Stop! Stop! I'll come take you," he groans, and I hear the speaker click.

I have precious seconds before he enters my cell with his cuffs. I yank my jumpsuit up and cover myself. The bullet rests in my fingers as I stand beside the door, waiting for him to come for me. The door hardly has the chance to open before I'm forcing the air around the bullet and shooting it forward with all the power I can muster. It strikes him in the leg, and he crashes to the ground, gasping in pain.

I kick his hand away from the dart gun, then rip off his hood. The whooshing of air in his lungs calls to me, and I find the dots of oxygen and pull them as hard and fast as I can. He chokes and goes limp. When I release my hold, his lungs inflate, notifying me he's alive. I haven't much time before someone else comes to the control room and sounds the alarm. I drag his body into my cell and remove his suit as swiftly as I can, leaving him in his skivvies.

The suit swims on me, but inside it, I'm anonymous. Hopefully, no one will notice the guard has lost thirty pounds and at least five inches.

My hands tremble as I slide the stolen keycard over the green light on the panel door, sealing the man inside. I've no idea if the tranquilizer gun can even defend me from anyone who figures out I'm not Trevor, but at least I look the part at first glance.

The rubber hall is eerily silent. A quick slide of the card over the first two doors reveals nothing but scientific equipment. I swing open the last door and see file boxes filling the room, stacked to the ceiling. I release the door from my grasp and prepare to move on when the hall light filters over one of the names on the side of the box.

Lucas Tress.

My fingers find the lid, and I flip through the medical records as fast as I can, searching for some clue in the dim light. All I find are a bunch of scientific numbers and garbage that makes no sense. Voices in the hall startle me, and the papers in my hands scatter to the ground. I dart for the door and push it almost closed as the voices grow louder.

"Are you sure that's what he said?"

"Yeah, I asked him twice for confirmation." His voice wavers with anxiety. "He says he has to remove the evidence he was ever linked with the family."

"That's too bad. They seem like nice people."

My heart rages out of control. I want to burst from the room and make these men pay for their knowledge, but of course that won't help my situation.

"When does he want it carried out?" asks the first man as they pass my hiding spot.

"Daybreak."

Fear grips my chest and my throat closes, a panic attack hovering around the edge of my consciousness.

"What about the informant?"

"Who, the boy?"

The nearby door slides open. "Him too. They're all to be disposed of."

As soon as the door clicks shut, I push my way from the closet, leaving the papers on the ground. I have little time before they find out it's not me in the cell.

I race down the hall and dart through the plastic decontamination panels at the end. The key panel blinks green when I swipe the card, and I open it carefully to reveal a long hall with an EXIT sign at the end. Resisting all temptation to dart for it, I tug the door shut. At least outside my rubberized prison the exits are clearly marked.

I shove open the next door and see two more doors at the end of a short hall. The blood races in my veins, and my heart can barely keep the pace I'm thrusting at it. The first door slides open sideways, and when my eyes adjust, my blood freezes, stopping my heart cold.

Drew!

His rest appears peaceful and that makes my anger boil like molten lava. I want to lunge forward, grab him by the collar, and shake sense into him. He is the reason we're all in this mess right now. However, as I watch him lying there, my exasperation melts. I may not remember this boy, but he is my brother.

"Drew." I shake him lightly, trying not to scare him. "Drew, wake up."

He shifts under my grasp and turns, seeming annoyed rather than frightened when he takes in the rubber mask I'm still wearing.

"What?" he says in a dreamy voice. "Is it already morning? What do you need now?"

I tug my hood off so he can see my face.

He reels backward once he realizes it's me kneeling before him. "What are you doing here?" His face fills with unnatural fright.

"Drew, you guys are in danger. You have to help me find Mom, Dad, and Tanner."

He scoots away and yanks the covers to his chin. "How are you here, Braidan? Did you kill more people?"

I feel my forehead crease with irritation. "No, Drew, I'm here to warn you. Regardless of what you've done, I still care about my family."

His lips pucker with displeasure. "Yeah, well Adrien says we'll all be fine once you're taken care of."

"How exactly do you think he's going to take care of me, Drew? Did you think about that?"

His face twitches as he seems to ponder my words.

"Drew they're going to kill us all. Do you realize that?"

He's up on his feet before I can say another word. "Liar! Adrien said we'd all be safe if we came here! He said he'd make me the same as you!" He holds his hands over his ears.

"Drew." I grab his arms and pull them away from his head. "You have to believe me. I just overheard the guards. We haven't much time." Tears well in the corners of his angry eyes. "I don't know what I did to you to make you hate me so much, but I'm sorry. I didn't ask for this. I wish I could go back to how it was before Saber Corp, but I can't. I can't, Drew. I need you to trust me."

Tears tumble down his cheeks as he throws himself at me. I'm about to fight him off when I realize he's wrapping his arms around me. "I'm sorry, Bray." His voice quivers. "I'm so sorry. He... he threatened me. I didn't know what to do. He said we'd be okay. I..."

"What's done is done, Drew. Do you know where Mom and Dad's cell is? Is Tanner with them?"

He wipes his face as he backs up. "Yeah. They're across the compound."

I'm dragging him away before he can even get all the words out. "We have to go. It won't be long until they realize I'm missing."

"How are we going to get through the compound without them seeing us?" His quiet pleas make me want to take him in my arms and comfort him.

I throw the mask over my face. "I'm just escorting you. That's all."

Drew grins. "That's a good idea. You're smart, Bray."

"Come on, kid."

Drew nudges me in the right direction as we come to a fork and pass through several keyed doors before entering a long, dark hall. "The fourth door," he whispers as we pace down the hall. I can't help myself from running. My heart's going to explode if I don't get there. I swipe the card and fling the door open.

Mom jumps and whacks Dad's back, fright registering full in her face, while Tanner sleeps on a small cot at the left. I'm frozen in the entry for a moment, peering into their faces, before Drew pushes his way past. He's darting for Mom's arms almost as soon as he clears me and the doorway.

"I'm sorry," he wails against her.

She calms him, seeming confused why a guard is standing in their room allowing Drew a three a.m. visit.

As soon as I pull my hood off, Dad is on his feet embracing me. "What's going on? How are you here?" He grasps the sides of my face. "Are you okay?"

"Yeah, Dad. I'm fine." I search through the gamut of emotions he's displaying. Love, anxiousness, fear, uncertainty. "You guys have to get out of here. They said at daybreak..." I can't even say it, but he reads it in my eyes.

"How did you get free? Did you...?" He gulps hard, and I realize it's what everyone assumes I've done.

"No, I just injured the guard and knocked him out. I'm sure he'll be fine, but we have to get out of here."

Dad darts for the door. "How long have you been out of your cell?" he asks, checking the hall.

"At least fifteen minutes." I yank off the hazmat suit and toss it in the corner. "Drew and I snuck past the cameras, but there's no way we'll all be able to hide."

"The control room is usually manned by only one person at this time of night," Dad says, motioning for the dart gun while averting his eyes from my face. "If we can take out a couple cameras, we might be able to find a way out from the roof."

My gaze narrows. How could he know this?

Mom shakes Tanner awake. He's groggy, but when his face twists toward me, his eyes widen and he bounds to his feet, crashing into my embrace. "Braidan! I thought I'd never see you again." His words come out in sobs.

"I'll always come back, Squirt." The room goes completely silent with this promise I have no right giving to anyone, let alone my eight-year-old brother.

Dad shifts his glance to Drew, who is obviously fighting his emotions. "We haven't much time before they find you're missing. They have to check in every thirty minutes from every station, otherwise they'll send out security reinforcements as protocol." He waves us forward.

"Dad, how do you know all this?"

He twists toward me, and I see his disappointment, but it's not for me. "I used to work for Adrien Saber."

The weight of his words falls heavy on my heart. This is why they couldn't pull me from the program. Saber had my dad in a deadlock, probably threatening them with death if they tried to run. And when they did... "Dad, Adrien said Michael Bailey was still on his payroll when I was in his care. Is that true?"

"Michael Bailey might not be my favorite person in the world, but you can't believe anything Adrien Saber says. He is a money hungry jerk who has no one's best interest at heart. He will say anything to accomplish his desires. I know. I've lived through it. Now, we've got to go."

Dad motions everyone forward, and we creep through the halls swiftly. He halts us and peeks around a corner. "Camera."

It's my job to take out the visuals. Calling forth my abilities, I sever the wires, thrusting the camera into darkness. We race down the hall, and Dad waves the keycard I've given him over the panel. When it blinks red, my breath catches in my throat. He tries it again. Nothing. Tanner begins to cry, but Dad motions us down the hall to another door.

This one allows us entry, and I breathe again.

The fact Dad knows the facility so well nags at me as we follow him through a maze of doors and climb a flight of stairs. The next door opens easily, and Dad races through but stops so abruptly I run into his back.

My stomach clenches when my eyes drift over his shoulder and focus on the room of two-way mirrors.

I know these mirrors. These rooms. These memories. The flashback strikes as soon as I see a child lying on a cot behind the tinted glass. Only now I'm that child, beating on the window, longing to be free. My face presses against the panes, and I see my father pleading with Adrien. Dad's face is red and blotchy from crying -- begging, gesturing, screaming -- for me.

Blink.

I'm going to puke.

Dad rears around and grabs my arms. "Braidan, I didn't want this for you. You must believe me."

I hold back the bile rising from my stomach. I know he's telling the truth, but if I open my mouth, I may lose it, so I just nod and press back the tears.

"Someone's coming!" Drew hisses, pulling the door closed.

We all scatter, but there's nowhere to go, save the locked rooms with possibly more hybrids trapped inside. Dad moves us to the side so we aren't the first thing they see.

When the door opens, light filters through, silhouetting the marshmallow frame of the man entering the room. The speed of his approach makes my heart jump into my throat. Three rushed steps in and Dad lunges forward, sticking the dart gun into his kidney.

"Don't move or I will blow a hole in you the size of your fist."

He raises his hands, dropping his own dart gun.

"Now, walk to the center of the room." Dad's tone is sheer disgust, as if he'd kill the man, given the chance. "On your knees."

The blob falls to his knees, hands still raised. "Please, I'm here to help." The voice pings in my mind, and I leap forward.

Mom grabs for my arm, but not quick enough. Dad calls to me, but I'm not listening. I rip the hood off, and sobs of joy erupt in the room when I reveal Lucas' face.

I grasp at him, tears falling down my cheeks as he embraces me. "How...? What are you doing here?"

"I came to help you escape," he says so arrogantly I'm not sure if I should slug him or kiss him.

Dad helps Lucas to his feet. "Luke, you have to help me free these kids."

Without hesitation, he darts for the other side of the room, swiping his card over the panel on the door. When it blinks red, my heart plummets to the floor. Dad swipes his and gets the same result.

"Dad, why isn't it working?" I try to keep my tone even, despite my growing anxiety.

"They must have restricted access."

I dash to the window and press my face against the darkened panes. Maybe I imagined the child. Maybe there is no one in there. Maybe they really have given up on this project. Maybe— The thoughts take me captive as my eyes adjust and I see the frail eight-year-old frame of a little girl.

Blink.

I see myself curled up on the same cot. I'm so scared and alone. This man, Adrien, says it's for my safety, but I don't believe him. He's already threatened my parent's lives if I talk about what's going on in the program. Fear radiates through my bones and morphs into intense anger as the scene dissolves.

Blink.

I'm once again pressed against the glass. Panic races through my bones at the thought of the horror these children have endured. Their parents have probably been told they're dead or vice versa. I fight the rage coursing through me like lava. It will do no good here.

Dad and Lucas try every door, but all the panels blink red. I'm frozen in fear, my heart breaking into pieces with every blink of the red light. I count the windows in the room and gasp. Ten. There are ten. Fire breeds in my veins. I glance at Lucas and realize he has reached the same conclusion. Saber Corp is rebirthing the hybrid program using the same serum and the new strings of DNA they extracted from me.

"Dad, we have to get them out." My voice shakes with hysterics.

He runs his hands through his disheveled hair. "I don't think we can, Bray, unless someone goes back into the compound and finds the right access card." He swivels his glance to Lucas, then back to me. "And I don't think that's an option."

I'm about to object when the shortwave radio attached to Lucas' belt buzzes to life. "Check in."

All the stations start responding in order.

"We have to go!" Lucas grabs my hand before I can respond.

The halls blur by as my heart rips from my chest for those children trapped in Saber's clutches. The numbers of the guards checking in tick through the stuffy hall air, and with each one our fate seals a little tighter. Number twelve doesn't respond. The alarm is going to sound any second.

"Sorry. Twelve. All clear."

We race down a flight of stairs, and Lucas pauses at a door panel.

Red again.

My breath catches in my throat.

"Fifteen. All Clear."

Dad swipes his card.

Green.

We release our pent-up breaths.

The radio is silent. We all stare at the machine in Lucas' hand.

"Sixteen?" The voice calls over the radio. We made it just in time.

Dad cracks the door, letting the cold morning air infiltrate the cramped stairwell. "Stay in single file, and whatever you do, if I say run, don't stop running. You got that?" He's frantic as he spits out commands. He waits with his hand up, watching for a clear path.

I yank Lucas back. "We can't leave these kids here. We can't. You know what he's doing to them. You know." My voice is low but anxious.

He grabs me, trying to calm the panic rising in my chest. "I know. I know. Michael is working on something right now."

I gulp back the saliva. "Michael Bailey?"

He nods, his eyes searching mine. I can tell he's holding back something more he needs to say. Before his lips move, I already know the answer to my next question.

"Where's Ian?" My thrumming heart pounds my head, and I barely hear his response.

"Sam's got him. He's in real bad shape. They didn't expect him to live through the night."

"Last call... Sixteen?" Barely three seconds before it buzzes to life again. "Commence lockdown."

"Braidan?" My father's frenzied voice breaks my trance.

I'm so numb I scarcely feel Lucas prod me forward. Tanner, Drew, and Sheila have already darted from the building toward the nearby trees. Dad yanks me forward and slams the door behind me.

The chill in the early morning air buzzes around me, teasing my senses, coaxing me awake. Lucas said Ian was in bad shape, not that he died. He can't die. Ian is a fighter. He will live. He has to live. Tingles of hope shoot through my limbs, bringing every cell to life. I hardly realize I'm moving before I'm entering the tree cover.

Dad stops in his tracks and faces us. "Braidan, you have to go with Lucas."

"What? Why?" The hysteria bursts over my lips. I can't imagine my family's safety without my abilities to help them.

"You have to stop Saber. Go with Lucas. Find Michael. We'll be fine," he says with certainty of their escape. I'm not so sure. "I'll check on Ian."

Lucas tugs on my arms, prying my hands from my father's grasp. "You guys get to safety."

The door bursts open behind us, and Lucas jerks me sideways as dad disappears into the forest. A gunshot blast echoes through the air, and I freeze, ready to turn around and go after my father.

Lucas flips me around as if he's read my mind. "No, Braidan, they'll be fine. McCready is waiting for them at the cross. It was always the plan if they were captured. We have to make Saber Corp follow us, not them, to give them time to make it there."

I suck in an uneasy breath, trying to gather my nerves. "What do we do now?"

The grin that plays across Lucas' face sets my mind to work, and the landscape bursts into dots. I see men creeping around the side of the building toward my family.

"We need a diversion." His words pierce my heart, making the landscape blink in and out. I bite back the pain of the memory of my last diversion and close my eyes, refocusing the ache into energy for the molecules around me.

The computer in my head clicks forward and in two seconds analyzes everything around us. I waste no time ripping through the trees nearby, toppling them onto the guards and providing a barrier for my family. I lift the transformer from the roof and slam it down into the pavement. Sparks erupt in a fireworks display worthy of the Fourth of July.

Another gunshot rings through the air, and I focus on the sound waves. The molecules shift in slow motion as I pull the energy from the bullet, leaving only a hollow metal casing tumbling to the ground at our feet.

"Let's move," Lucas says, tugging my arm.

But I can't. The need for vengeance captures me. These men need to pay for their crimes against the innocent. Against the children. Against their country.

My skin is red hot as I stalk forward, sure I must be glowing from the rage. Men dart in every direction when they see me step into the clearing. They are afraid of me. Good. They should be. I lift my hand and fling anything I can at every living person within my eyesight. Each one goes down with one fell swoop, and I'm pleased.

"Braidan!" Lucas screams from beyond my range of fire, trying to convince me to return to him.

But I can't. The urge to annihilate these men bubbles through me like a pot of boiling water that can't be cooled.

More guards rush around the building and lift their guns to aim. I can't help but laugh as their bullets rocket toward me. With one motion, they're all lifeless. More shots ring from every direction, and I twist and pull the energy from the metal.

A sharp pain pierces my thigh and inches its way up my leg, dissolving the heat rupturing my sanity. I grasp at my leg, and my wits return. More shots ring through the morning air, and instead of pulling their energy, I dodge through space and time, narrowly avoiding them.

Lucas grabs me and hauls me through the bushes, cursing every step of the way.

Pain radiates through my leg, but I press forward as fast as he's pulling me. I hear the men's calls and the newly released dogs tromping through the brush behind us. My mind reels with my murderous actions. A wildfire of rage surged through me, and I could do nothing to stop it.

No. I didn't want to stop it. And that scares me.

I grasp the wound, seeping with blood, and grit my teeth as I run. The throbbing fuels my steps, pushing me faster and faster across the landscape, clipping Lucas' heels.

It's not long before the howling dogs are nearly upon us. We pick our way less carefully and plow through the foliage. Twigs and branches leave painful scratches in their wake, but we continue, pressing through the twilight toward our freedom.

The *whiz* of a car penetrates my ears, and I realize we're nearing a road. Exhilaration and fear mix in my chest as I stumble through the brush, almost slamming my face into an electric fence. My limbs shake, and I question whether I can go a step further.

"Over here!" I jump at the hushed call coming from a new voice.

Seeing my hesitation, Lucas scoops me into his arms and hurries toward the man crouched near the other side of the fence. The man pulls back on a gap of metal, hands covered in thick rubber gloves. Lucas lowers me to the ground, and I fall to my knees, pain shooting through my body. The buzz of electricity raises the hairs on my arm, unnerving me as I press my small frame through the narrow opening.

"Quick!" he commands Lucas, who shimmies through behind me. "Come on. Come on."

Once Lucas is clear, he seals the fence with zip ties and motions for us to move. Lucas picks me up again and scurries down the side of the road. The half-mile or so seems like fifty as we race alongside the scarcely traveled road. Every time a car nears, we dart into the bushes and wait it out. I have this uneasy feeling it will only be minutes before one of the cars is occupied by Adrien Saber.

A satisfied sigh escapes my lips when an empty vehicle at the side of the road comes into view. The man doesn't hesitate to jump in and bring the engine to life while Lucas places me in the backseat. The door barely closes behind him before we're rocketing down the road, away from the danger of Saber Corp.

"What about my parents and brothers. Did they make it?" I grasp the seat in front of me, hoping the stranger has some news.

He waves a small device in his hand, which hisses to life with a crackle. "Update?"

"Package received," he says with a wide grin before throwing the radio back to the seat. "The trackers followed you as planned, and your family has already been picked up by the convoy on the other side of the compound."

I let myself relax against the backseat, then cringe when the slight movement radiates pain through my leg.

"Was she shot?"

"Yeah. I'm afraid she left a trail of blood in her wake."

He shakes his head. "It doesn't matter. My intel tells me they already have what they need from her. They won't worry about a little spilled blood." He reaches over the back of the seat, grabs a backpack from the floor, and hands it to Lucas.

"You need to get that bullet out, posthaste." He peers at me through the rearview mirror. His familiar eyes send chills scurrying up my spine.

"Michael?"

His eyebrows furrow as he seems to be briefly taken aback. "How do you know who I am? Have your memories returned?" He searches my eyes for answers.

I pull in long, labored breaths. "Not all of them. I've had a couple flashbacks…"

Lucas tears my soiled pant leg apart to view the wound. He opens the backpack and reveals medical supplies. From anesthetic to catgut for closing wounds, to gauze, tape, and bandages. When Lucas flops the bag open, the name scribbled on the inside twists like a knife in my stomach.

Ian Bailey.

My eyes flutter to the mirror again, and Michael turns away. This man has risked his life yet again to save me, and his son has done the same. How could I have ever believed

Adrien? My dad was right. He would say anything.

"The bullet is too deep for me to grab," Lucas says, ripping open a gauze pack. "You're going to have to pull it out, Bray."

"What?" I release a shaky breath, debating whether he is serious. "I don't know if I can do that. I..." The wound seeps red, turning my stomach. "I'll pass out."

"No. You can do it," Lucas says, grasping my arms.

Michael clears his throat. "I will talk you through it. Just be slow and deliberate. You need to close any blood vessels or arteries first, so you don't bleed out."

The sigh built up in my chest tumbles over my lips as Lucas draws out a bottle of antiseptic. With a quick twist, he pours the contents over the puncture. My leg burns, and I draw in a sharp breath through my teeth.

"You can do it, Bray," Lucas encourages.

I nod, allowing my mind to wrap around the wound. "The bullet is nestled against my bone."

"That's great news." Michael runs a hand through his hair. "Well, it's good news it didn't fracture the bone, not that it's in your leg. Can you see any burst vessels or fresh blood leaking around it?" He grips the steering wheel so tight his knuckles turn white.

"There's a small trickle of blood just above it, still flowing."

"See if you can seal it off and look for any more," Michael

says with confidence.

Lucas squeezes my hand, and I refocus on my leg.

My lungs fill with the stale air in the car, and I mentally prepare myself for the pain I'm about to endure. I press through the fear and grasp at the fibers in my burst vein, stretching them across each other until they grasp hold and the blood stops.

"I did it." Relief exits my chest, and I want to cry.

Lucas' smile reaches his ears, and Michael lets out a big sigh. "I knew you could. Once you've made sure nothing else is leaking, head for the bullet."

A quick check around my leg shows me the bullet made a clean entry and most of the damage has already clotted.

Lucas squeezes my hand and nods.

I push the pent-up energy from my lungs through my nose and turn my focus to the bullet. When the slightest motion streams a ricochet of pain through me, I know a flashback isn't far behind. I've released everything in hopes of soothing the pain when it strikes me like a lightning bolt.

"Are you okay?" Lucas asks, concern thick in his voice.

"If I do this, I feel like I'm going to have another flashback. It seems they're connected with intense pain or emotion radiating through my body."

"Okay?" he questions, not seeming to understand my fears.

I twist and study him.

"Braidan, all your memories are going to come back now. There's no use being afraid of them."

Tears collect in the corners of my eyes, and I lean my head back against the seat. "I had no idea what I was asking for when I said I wanted to remember. This is all too much," I say, barely loud enough for him to hear.

Lucas pushes the hair away from my face, his touch making me shudder. "It was time."

I tip my head sideways. All the anger, resentment, and fear has melted away leaving only affection.

Michael clears his throat. "Everything will make sense soon. Just concentrate on getting that bullet out." His tone is even and fatherly, but when I look up, he's watching the road, not me.

I close my eyes and allow my mind to roam over my knowledge of Michael and in turn, Ian, wondering if I can call a specific flashback forward or if it will be something random. I want to know more about the Baileys. I want to know how close I'd come with Ian.

Lucas' hand closes around mine again, and I fight back tears. I can't believe Ian's hurt, possibly dying, and I'm holding another boy's hand in the back of his father's car.

A tear dribbles down my cheek as I grasp at any memory, frantic for something. Anything. Ian's face pops into my head in short little clips, bouncing around my mind like a ping pong ball smacked into a seamless room. I fight to catch the picture and gasp when I've caught the edge of it. I coax it forward, but it won't move... yet.

With another piece of my mind, I draw the metal slowly from my body. Pain shoots through my limbs, scrambling my mind, causing me to lose hold of the scene. I struggle against the pressure of the pain and try to call it back. My mind's eye stares into Ian's face, and I fight the writhing trying to take over my trembling body.

Come on. Come on.

As if listening to my command, my mind blinks, and I'm in the back of the same car. Michael's driving. I twist to look at the boy beside me. Ian.

The wind whips our hair around in the summer breeze coming through the windows. His eyes flit to mine, and his deep dimples pull into a sorrowful smile.

I slowly draw the metal from my leg, half my mind focused on the flashback and half on the pain.

"I promise I'll never forget you," I whisper into his neck as I nuzzle closer. "No matter what happens. I can't. You've helped me so much."

His arm rests around my shoulders and tugs me closer. I wrap myself in him as my tears fall. His lips trace the side of my face, and he places his cheek upon mine. "I'll find you," he whispers. "They can't hide you forever. I'll find you." He backs away and stares deep into my eyes.

He means it. He will find me.

Screeching tires shatter my flashback, and I wince at the intense pain radiating from my leg.

Michael yells at the car in front of us and corrects the wheel. "You two okay? That guy came out of nowhere."

I watch the car swerving around the opposite lane in the early morning light as my heart rate slowly returns to normal.

"Stupid drunk," Michael says, focusing on the road again.

I wipe the perspiration from my forehead with the back of my arm. "It's almost out." I lock my jaw and wrap my mind back around the bullet, finally yanking the metal free. It thuds softly on the seat and falls to the floor.

Blood flows freely around the space so I tie up the threads, then focus on my muscle. I weave it tightly over and over again until I'm sure my cells have taken hold. I watch while I heal, marveling at the progress with which my body can accomplish this.

"Is this normal?" I ask when I notice Lucas peering down at my leg.

"Definitely normal for you, but not for the other hybrids."

"So, I really am different from the other hybrids?"

He nods. "Yeah. You're the only one I know of who can do this."

The sound of shattering glass ricochets through the small car, and I duck instinctively, covering my face.

Michael swears and punches the accelerator. "We've got company."

Lucas grabs my arms. "You okay?"

When my head pops up from the back seat, the sickly blue SUV turns my blood to fire. This has to stop.

20

Shots ring through the air, piercing the car windows and bouncing off the metal.

"Why are they shooting as us? Don't they want me alive?" I scream, burrowing my head between my legs.

"They already have what they need, Braidan. You're a security risk now. All of us are," Michael says, still focused on the road, trying to speed away from our pursuers. "Just stay down and hold on."

Lucas pulls me close and leans over, shielding me from the shattered glass. The smash of metal and jerk of the car tells me the SUV has caught up. I shut my eyes, resisting the urge to scream. The burst of dots encircle me, and I realize I don't have to see the vehicle with my eyes to damage it.

The urge to explode the gas tank races through my head, but I fight it. I have to control my emotions. I have to harness the power throbbing through me. I clench my jaw and tighten my muscles, fighting against the riptide in my soul.

The screech of tires travels through the small car as my

body flies forward to the left.

Tires.

With quick focus, I yank off the hubcap and begin to work on the SUV's front tire lug nuts. Because they're pure alloy it would take too long to melt them, so I resort to untwisting each nut. The first one shakes free and tumbles to the asphalt, sending euphoria surging through me.

When the final nut falls off, I expect something to happen, but the SUV doesn't even seem fazed by the missing parts. My mind clicks forward and weighs the physics of my actions. I see the speeding tire and the centrifugal force keeping it attached. But with one quick jerk of the wheel, the tire twists free.

"Michael, make a quick turn to the right!" I say, pushing Lucas off.

"No, stay down," Lucas says, struggling against me.

"No, just do it!" I shriek, prying myself from his grasp. I rest my hands on the door and seat, ready for the force of the turn as I watch the tire wobble. "NOW!"

Michael yanks the wheel to the right, down a small road.

I sit straight up and watch as the SUV repeats the action, hoping it can follow. The force sends the tire spinning from the vehicle, and the SUV flips several times before coming to rest in a dusty cloud.

Lucas and Michael both laugh. "Good job, Braidan." Michael is obviously pleased.

We drive well into mid-morning before I feel the car slow. Lucas shifts in his sleep and leans against the door as I push myself up to peer at our surroundings. Large wind turbines twist through the air, pushed by unseen forces. Fields of vineyards flank either side of the road and signs for Napa Valley plaster every billboard

"Why are we in Napa?" I ask Michael when his eyes swivel to mine.

"Safe house." He turns left up a dirt road.

"Safe house? How did you know you'd need a safe house?"

"When you work for someone like Saber on a project where people are dying, you have to have a failsafe. This is it." He stares at me through the mirror, his expression equal parts relief and sorrow.

"Michael, thank you for coming after us." I'm unsure how to express my gratitude.

"I felt somewhat responsible for your predicament, so it's the least I could do."

"How are you responsible?"

"It was with a breakthrough of mine that this whole program began." His hands knead the steering wheel, and he releases a labored sigh. "I felt I should keep my findings to myself, but I was a man full of pride. I wanted to be recognized for my achievements."

The road narrows and leads us into a mass of tree cover,

shrouding the car in darkness. The cool cocoons around us, and a chill scurries up my spine.

"Have you heard any news about Ian?"

He looks away. "No news yet."

"I'm sorry."

"Braidan, Ian would have done anything to save your life. He knew the chances you two would ever be together again were slim to none. He also knew you couldn't fall into the wrong hands."

Tears well as he speaks, and all I can do is nod.

"You can't feel guilty about what happened." His eyes find mine now. "He would've defended you to the death. What he did saved not only your life but dozens of others. And you never know. He could pull out of this in top shape. He's a strong boy."

I nod, gulping back the enormity of his words. "Saber has more kids in his lab."

"I know, Braidan, and before this is over, we will stop him from doing this to anyone else." He offers an encouraging nod as Ian's words from the park wrestle in my head, colliding with contradictions.

"Was Ian the first hybrid?"

He nods at my question, still deep in thought. "I found the first anomaly in his blood quite by accident. He was a pretty normal child, with no real markers to indicate I should even consider him as a test subject. I wouldn't have even bothered to check for the extra strands of DNA had he not insisted on being tested at age eight. He wanted to feel like part of my work, and when his blood came back a match, it opened up a new alley for us. Then, coupled with the case studies released regarding the reactivation of junk DNA, he became a valid subject for us to try the vaccines on."

"So the vaccine Saber was shooting into all of us reactivates these dormant or junk DNA?"

Michael nods. "At first, it just made Ian smarter and more skilled at whatever he put his mind to. We'd allow him an instruction hour, and at the end of it he'd have the skill almost completely mastered. Saber really got behind this and was going to try and sell it along with all of our research, but he wanted to do a blind test first on another group of more normal individuals. He picked a town with the most children per capita with the extra strands and began to add our hybrid-vaccine to a common childhood vaccine. When it worked, Saber believed he would be a millionaire."

The road winds upward, and Michael shifts the car into overdrive as we pick our way up the rocky mountain slope.

"But Saber couldn't settle for the millions he would be able to make, could he?"

Michael shakes his head. "I tried to press him for FDA approval before our next round of tests, but he was too greedy. It wasn't long after he hired a team of new scientists that we discovered if we mutated the vaccine first it caused unchartable results in our tests. Not only would the vaccine activate the dormant strands, but it would hyper-stimulate them to affect everything in the host's cells, mutating them into something completely new."

I study his face in the mirror as he grimaces.

"This in itself was a fascinating find, but when we injected the mutated vaccine into a living host, the results were devastating." He fights the tremor in his voice. "The hybrid died a horrifyingly tragic death, but Saber played it off as an accident. He was so hungry for more." His eyes trail off into the distance as a large cabin comes into view. "At that point his lust for power and money overtook him. He would do anything and everything to make this new serum work in a host."

"That's why he was collecting our blood, wasn't it? So he could test on it without losing us?"

He nods. "However, when he got the results he wanted from blood samples, he began to test on live hosts again." Michael's eyes grow dark. "I've lost count as to how many children were sacrificed for his greed. It wasn't long before the investigations began and he couldn't afford to have our findings come to light."

"That's when he faked our deaths, isn't it."

Michael nods as he pulls past the abandoned house and heads into the covered shelter where a dusty old truck sits in the other spot. "I pulled out of the program soon after finding out what he'd planned for you children."

"What was his plan?"

Michael puts the car in park and turns off the engine, turning his body in the seat to look at me square in the face.

"He was sacrificing you all, one by one."

"When they injected me with the mutated serum on the plane, I was their last hope, they said."

He lifts an eyebrow as he considers me, then nods. "Indeed, you were the last hope for this project. The others either died from the procedure or there was no change to their DNA strands within the blood studies." He glances at Lucas, then back to me. "If it didn't work on you, they were out of options."

I consider Lucas. "He's had the extra vaccine?"

Michael nods. "Everyone in the program has."

"Why was I the last?"

"Saber knew you were different. When the readings came back on your code, they were different, but we couldn't figure out why. He wasn't willing to sacrifice you yet. He wanted to make sure he tried everything first."

"Why on the plane?"

"After another child died, I told him this was enough and I was calling the FDA. I should have made provisions for you first, because in that same hour he vanished with you in tow."

"I've only had a flashback of the moments after it worked. What happened at that point?"

He chuckles and wipes his hand over his face. "You were pissed and rightly so. You attacked the Saber Corp Labs, where the remaining hybrids were being kept, and released them. Each of the parents was then warned that if they didn't put their kids in hiding, Saber would come after them."

I draw in a deep, shaky breath. "What I don't understand is if Saber had your research and knew the children with the extra strands would react that way, and those with mine would react the way I have, why was he searching for me or any of the others? Why not just inject more children and create new ones?"

Michael's eyebrows bob up and down. "Problem is, I may have fudged a few codes before I left, so he wasn't able to replicate the vaccine without the information here." He taps his temple and grins. "What he has now is very closely linked to a common flu vaccine."

The laugh emerges, startling Lucas upright.

"What's going on?" He rubs his eyes and grabs the back of the seat. "Where are we?"

"Safe house." I tug the handle and step into the crisp air.

Michael sticks the key in the door and turns the knob. He draws out a gun from the cargo pocket of his pants and checks the clip. "Stay here while I sweep the house."

Lucas curls his arm protectively around me as Michael disappears. I don't dare speak a word.

Butterflies tumble through me until Michael pokes his head back out. "All clear. Traps have been dismantled, and no one has been here since I left."

The cabin is large and decorated like a hunter's vacation home. The heads of every type of creature are mounted to all the walls, and cobwebs cover everything, along with half an inch of dust. Michael shows us around as we follow.

"So what happens now?" I lean on the kitchen counter while Michael forges through his pantry, checking the contents of the cupboards.

"We wait for word from McCready."

"What? We can't wait. Saber has those kids. He's going to move and hide them. He has to know we've seen the rooms."

Michael pats down the air around us as Lucas rests his hand on my back. "It shouldn't be long, and besides," Michael says, pushing the pantry shut, "I have an insider who will notify me of their location if they're moved. But I have it on good authority the FBI is watching Adrien like a hawk. If he attempts to move a bus full of children, someone will see, so his hands are tied right now."

He shifts his glance to Lucas and clears his throat. "None of the food here is edible. I have to run back into town. Braidan, there are clean towels in the hall closet along with some of your old shoes and clothes you left behind. Why don't you get in the shower and try to rest. We need to be ready at all times to move," he says, motioning for Lucas to tag along. "Do you know how to use a nine millimeter?"

Lucas nods.

I follow them into the living room, and Michael heads to the cabinet. He punches in the code, and the lock clicks open. A quick pull reveals an arsenal of guns. Michael tugs one from the confines and slams a clip into place with the heel of his hand. He checks the safety, then offers it to Lucas.

"Shoot first, ask questions later. When I come back, I'll knock on the front door but come to the side. Under no circumstances open the front door for anyone. Not even me. Got it?" He looks between Lucas and I, then grabs another ammunition clip and hands it to Lucas. "Just in case."

The knot in my stomach twists as he shuts the case and locks it again.

"If I'm not back in forty minutes, consider this safe house compromised. There's a jeep up the mountain with a key hidden in the wheel of the rear passenger side." The way he looks at Lucas makes the butterflies turn to worms as they weave in and out of my gut.

Lucas nods and tucks the gun in the back of his jeans. "Where's the rendezvous point if something goes wrong?"

Michael flips a card from his pocket and hands it to Lucas. "McCready will be available at that number tomorrow at fourteen hundred on the dot. If we miss the window, we'll have to wait for two more days, same time."

I grasp Michael's sleeve as he turns to go. "You sound like you think you aren't coming back."

Michael looks down at my hand. "Braidan, we're playing a different game now. We've got to plan for the worst, because we've got no idea what will happen five minutes from now. We've got to be prepared for all phases."

My hand looses his shirt, and he darts for the door. "Thirty minutes," he says, and seals us inside.

The hot water filters over my sore muscles, and my hands find the wound on my leg, now only a small white mark on my skin. Even as I stare at it, the pigment changes, blending with the rest of my body.

Tears come from nowhere, and I let them fall, thinking about everything the past forty-eight hours has afforded me. My memories will return, and with them, anger and resentment toward the man who reactivated my dormant strands of DNA. I have to find a way to control the surging rage, otherwise I will be my own worst nightmare.

My thoughts linger over Ian and the urgency of his lips on mine. He knew he might not ever get the chance to kiss me again, and that realization stung. The boy cared about me so much he was willing to be killed protecting me, and I'm the one that must live with the guilt of his actions. Because I'm alive, he's seriously injured or even dead.

The fester in my veins fuels the hot tears streaking down my face. I resist the urge to blast from the bathroom, take to the road, and find Adrien to make him pay. I grasp the wall on either side of the faucet and lean into the water, allowing it to batter my face with hot prickles. The fury simmers, but I channel it forward into the water, bringing the wrath upon myself. I grit my teeth and endure the pain due me. The pain I deserve.

If I weren't alive, Ian would be fine. If I weren't alive, Lucas wouldn't be in danger. Michael wouldn't be running for his life. And my family... my family would be living a somewhat normal life outside the hands of Saber Corp.

The idea hits me like a ton of bricks dropped off a building, and I stumble back into the wall. I have to save everyone in my life from hurting on my behalf. The tears come fresh, but I know it's what I should do. No. It's what I must do.

The terrycloth towel wraps around my body, offering false protection for my sanity. No one can protect me. It's foolish to think they could even try. I'm slipping into my socks when the soft knock on the door startles me.

Without waiting for an answer, Lucas pushes through. "How are you feeling?"

I shrug, staring at the floor. I don't want him to see the resolve in my eyes. My heart quickens in my chest as he sits on the bed and lays the gun on the nightstand.

"I need you to understand something, Braidan." He pulls his leg up on the bed, one foot still on the floor. "Whatever is going on in that head of yours, you've shared with me before. The feelings you have. The rage. I know it's there, and I know what it's telling you to do."

I chance a glimpse and see him staring at the space between his legs, not at me.

"You used to share everything with me before..." His eyes meet mine, and I see the pain he's trying to hide. "I know Ian means something to you. I accept that. I wasn't around, and he took a piece of your heart. I know he will always have it."

The tear slips down my cheek unchecked.

"But, I love you, Braidan. I've never stopped loving you. Even when we were apart, I loved you." He lifts his hand and wipes a tear with his thumb, his hand remaining on my cheek. "I don't want to replace Ian, but I want to reclaim the part of your heart that belonged to me once. I want it to be mine again." His thumb traces my jawbone.

I cover his hand with mine and twist my face into his palm. When my lips brush his skin, tingles explode over my body, and I pinch my eyes shut, wishing for the feeling to leave. But it doesn't. My lips find his as quickly as my body will move. I'm as frantic for him as he is for me. He rolls over on the bed, our lips never parting, and lies beside me, cradling my head. The hunger bursts from my body, and I grasp for him, eager to welcome him back into my life. To smother this guilt that has overtaken me.

He pulls back, his breath coming in quick, ragged pants. His eyes search mine as I play with the back of his hair, trying to tug him forward to me again. "I don't want to rush things," he says, but I can tell by his body language that he longs to move forward and remind me of his love.

"I want to remember, Lucas. Help me remember." I pull, and he eases forward, eyes moving from my lips to my eyes again.

"Braidan, we've never..." He squints as he chooses his words. "We decided to save that for our wedding night." His eyes twinkle when the words tumble out with much more remorse than needed.

The grin plays across my lips as the thought formulates in my throat. "And whose idea was that?"

He takes my hand from behind his neck and places a kiss on every finger. "It was ours." He places my hand on his cheek and closes his eyes, twisting his own face to place kisses on my palm. He draws in a deep, unsteady breath, and when he opens his eyes, his smile melts my heart.

While Ian may hold a piece of me, this is the boy I love.

A knock on the front door echoes through the house, and the blood freezes in my veins.

Lucas curses, jumps from the bed, and grabs the gun. He checks the chamber and motions for me to follow.

Another knock bounces through the living room, then slow deliberate steps resonate across the porch and around the side of the house. Lucas clicks off the safety, raises the gun, and aims at the door, his finger on the trigger, as I watch over his shoulder in complete panic. My mind bursts into dots as the back door jiggles. A man holds a paper grocery sack. I grab Lucas' arm so he lowers the gun, but only enough to watch the face coming through.

Michael pushes the door open and deadbolts it behind him. "Uneventful thirty-four minutes?"

I grin behind Lucas' back as he clicks the gun's safety.

"Why did you knock twice? I could have shot you," Lucas asks, sitting at the stool at the counter.

"I wanted to make sure you heard me if you were otherwise occupied." He glances from Lucas to me in a flash.

Heat creeps up my neck as I sit beside Lucas on the stool. Did he know something might happen while he was gone? The thought sends the butterflies scrambling for cover.

Michael draws out red boxes of processed food, setting them on the counter. "When you're hungry, these are our choices. I bought the corner store out of them. Hopefully they aren't expired." He flips one over and checks the date, then reaches into the brown paper bag again. When he sets the instant oatmeal and package of brown sugar on the counter, I can't help but smile. "You still like oatmeal, Bray?"

I pull in a deep cleansing breath. "I think so. Thanks, Michael."

He nods and turns his attention toward Lucas. "Why don't you head for the shower, and I'll keep watch. Braidan, you need to eat something and go rest." His tone is fatherly again, twisting my heart in my chest.

"Is there something you're not telling me about why I should be resting?"

Michael averts his glance to Lucas, who's leaving the

room. "It's just a good idea."

I can tell by Lucas' body language he agrees.

"Michael, what were we training for when I was with you?" I ask when we're seated at the counter with our black, plastic trays steaming in front of us.

Michael pushes his food around the tray before clearing his throat. "We were exploring the limits of your telekinetic abilities."

"My parents sent me to you so I could explore my abilities?"

He jabs his fork into the brownie in the small cup. "They sent you to me to help you prepare for when Saber Corp found you." He sticks the brownie in his mouth.

"When, not if."

He nods.

"So what's wrong with me, Michael? Why do I have these fitful surges of anger pulsating through me at the drop of a hat?"

"Only anger?" His eyebrow rises to his hairline.

I slam my fist to the counter. "Every emotion feels out of control at one point or another. One minute I want to rip someone's face off and the next..." I've been too blunt, and his face shows it. "I just want to know how to control it."

"Well, we were controlling them pretty flawlessly with the amalgam."

"Only you turned me into the walking dead, with no memory of my yesterdays. How was that decided as the best option?" I refuse to hide the disappointment oozing through my words. "I mean how can that even have been an option?"

Michael sets his fork on his tray and presses his fingers together in front of him. "Braidan, what I'm about to tell you may come as more of a shock than you can imagine, but if your memories return, the shock of finding out that way might be greater than it is now."

My heartbeat thrums in my ears, and I have to will my pulse to quiet so I can hear his words. "What did I do?"

His lips are a fine line of worry. "In one of your moments of rage, you took an innocent life."

Acid creeps up my esophagus, and Drew's words assault my mind. 'Did you kill more people?' I cover my mouth and shake my head. "No." The word barely rasps over my lips as the feeling of loss rockets through me. "I couldn't have I didn't. No."

Michael's heavy arm is now on my back as he prepares to deliver what will surely be a blow to my soul. "You had a sister."

22

Blink.

The flashback starts before I even realize I'm in it. A series of emotions take over my mind as I storm through the house. I don't feel in control of anything, but neither am I frightened. I embrace my feelings and race through each room, searching for a place to hide. Luckily, my family is at Drew's soccer game, so they won't experience the fracture in my soul. I don't know what has come over me, but I am angry.

So angry.

I want to hide myself away until the fury passes. It's getting hard to hide now that I'm home again, but the things Saber Corp did to us make me fume. He shouldn't be able to get away with it. He shouldn't.

I find myself in the kitchen, ripping through the cupboards, looking for something to take my frustrations out on. I catch my reflection in the toaster and curse at the blonde chunk of hair reflecting back, a reminder of what I am. I slide the toaster across the counter, and it crashes to the floor. I grab open a drawer, then slam it shut as hard as I can. A knife topples from the butcher block in front of me.

Panic gushes through me as I finger the black handle and run the sharp steel blade over the tip of my finger. I barely wince at the red dribbling from the slice. Instead, I concentrate on the fibers and pull the skin back together, fury still seething through my veins.

Creak.

I jump and flip around, flinging the knife at what should be Saber Corp. Only it's not Saber Corp, and when I register the face in front of me, I scream. It's my own.

The girl topples sideways with a look of terror as she attempts to pull the knife from her chest. I run and take her in my arms. Blood spills all over my hands and the floor.

The scream from the front door makes me look up to see Sheila and James standing horrified in the opening. Sheila collapses to the floor, grabbing a young Tanner to her chest. Drew stands behind them, face wrought with disbelief.

Blink.

Michael has me in his arms, comforting my sobs.

"It's not your fault, Braidan. It's mine. If you want to blame someone, blame me." Tears of his own tumble from his cheeks. "I'm a greedy man. I should have never created the program."

I release a loud, visceral scream and fling my arms at him, wishing him dead. Wishing I could erase every flashback I've seen. The tears come harder as I realize that even if I couldn't remember, they would still be true. I relax and let the intense sobs break through my body.

Michael has hold of my wrists and pulls me into his embrace. "It's not your fault, Braidan. It's not. It's not your fault. I'll fix this." He strokes my hair as he holds me, trying to comfort a murderer.

~

I wake, tucked into the same bed where Lucas and I shared our embrace. It's dark outside. My face feels puffy from crying most of the day and into the night. I feel spent, and when I rise to use the bathroom, I have to steady myself with the wall.

I don't deserve Michael's help. He risked his life for me on more than one occasion. All for a murderer. Does Lucas know what a horrible person I am? Surely he doesn't know. He wouldn't stay with me if he knew. He would—

The chair in the corner of the room squeaks. I flip around and see Michael, shotgun across his lap, his eyes fixed on mine. "Don't you get any crazy ideas about leaving," he says softly, like he's been reading my mind. "We are going to fix this."

I wrap my arms around my wary body. "I don't deserve this kindness, Michael. What I've done--"

He stops me when he stands. "What you did was an accident. And it killed you every waking moment of your life.

It was me that got you into this mess. It is me that is going to find a way out. I promise you, Braidan O'Donnell, I will fix this. No one will live with this pain anymore." He's standing in front of me now, his eyes trained on mine. "Everything will be better soon, Braidan. For everyone. I swear it."

I force myself to nod. I have no idea why I can't believe him, but I can't. How can any of this ever be fixed?

"Listen, I'm going to get Lucas. He has the next watch while I sleep for a few. Are you going to be okay for now?"

I nod.

"Try to rest." The words float over his shoulder as he leaves the room.

I'm just laying my head on the pillow when a very groggy Lucas steps through the door.

"What did I miss?" He sits on the bed next to me and pushes a lock of hair from my face. When his eyes rest on mine, I know he can tell I'm wrestling to understand.

"Do you know?" I ask, staring straight into his eyes through the dim light filtering from the bathroom. "Do you know what I did?"

He nods, still fingering the lock of hair.

I shake my head as a tear slips down my cheek onto the pillow. "I understand why they drugged me. I probably welcomed it."

Lucas presses back another lock of hair and traces my jaw with his finger.

"I probably begged for it."

He pulls in a deep breath and nods. "I don't think you were opposed, no."

"I saw the flashback." My voice shakes. "She was my twin, wasn't she?"

He nods.

"But she wasn't in the hybrid program, was she?"

He shakes his head and seems to consider his next words carefully. "Braidan, we're all twins. The anomaly is only in identical twins. Though they should be exact replicas, one of the twins has extra DNA strands lying dormant in a few chromosomes."

"Ian was a twin?"

He nods. "His twin and their mom died in a car accident when he was younger, which left Michael as a widower committed to science and raising his only son."

"How do you know all this? I thought you didn't know Ian or Michael."

He sighs. "When Ian got worse, I knew I needed to find his father, so I dialed the last number called on your phone, and it was Michael. It's proven to be valuable to have him on our side. I don't think I could have gotten into Saber Corp without his intel. And I certainly wouldn't have been able to get us to safety. I owe him my life... and yours."

I push out a slow, steady breath and move my hand under the pillow. "He blames himself for all this."

Lucas nods. "I know he does."

I'm quiet for a long time as I consider my next words, wondering how to formulate my need for help. "Lucas?"

"Hmm?"

"Have I ever asked you to help me figure out this emotional turmoil before?"

"No. You always claimed you could do it on your own."

I twist to my back, and his hand traces down my arm. "I can't do it alone. I'm afraid of myself and what I'm capable of. What I felt back at Saber Corp was monstrous. What I experienced in my flashbacks is uncontrollable. I don't want to feel that anymore."

"I know, Braidan. I know. Michael told me last night he's been working on a new serum that targets the emotional part of one of the strands. He thinks he might be able to deactivate the one causing all this."

Anticipation quivers in my heart with the first glimmer of hope I've had in days. "Do you really think it's possible, Lucas?" Relief washes over me, and I allow my eyes to flutter closed.

"Anything is possible, Braidan. Now rest. I'll be here when you wake." He places a kiss on my head, and I feel him rise and take his place in the chair.

I will sleep. I need my rest.

25

I feel a poke, and my eyes open to the face of Lucas

"Wake up, princess," he says, poking me again. "Your porridge awaits."

The night's terrors aren't lost on me as I get ready to face the day. However, the hope of what might be waves through me as I stand at the counter in front of Michael.

"Lucas tells me he let you in on the plan," he says, spooning some brown sugar into his bowl of oats.

"Yeah. Do you think it will work?" I rip open the oatmeal packet and dump it into my bowl.

"It's worth a shot. I don't believe it will take away your memories, but it might deactivate some of those troublesome traits."

I turn on the faucet and add water to my bowl. "Will it deactivate all of the extra traits?" I place the bowl in the microwave and spin on my heels when I notice the room is silent.

Lucas and Michael are staring at each other and turn to me when they realize I'm looking between them.

"Thing is, I don't know. I've not had anything to test it on. My prelims came back with deactivated strands, but they weren't used on living hosts." He pushes his oats around the bowl and glances up at Lucas, who is staring at his own bowl. "Braidan, the serum is risky, just as the others have been. Your life could be endangered when we inject you with it."

"It's worth a shot though, right?" I ignore the beeping microwave behind me. "I mean what's the worst that can happen?"

"You could die," Lucas says through clenched jaws.

Michael stares at his bowl.

I gulp back the breath I'm holding. "If I die, it's meant to be."

Lucas jumps to his feet, and a string of profanities tumbles from his lips. "You better hope to God she doesn't die, because I will personally take it out on you!" he screams with his finger in Michael's face.

"Just stop!" I yank open the microwave to cease the infernal beeping. Aggravation pokes at my mind, and I want to throw the bowl of oatmeal across the room. "It's worth a shot." I glare at Lucas, daring him to contradict me.

His eyes narrow as he grabs the gun beside his bowl and storms from the room.

"It's worth a shot, Michael. It is. I can't live my life like this."

"I know, Braidan. And for the world's sake, I hope this works."

The hike up the mountainside is steep, but Michael picks through the underbrush, following some unseen path. Once we're in the jeep, instead of going down, he takes the high road and switches into four-wheel drive, powering further up the mountain. The rocky terrain makes my head nearly smack the roll bar several times before he turns off the road and heads straight up through the trees. I grip the metal rod to my right and am tempted to ask him if he's lost his mind until I see the lightly worn path in the brush.

We hit the top, and the trees open up, and we travel across the mountain ridge. The early morning light peeks over the horizon, illuminating the vineyards below and casting a warm glow over the land. The turbines I saw yesterday barely turn in the still morning air. Over the valley to our left, several brightly colored hot air balloons lift into the sky. Serenity passes over me like a cloud encompassing a full moon. Whatever happens today, it will be all right. I will be okay.

The trees obscure our view of the valley again as we head down the opposite side of the mountain. We drive only another minute or two before Michael slows and a small building comes into view.

"Where are we?" The anticipation in my body makes my voice squeak. Lucas grabs my hand.

"My lab," he says, allowing the grin to play across his face.

"It's not big, but it works for sensitive research. Only one road in." He points back behind us. "And I can see who's coming from a mile away."

I twist my head back and see the dirt road through the trees across the top of the mountain.

Michael uses the biometric control panel on the side of the door to scan his entire hand. The lock plays a series of tunes before he twists the knob. The lights flicker on at his command and reveal a complex lab filled with scientific equipment and DNA charts plastered in every available space on the walls. Each chart has handwritten notes and pictures of people I know I should recognize but don't.

Ian's picture pierces my heart, and I turn away, taking in the rest of the lab. Test tubes, beakers, bottles, and microscopes sit neatly on the backs of every counter and in every glass-covered cupboard. Affixed to the far wall is a large, clean whiteboard with every color of dry erase marker. If the whole lab wasn't clear of dust, I'd think it hasn't been used for months. But as I run my hand across the counter, it's smooth, as if it were wiped moments before we entered.

Michael brings the computer to life with only his voice. "Wake. Pull up data for hybrid-mutation 443206."

The number jogs around in my head, and I quickly realize it's mine. "You have my number memorized?"

"I have everyone's memorized."

"Morning, Dr. Bailey. Retrieving data now."

The whiteboard on the far wall blinks to life, and black

text scrolls across it, along with charts and other numerical data. Michael sets to work, reading the numbers and sifting through the charts.

Lucas reaches for my arm, causing me to turn. My eyes land on a gurney on the opposite wall, complete with thick straps to hold its captor steady. Lucas' trembling tells me he has the same unpleasant memories as I recall about such a contraption.

I suck back a breath, calming my nerves. Things will change this day. They have to change.

Michael walks to the wall nearest the centrifuge and opens a cupboard, revealing a black fireproof safe. He opens it with a few button clicks and another voice command. The contents of the safe are only one syringe, which he draws out carefully. He walks to the centrifuge and inserts the vial before setting it in motion. He turns and pushes his glasses to the top of his head.

"I need to start an IV. In the past, our test subjects responded more fitfully when it was injected directly into their blood stream instead of a large muscle group. This also might help us cut off a bad reaction," he says, glancing at Lucas, "should something go wrong."

I nod as he lifts his hand and points at the gurney.

"I hope you understand why we'll need to strap you down."

I sit on the sheeted stretcher and nod again.

Lucas sits in a nearby chair and scoops my hand into his,

reassuring me he won't allow anything bad to happen.

With a quick pinch, the catheter is in my vein. Michael hooks a bag of saline to the nearby pole and asks me to lie down, which I do without hesitation. I want to get this over with. The rip of Velcro grates on my nerves as he opens the bindings and slips my hands in them. Another large strap drapes over my chest and presses down, giving me a sense of security rather than despair. Several more bind my legs and ankles. The last secures my head to the board before Michael turns for the vial.

"You don't have to do this," Lucas says, leaning over to peer into my eyes. "We can figure something else out."

"I have to do this, Lucas."

Michael is at our side again, and he's gloved, syringe in his hand pointed up. He lets out a long, almost cumbersome sigh and looks into my face. "You ready?"

I don't like the way he says it, but he's probably as nervous as we are. I bite the edge of my lip and take in Lucas' face, marred with sheer terror.

"I love you, Braidan O'Donnell. Don't leave me."

My eyes dart to Michael, who has turned away. I want to tell Lucas I love him. I want to tell him I'm doing this not only for me, but for him. But the words fight on my tongue, knowing they will pierce Michael, and I just can't do that.

Michael's eyes meet mine, and I see the tears collecting there. I nod and shift to Lucas, begging him to read my mind. To know I love him too.

Blink.

The flashback hits almost as soon as the serum enters my veins. I'm in Michael's house. I've just come in from outside and am getting a soda from the refrigerator. I'm just about to pop open the top when I hear a muffled voice from down the hall. My feet carry me toward the voice, thinking Michael called me. I freeze at the conversation.

"No. I'm trying to see what her capabilities are. Her parents believe I'm training her in case she's ever found." There's a pause, and I vaguely hear the squawk of the other person on the line. "Nothing we didn't already know, though her rage seems to be quelled when her attention is diverted, which works out well since she's hit it off with my son, Ian." Another long pause.

"No, I can't let her fall into Saber's hands. I'd rather end her life than let that happen. Yeah, I think I'll track all the remnants of the program down. I've always maintained that if I can't stop Saber, I can take away his toys. Yeah, even the ones who don't have the mutated genes. We can't risk this information falling into the wrong hands."

My breath catches in my throat as I step backwards, away from the hall. I bump the end table, toppling the lamp, and hear Michael say he's got to go. The lamp crashes to the floor, and I'm picking up the broken pieces when Michael shuffles into the room.

"What happened here?" He sounds angrier than I've ever heard him, and I don't dare look up.

"I was rushing to the bathroom and bumped into it. I'm

sorry, Michael."

He kneels on the floor next to me and grabs my hand. "Don't worry about it, Braidan, it's only a lamp."

I hesitate, staring at the hand over mine, before I sit back on my heels, slipping myself from his grasp. My eyes flit to his and see a genuine smile on his face, much like my father's. Hurt thumps in my veins. I need to leave the room before my fears betray me.

Blink.

Back in Michael's secret lab, my body quivers. Fire tracks rapidly up my arm, and my cells rebel, fighting the concoction. Lucas is holding my hand, and Michael is standing over me, slowly injecting the serum into my body.

He's killing me. He's afraid Saber is going to find me, and he is going to kill me. And he'll possibly kill Lucas next. A scream builds in my chest, but as I open my mouth Michael sticks a bite stick between my jaws.

"It's okay, Braidan," he says, running his hand over my forehead. "It's almost over. All this pain. It's almost over."

I thrust my tongue against the bite stick and try to push it out of my mouth, but my jaws clench, locking it in place. I feel my cells fighting against the concoction he's injected into my veins, and I'm certain it's going to kill me.

Michael's face twitches as he stares at me. I see the pain in his actions but also his resolve. The lab bursts into dots, and the idea slams into me like a freight train as my body fights the tremors. I wrap my mind around the red dry erase

246

marker, and it flies across the board as I scrawl words in the blank spaces for Lucas to read.

H-E-I-S-K-I-L-L-I-N-G-M-E.

When the last letter forms, I release my mind, and the marker drops to the ground.

Both of them turn to see what made the noise. Lucas twists back around to me, his eyes telling me he didn't read the board, but when Michael's face focuses on mine, I know he's seen it. He plunges the syringe, releasing what remains of the serum.

"Watch her carefully now," he tells Lucas.

My body shakes more violently, and Lucas grips my hand, squeezing it in short pulses. I realize he's speaking to me in Morse code.

Are you okay?

My mind clicks forward, and I squeeze his palm, hoping to get out the message before it's too late.

Dot. Dot. Dot. Dot.

Dot.

Dot. Dot.

Dot. Dot. Dot.

Dash. Dot. Dash.

Dot. Dot.

Dot. Dash. Dot. Dot.

Dot. Dash. Dot. Dot.

Dot. Dot.

Dash. Dot.

Dash. Dash. Dot.

Dash. Dash.

Dot.

Lucas' eyes go round as he registers my statement. He slowly releases my hand, standing to his feet.

Michael turns his head toward him, while he tries to remain emotionless, but when Lucas' eyes dart to the whiteboard, Michael lunges for him.

Glass shatters around me, and I hear a series of punches landing on their target. Grunts of pain echo in my ears, and I have no idea who's falling to the ground as my body continues to shake uncontrollably. A gunshot resounds in the laboratory, and my breath catches in my throat as the scuffle ceases.

Panic sears my senses as I hear someone shuffling toward me. When Michael's face enters the rim of my view, I want to puke through the seizures. With a satisfied smirk he reaches up to the dial on the tube, turning up the juice.

"One down. Two more to go."

Fear flashes through my eyes.

"Oh, didn't you know? If Ian isn't already dead, he will be shortly. I'm doing you a favor, Braidan. I'm doing the world a favor. And when I'm done, the world will be a better place." His eyes are wild, like he's completely lost his mind. He glances to the bag. The injection is nearly complete.

"Goodbye, Braidan." He arches his eyebrows as I try to shake my head back and forth, pleading with him. But he only stares into my face, watching the serum seep into my veins, killing my cells.

An alarm pierces the air before a loud blast rips through the small laboratory, throwing Michael forward and yanking the IV from my arm. The roof hangs in shreds, and the morning light pours through the bare beams. Chaos swarms around me as I hear men yelling amidst gunfire.

My body still shakes violently, and I realize it might be too late. Enough of the mixture has been deposited in my veins that I will die anyway.

"McCready, over here!" The familiar, panicked voice bounces around my ears, but I can't remember who it is through the haze taking over my brain. The face that comes into view brings tears of relief.

Ian.

Ian rips the bite stick from my teeth, but my quivering body won't allow words to leave my throat.

Another face enters my vision. It's Sam. "Get the hemopurifier over here!" she commands, pushing open my eyes to check my pupils. "She hasn't got much time!"

There's a flurry of commotion as I struggle to remain coherent and attempt to grasp the situation. Ian has my hand, but all I can think about is Lucas. He's been shot and is possibly dead.

Ian pulls the straps from my head, and I'm able to turn. I frantically search for Lucas, but a man obscures my view, rushing forward with something like a dialysis machine.

"This is going to hurt," Sam says, pushing my head to the side.

She shoves a needle into my neck, and immediately I feel the evacuation. The machine clicks on, and I realize Sam is straining my blood for the serum, trying to remove the toxin from my body. Within seconds, the tremors cease, and I feel my cells come to rest, preparing to regenerate and fix the damage. I close my eyes and welcome the healing.

The voices in the room around me are static to my senses as I concentrate on the reactivation of every deactivated DNA strand. My mind flips through each strand and labels it in my head as my body goes to work on repairing. My cells pass the strand through them in an assembly line, repairing the parts needed to function properly.

Once the emotions are labeled, my body pauses, and the CPU that is my brain clicks through the knowledge of the turmoil my emotional upheaval has caused me. It knows I need emotions as a human, so it won't rest on the termination of this cell cluster. Instead, it routes and reroutes until it finds an answer.

My body attacks the cluster, and I feel the tug and push of emotions as it deletes then stretches the remaining cells before moving on to the next cluster. In ten minutes and with the help of the hemopurifier, my body has fixed itself. I draw in a deep breath, preparing myself for whatever is to come, as my mind flickers clear.

Ian's in front of me still when I open my eyes. "How are you feeling?"

"I'm better," I say, feeling the ache in my limbs dissipate with every breath.

"Let's get this out of you," Sam says, drawing the needle from my neck.

Ian rips open my bindings, which fall from my wrists and torso, allowing me to sit up. I'm barely upright before he has me in his arms, breathing into my hair his thankfulness that they arrived in time.

I want to push him away. I want to find Lucas and make sure he's alive, but I don't. Instead, I wrap my arms around him and cry into his shoulder. He has just saved my life yet again.

"Don't go too fast," Sam says, still winding up the tube.

251

She sticks everything in a bag and throws in the small hemo tube, then seals it. "Burn it, immediately." She hands the bag off and pats my knee.

I twist to search the room for Lucas. My heart beats hard against my chest at seeing a pool of blood collected on the ground near the door. Michael's body lies motionless, but no others remain. "Sam, where's Lucas?"

The words have just rolled off my tongue when a figure steps through the rubble. My heart leaps as Lucas enters the room. I want to race to him, to tell him I thought he was dead, to tell him I love him. But his eyes shift from happiness to pain as he bites his lip.

It's then I realize I'm still in Ian's arms.

26

"He's got my blood. Do you know what that means?" I try not to yell at Colonel McCready over the table, but my temper soaks every word. "He's planning to sell this technology to the highest bidder." I glance around the room of military personnel, waiting for them to come to the same conclusion I have. "Meaning terrorists or anyone that can give him what he wants."

McCready shakes his head. "I know he's not the most ethical guy, Braidan, but I don't think he's going to sell his findings to anyone outside the United States. The U.S. Government has had him under their microscope for years, and they've had no reports that were less than ideal."

"And his hybrid program was ideal?" I cross my arms, disgusted at what I'm hearing. "This is B.S." I slam my fist into the table, making the lady next to me jump. "You have to find those children."

"I'm telling you, we've searched every facility registered to Saber Corp. There's no evidence he has or ever had any children in his facility."

Outrage fills my chest. "So, I'm just making it up?"

McCready lets out a long sigh. "Braidan, I assure you, if we had any evidence your accusations were true, we'd have him in custody. But we've found nothing."

"Then he's moved them somewhere not registered to Saber Corp Industries. Did you check all his employees? Like Michael Bailey?" My words are furious as I yell across the room. "And what about my blood? Did you find and destroy it?"

The silence in the room is deafening as I watch McCready glance sideways at the officer nearest him. His unspoken words turn the blood in my veins to ice. They don't want to destroy the findings they want them for themselves. Which means, they might know where the children are and plan to capture them for research. I want to vomit at the thought.

I stand straight up and glance between each person in the room. Every single smug look confirms they are planning to use the information for their own benefit.

Resentment tries to overtake my sanity, but I shove it down and breathe out evenly. "Just tell me you have something planned. Anything." I pretend to plead as I can tell he's been told to pacify me.

"Braidan, we will do everything in our power to rectify this situation." He nods, and the door swings open so Sam can usher me out. She's dressed in the BDUs I now realize is her work dress.

I'm silent as they escort from the room. Ian and Lucas,

who are sitting in the waiting area, rise when we come through the door. Their crestfallen expressions tell me they know things didn't go as smoothly as we'd hoped.

Sam stands in the doorway, watching us as I shift glances between the two boys. The awkwardness of the situation is not lost on me, but I push it away as I think about the kids. I have much to tell the boys, much my mind has already planned, but can I trust Sam with such information?

"Bray," Sam says with uncertainty. "I know it's hard to believe right now, but they will do everything they can to stop Saber."

I twist toward Sam and stalk up to her. "What about those kids, Sam? You know what they're going to do if they get their hands on them?" I search her face as she contemplates my words.

She knows.

Sam's eyes dart to the camera nearby, and she hardens her brow. "Braidan, there's surveillance in this room. I suggest you not say anything you don't want overheard." Her eyes flare at the last part, and she sits down awkwardly in the nearby chair.

I stare at her a moment before she glances at the camera again, and I realize she's trying to send me a message. My mind erupts into dots, and I cross my arms, pretending to stare her down. Focusing on the microphone, I push molecules over the top, creating static to the listener.

"Go," I say softly.

She shakes her head and stands. Her mouth moves, but no sound escapes. She pretends to tell us something, but when the word glides from her lips, I want to kiss her.

"Chicago."

I lift my brows and release the static. Sam clears her throat. "So, you're just going to have to trust him. If there are children to find, they'll be found." Her eyes flare again, and she nods at the boys, who seem to comprehend the situation. She checks right and left as she steps toward the door.

"The escort will be here shortly to bring you back to your holding room. Boys, you're going to have to leave. I'll give you a few minutes to say your goodbyes." She hesitates, hand on the knob. "There's a guard behind this door, so don't try anything." Throwing a fleeting glance to the opposite door, her face flickers with a smile. When she disappears from the room, my eyes land on a piece of plastic where she was just sitting.

Her security pass.

In mere seconds, I've fogged the camera and we're pushing through the unguarded security door, stepping into the lobby of the San Francisco Federal Building. Lucas tosses the security pass in a nearby plant as we head for the street. I almost expect to meet some kind of opposition outside on the sidewalk, but only sunshine awaits. Lucas guides us to an idling bus and fumbles with his wallet to deposit money into the turnstile. I watch the glass doors, barely daring to breathe until the bus pulls away from the curb.

"Chicago. We have to go to Chicago. The kids are there."

I run my hand through my hair and bite my lip.

"It's too dangerous," Ian says, sitting in front of me. "Let me go. I'll bust them out."

Lucas glares, "No, I'll go."

I shake my head. Ever since Michael's lab, Lucas has been distant, as if allowing Ian to creep in and take back the piece of my heart. It angers me, but I've got greater things to be furious about. "Look, we all have to go. Saber is ruthless. We know that."

"Some more than others," Lucas says, earning a glare from Ian.

"Just because I was never a sock puppet doesn't mean I wasn't tortured enough on my own," Ian spits the words.

I hold up my hands between the boys. "I'm not going to bring either of you if you don't knock it off. I realize this whole situation is awkward, but there are children who need our undivided attention. We have to get them out. Save it for Saber."

∼

"Dad?" My voice shakes. "It's me."

"Braidan? Where are you? Sam said you escaped from the Federal Building?"

"Yeah, we stole her security pass. I had to get out of there. How are you guys? Everyone safe?" I lean against the plastic glass lined with graffiti.

"Yeah, the government put us up in a great place... I can't tell you where over the phone, but yeah, it's nice, and we're safe. You're safe?"

"Yeah Dad, we're all okay." A pause and several clicks alerts me to the trace on our call.

"Bray, you're not planning anything are you? McCready said they will take care of it."

My heart twists in my chest. "No, Dad, I just need a break." I hope he can't sense I'm lying. "I wanted to call and check in and let you know we're headed to the Los Angeles area. Lucas has some friends there we can stay with, so you won't hear from me for a while. I need some time to sort through all that has happened."

"Braidan, I don't know if that's a good idea." I hear the worry seep into his voice.

I know my time is limited, so I'm rushing through my words now. "Dad, it's got to be like this. I can't live locked in a facility for the rest of my life. I need time for people to see that whatever was broken in me is fixed, and I need time to deal with the consequences of my actions. My memory is almost completely back now, and I don't like who I was... but I control who I will be."

"Braidan, we love you. We know it was an accident. Please don't allow yourself to hold the shame or guilt of any situation, let alone that one. Accidents happen."

I suck back a sigh that wants to escape. "I know, Dad.

Love you too. Give my love to Mom and the boys. I'll try to check in again soon."

My hand hovers on the plastic receiver of the payphone after I've hung it up. I lean my forehead on the back of my hand, realizing that might have been the last time I speak with anyone in my family. We are willfully heading into a war zone, a zone whose dictator wants me dead and out of his way.

The shuffle of feet makes me stand tall. "They're fine. McCready has them in a witness protection program."

"That's great news, Bray." Lucas hands me a bottle of water. "Did you mention Los Angeles?"

"Yeah, and I could tell McCready was listening." I pull in a breath and twist the cap off a bottle. "That should put him off the scent for at least another day or two." The water flows over my tongue and splashes my throat with its bone-chilling cold. "Where's Ian?"

"He's clocking in. It's dumb luck that Chicago Catering Company was hiring. Had we not seen their van pull into the facility, we might still be searching for a way in."

"Luck or a trap. What if Saber is luring us?"

Lucas shakes his head. "I don't think he has a clue we found them already. But regardless, we'll be on our guard."

"What if someone recognizes us?" I tug the hat further over my head and push the dyed hairs behind my ear.

"No one would believe you were ever a redhead. Blonde looks amazing on you."

He runs his hand over his own head, inspecting the short locks. The buzz cut makes him look much older than seventeen, as if he were leaving to enlist in the next week. His grin turns lopsided as he stares. Then he pulls me against his body and places a kiss square on my mouth. Tingles shoot from my lips all the way down to my toes as my emotion swell. Emotions I can now control.

"I'm sorry I've been so distant. Things are so weird right now."

I sigh and press my forehead against his. "I know. And I'm sorry." I tug on the short hair at the back of his head.

"Let's get married after this is all over," he says, staring deep into my eyes. He's dead serious.

"Luke, I…" I hesitate at the hurt flickering in his eyes.

He releases me and steps back. "No, it's okay. I get it."

"Lucas, it's not that." I try to grab his hand, but he steps away. "I'm just in a crazy place right now. With all my memories returning, I…"

"No really, it's okay. You don't have to explain. I knew better." He releases a sigh and tips his water back over his throat. "Let's just get those kids out." His eyes find mine, then shift to the street.

"Lucas?"

He grunts.

"I want you to know you mean more to me than I can ever imagine a person meaning to anyone. But right now, I

260

have to focus on those kids. We have to save them."

He turns away with moist eyes, and I can't help but feel he doesn't believe me.

～

The evening chill breaks over the land, bringing desperation. Ian pulls up in the white catering truck, and we jump in the back, tucking ourselves behind the seats.

"I brought some cargo blankets," Ian says, turning left, inching closer to our destination. "You might want to cover yourselves. Twice this week the guard has opened the back to check, like the peanut butter is going to run away."

Lucas grunts. "Or like you're sneaking someone in?"

Ian ignores the comment and turns down the last of the streets. "I see the gate. You ready for this?"

"Ready as we'll ever be." I pull the scene into dots and sigh. Fortunately, only two guards are standing at the gate when Ian brings the truck to a halt.

"Evening. I'm here to make today's delivery." Ian leans on the door and hands him the paper.

"Did anyone stop you on your way in?" The man shoves the paper back into the window.

"Nope." Ian stays relaxed, and I'm grateful he's warned us of the order of questions he'll be asked.

"Have you been in possession of this truck since it was loaded?" The guard sounds bored as the other uses a mirror to check the bottom of the van.

"Yes, sir."

The guard nods. "All clear." He motions at the gate, which creaks open. "Have a good evening," he says and waves us through.

Ian follows the road up and around, and it's everything I can do to not hyperventilate under the cargo blanket. I can practically feel the children's presence as we draw nearer to the facility. I seem eerily connected to each one.

It's at least five minutes before Ian clears his throat. "There's a road right there," he says, still following our desired course. "That's where I'll ditch the truck."

I make a mental note as the crows in my belly flap for release, but I keep quiet.

"Two guards on the docks," he says, though he knows I can see them. "Stay still."

The truck lunges to a stop, then Ian backs into the bay. He barely waits for the engine to die before hopping out.

"Evening," he says, shaking hands with the two guards as if they were old friends.

"More peanut butter?" The first guard says, heading for the dollies on the bay.

"Of course. You guys seem to be going through it like water."

The back doors fling open and guards begin to shovel the food out of the back. I hold my breath as the second guard reaches within inches of my foot.

"Here, I'll get that." Ian jumps into the truck and pushes the last case toward the back.

"Thanks," he says, tipping the box onto the dolly.

"Hey, do you have a restroom I can borrow?" Ian asks as he slams the rear door shut.

"Sure, follow us through the bay. There's one just down the hall."

The plan works seamlessly, leaving Ian inside with no guards watching the dock. I focus on the camera and fog the lens with the humidity in the air. After the camera has tried to refocus several times, I'm certain it's fogged over enough for Lucas and me to slip by.

The truck door snaps closed, and we rush through the dock, the landscape a colorful array of dots. Once out of the camera's range, I defog it with a quick flip of my mind and hear the mechanism focus back into place.

Perspiration dapples Lucas' forehead as I scan the long, narrow hall for any other cameras. We make our way down, hoping to find Ian before raising any alarms. My vision maps the area in front of me, and I see the two guards pushing the dollies toward a set of double doors, Ian following closely behind.

"Here you go," one says. "I'll be right out to escort you back."

"Sounds good, thanks," Ian says and presses his way into the small restroom. After the door closes behind him, he smashes his ear up against the panel and waits for the double doors to swing shut. We're dashing to him as he exits the bathroom.

"What are they doing?" Lucas says, twisting his head to peek down the hall.

The dots in my vision move seamlessly. "They're unloading the dollies now."

"Any other security?"

I scan the area and only see a microwave drawing power. "No. And no cameras down the remainder of this corridor. Want me to take the guards out in the kitchen? They'll never know what hit them."

No sooner does Lucas nod than the soft *thunk* of bodies falling to the floor echoes down the hall.

"Dang, that's cool," Ian says, grinning from ear to ear as he flaps open the door for us.

The boys hurry to the two men lying on the ground in a heap, strip them of their uniforms, then bind their hands with the zip ties from their pockets.

"There's a pantry over there," I say, strapping the silver tape over one mouth. I feel terrible seeing the older man with large stubble covering his face. "He really should have shaved today." I press the tape into place, cringing at the thought of it being removed.

Lucas picks up the first man. "Hindsight is 20/20, I guess." The half-naked man groans as Lucas drops him in the pantry.

I yank the air from his chest once more, causing him to faint again. "That one's a fighter. Maybe you should tie his feet too."

Without hesitation, Lucas links two ties together, strapping them to the guy's ankles. "Let's get this other one in."

"Be careful," I say, as Ian hikes the guy over his shoulder.

He scoffs at my warning and practically drops him on the first man's lap. "That'll be interesting when they come to." Taking one more zip tie, he fastens the two men's hands together.

Lucas and I pull on the stolen uniforms as Ian unloads the rest of the items on the dolly. I tuck my hair under the collar and pull on the security hat.

"I'll push this dolly back out."

I nod, trying to ignore my tumbling stomach.

"I'll ditch the truck back at that access road. I think we'll have at least till morning before they realize it shouldn't be there." Ian hesitates at the edge of the kitchen. I want to rush to him and wrap my arms around him, but instead, I stay rooted to my spot.

"Please be careful. Meet us back at the docks as soon as you can."

He nods, then turns and glares at Lucas. "Keep her safe."

"I will, man. You stay safe, too. We need you in here." For the first time, the façade breaks between them. I see Ian wrestle with his attitude before twisting on his feet and disappearing through the door.

My vision bursts into dots again, and I continue to report his location until he's safely in the truck and driving away. I pull in a hefty breath and turn toward the other boy standing in the kitchen. His face says he's well aware of my feelings for Ian, still.

"Lucas, I--"

"Braidan, I told you it's okay," he says, buckling the gun belt around his waist.

I want to scream at Lucas to shut up, but something keeps me silent as I watch him fumble with the clip.

"I just want you to be happy. And I mean that. If you want to be with Ian, then I'll back away and not interfere." His eyes find mine, and I see the truth behind his words. "I just need you to know I'll always be here for you, even if all we can ever be is friends."

I don't realize I've moved until I'm in his arms, pressing my lips against his. I taste the saltiness of tears, and I've no idea if they're mine or his.

"I love you, Lucas. I've never stopped loving you. Even when I didn't remember who you were, my body knew it loved you. Knew it needed to remember you." My lips find his again, and I pull him to me, desperate for the moment to never end.

He embraces me and presses his face into my hair. His happy sighs echo off my heart, and I know we're one again.

He steps back, holding my cheeks and wiping the tears with his thumbs. Fire has lit in his eyes as they focus on mine. "You ready for this?"

I nod and inhale an unsteady breath. "When this is all over, I'll make sure Ian knows all we can ever be is friends."

Lucas nods and motions at the gun belt still sitting on the counter. "Don't forget that."

I reach for the weapon and freeze at seeing a real gun sitting in the holster, along with several clips of ammo and other tools.

Now that my memory has returned, I recall taking target practice with Ian, but I'm rattled to think before this night is out I might have to shoot at living beings. I strap the belt around my waist and adjust it to the right spot on my hips.

"You look good," he says, eyeing me.

"I look like a guy." I tuck my shirt down tighter.

"That's a good thing, considering it's a guy you're replacing. Any sign of Ian?"

I scan the terrain outside, resisting the urge to panic. "Not yet."

"Don't worry. He's just being careful. He'll be here."

The radios in our belts roar to life, and my breath catches in my throat. "Check in."

My heart pounds as I realize we've no idea what station the guards were. "Did Ian tell you?"

He shakes his head, panic full on his face. "We'll wait for a missed check-in and pray it's the right one." He grasps the radio and brings it near his mouth.

We listen intently as the check-in begins and wait for someone to miss it. At seven, there's silence on the radio. Lucas' hands tremble as he brings the radio to his lips. As he's about to click the button, it buzzes to life.

"Seven. All Clear."

The numbers tick up until stopping again at twelve.

"Twelve?" The voice bumps around in my head, and I know it must be us, but Lucas waits, just in case. "Twelve... last call."

I gulp hard as he depresses the button.

"Twelve. All clear." Ian's voice carries over his shoulder, and Lucas almost drops the radio.

I resist the urge to punch Ian's arm as we all move back against the wall into position. He's suppressing a chuckle when I glare at him. "That wasn't very nice," I whisper, my heart still beating uncontrollably.

A quick glance at Lucas shows me he's pleased as well. "You two..." I resist the urge to punch them both.

"Let's wait for the all clear. Then we'll head in," Ian suggests.

The check-in goes to twenty-two, and once the final voice proclaims, "All clear," the tension lifts from my shoulders.

"You guys ready?" Lucas asks, taking the gun out of his belt.

My stomach flops as I massage my hands together, worried what will transpire in the next thirty minutes of my life.

Ian glances up at the nearby camera, and I drop my hands, resting them on the butt of the gun on my hip.

Lucas reads the distress on my face like he always has, and when we step into the hall shoulder-to-shoulder he nudges me, speaking softly. "Braidan, whatever happens, this was the right choice, okay? I want you to remember that and hold onto that fact, regardless of the outcome."

Ian nods his agreement. "We chose to do this on our own accord. We know what he's doing to those kids. They need to be freed. We would have come on our own if we couldn't get you out of the Federal Building. We'd already discussed it."

I look between the two boys as they nod at each other and then at me. "I know. I know."

What they don't realize is that I plan to remove them from the equation if I can. Take them out of harm's way, so they will live if I am to die. Or at least... I will die trying.

27

Our footsteps are light as we sneak through the halls of the Saber Corp Laboratory. I fog the cameras as needed, but the corridors are oddly silent. Fear courses through me at the possibility we've been given information on the wrong facility. That maybe Sam was misinformed, and now we will die, and the kids won't be saved.

I shove the thoughts away. I can't think like that. I can't believe we will fail before we've even started. Besides, the same electricity I felt when we pulled onto the facility grounds radiates through me now. I couldn't explain it if I tried, but I know those kids are here.

The door to our left pops open, freezing us, and a man steps through wearing a blue Saber Corp smock. My heart flutters in my chest, and I want to scream with the joy filling my veins. I recognize him. He is my final proof the children are here. Instead, I stare at my feet, hoping he won't recognize me.

"Oh," he says, seemingly startled as he pulls the door shut behind him. "Out on rounds already?" He checks his watch. "Well, I'm off for the night. Have a good evening." He spins on his heels and heads down the way we came, barely lifting his head enough to shuffle past us.

Once he's out of range, I tug on the boys' arms so they'll draw closer. "That's Saber's leading guy. He was there when I was captured last."

Lucas glances at the door he came from and nods. "Let's see if we can get inside." He swipes the first guard's card over the keypad.

Red.

He tries the second card.

Red.

He curses. "That would have been too easy," Ian says, running his hands through his hair.

"Let me try something." I stare at the pad and focus all my attention on the computer attached to the lock.

As I hoped, my mind clicks into hyper speed, analyzing the possible magnetic codes which might open the door. It pulls up possibilities, then uses the possibilities to reprogram the card in my hand. Each time it mixes the code, I swipe the door, but it blinks red. Nearing the end of my list, I swipe again.

Green!

"Got it!"

We rush through the door and snap it shut behind us. The lab is dim with only a few spotlights shining on projects on tables around the room.

"Let's destroy any and all blood samples, regardless of their label," I say, hurrying toward the steady whir of the centrifuge, while Lucas and Ian cross to opposite sides and begin yanking cabinets open.

The spinner slows to a stop, and without thinking, I reach for the metal trash bin and start slamming the vials of blood into the bottom. They crash against the metal, and blood splatters all over, painting the inside of the trashcan a sickly red. The scent of metal in the air draws the bile into my throat, but I keep trashing the vials without hesitation. More vials line the inside of a nearby tabletop refrigerator. I push them all into the can with a quick swoop. At least eighty vials of blood have been wasted at my hands.

"What is this?" I spin around at the sound of Lucas' voice. Familiar boxes line the inside of a closet.

"Those are our records," I say. "Is there a shredder here? We can't very well set them on fire."

Ian darts for the desk. "Bingo! And it's commercial grade. This baby will take at least forty pages at a time."

The buzz grates on my nerves as they feed stacks and stacks of papers through the machine. The reservoir fills before they've finished the first box. Lucas takes it out and dumps it on the floor.

I continue searching through the cupboards as they whiz through the boxes, each taking turns destroying the records Saber Corp has tried so hard to hide. Ian makes light of the situation by dumping the crosscut papers all over the lab tables before bringing the container back.

"I've checked everywhere. There's no more blood in here."

"I saw a bottle of alcohol under the sink." Ian points, still feeding papers into the shredder. "Pour it in the trashcan and mix it around. It should kill anything still viable in there."

I twist the lid off the economy-sized bottle of isopropyl alcohol and pour it into the trashcan. The thrill of success races through me as I hear the liquid slosh around, the shards of glass clapping into each other in a small, victorious tune.

"Should we take note of what records we've destroyed? So we know if we've got them all?" Ian asks as he tilts the box on its side to check the name.

"That's a great idea. I'll finish these while you find a pen," Lucas says, feeding more papers through the hungry machine.

Ian dashes to the desk and rummages through the drawer. Curses pour over his lips as he clicks something on the computer screen

My heart drops in my stomach. "What about the computer files?" There has to be some sort of unit the memory is stored in.

Lucas joins us at the computer desk as we search in vain for such a device.

"It must be networked. We have to find the server, and I'm betting it's also somewhere in this building," Ian says, slamming his hand against the desk.

"We're running out of time." My hysteria is hard to mask.

"Let's split up," Ian says, pushing to his feet.

"What? No!"

"Braidan, we have to," he says, pulling the cord from the wall.

"No we don't Ian, we can--"

"He's right, Braidan. We have to split up."

I glare at Lucas like he's lost his mind as he pats Ian on the back. "I can go, man," he says, unwilling to meet my eyes.

My heart rips from my chest, but I say nothing.

"Are you sure? It was my idea. I'll go," Ian offers, turning to Lucas.

"No, you stay with Braidan. Keep her safe and get to those kids. I know enough about computers that maybe I can find a virus and wipe out their systems." I'm barely holding it together as Lucas speaks. "Let's just take another scan of the lab and get those names written down. When we are sure we can't destroy anything else, I'll get moving."

I can't help but feel this is a bad choice, but I've no idea if it's just my fear of losing Lucas or my instincts telling me something is terribly wrong.

Ian scribbles the names from the boxes onto a sheet of paper and then frowns.

"What's wrong?" I ask, stepping up next to him. He offers me the paper, and I scan the names and freeze, realizing mine isn't there. "My records aren't here." I shove the paper in my pocket and scramble for the closet, hoping maybe we missed a box, but the room is empty. I resist the urge to slam the door. Has this all been a waste?

We scatter when the clicking of locks echoes through the small lab. I dart behind the table. With a single command, the lights flicker on, and I hear a gasp as the chaos of the lab is revealed. He darts for the control panel, where I finally see him. It's the same scientist we saw leaving this lab ten minutes before.

"Freeze!" Lucas steps from the shadows, gun raised, pointing it at the scientist. "Put your hands where I can see them and come away from the door."

He obeys, and when he turns, his eyes grow wide as he registers who's standing in front of him. "Please don't shoot!" The name on his smock says Dr. Morgan Graham.

"Where are my files?" I ask, stepping toward Dr. Graham. I'm shaking and can't decide if it's from fear or anticipation.

"I don't know." If I didn't know better, the look in his eyes would say he's telling the truth, but how can he be?

I'm at his side in an instant, gun pressed against his throat. Ian lunges forward but stops short as I wave him off. "Where. Are. My. Records?"

"You wouldn't kill me," he says, but the vibrato in his voice betrays his doubt. He doesn't know I've quelled the emotional battle in my body. He believes I can and will do it.

I press the frantic breaths from my lungs through my nose in pants, a growl escaping every time I exhale.

"Just kill him," Ian says. "We will find the records with or without him."

I narrow my eyes on the doctor as terror ripples through him in waves. "Works for me." I lift my gun and press it into his gullet.

"Please. Please. I have a family. Please. I'll tell you anything you need to know. Just let me live. Please."

"Where are her files?" Lucas almost yells.

Dr. Graham shakes his head. "You must believe me. I really don't know. Saber usually keeps them with him at all times."

My memory flashes back to him carrying the same folder almost every time I've laid eyes on him. He didn't trust anyone with the information.

"And he doesn't keep copies anywhere else?" I jab the gun harder into the man's neck.

"No. Not that I'm aware of. He is afraid information will leak on the discoveries."

"Then what are you testing in here?"

"Just pieces of your code. The only one who knew everything was Dr. Bailey."

Lucas curses. "Where's the server you network to through this computer?" He swings his gun toward the computer on the desk.

"I don't know." His voice shakes uncontrollably. "We aren't given that information."

Lucas steps up to the man, who attempts to step back, but I've got him by the collar, and he can't move. "Problem is, I don't believe you."

"It's in the basement, I think." His voice breaks as the words come out.

I click my tongue on my teeth a few times as I reach a conclusion. "Dr. Graham, here's the deal. Ian and I need access to those children, while Lucas here needs to take down the server. The way I see it, you have two options. You can help us and live, or you can die like the coward you are."

Dr. Graham's eyes flash from mine to Lucas, and a tear trickles down his cheek. "Children?"

I can't hide the confusion on my face. "Yes, children. Aren't you testing on other samples besides mine?"

He shakes his head violently. "No, only yours."

Lucas draws his gun back and taps the handle on his palm. "I saw the kids, Dr. Graham. It's no use trying to cover for Saber. Braidan and I both saw them."

"I really know nothing about any children. I'm only privy to information I'm given." He bites back the shake in his voice and clears his throat. "I don't work for Saber because I want to." He stares at close range, his thoughts lost somewhere else.

I release the doctor, and he lets out a deep sigh and wipes his face. "Saber is blackmailing me to work for him. I made some bad choices and somehow he found out and... well... I've tried to leave my past in the past. I've tried to be a better human being, but he still holds it over my head."

"Dr. Graham, Saber has at least ten children in this facility right now. You and I both know what he plans to do with those children. We need your help to stop him. We have to destroy all the evidence anyone like me ever existed." My eyes plead with him as I speak, and I can tell he feels trapped. "If we can stop him, you can live free from his blackmailing. Whatever you did in the past will be gone. No one has to know."

He gasps, and tears trickle down his face. "If that's possible... What can I do to help?"

"Can you gain access to the top security doors?"

He nods. "I can probably access every room in this facility."

I release the pent up breath and lower my gun completely, placing it in my holster. "There's an observation room we need to find a way into without being detected."

"All the doors in this facility are on a security panel. Even if you could get close enough, they'd track every step. If there are indeed children in this facility, they would be on strict lockdown, and no one would be allowed in or out at undesignated times."

"There has to be a way in." I rub my temples, trying to coax the monstrous headache tugging at my lobe to depart. The temperature in the room shifts by the second, and I know it has everything to do with my body and nothing to do with the thermostat...

Thermostat!

My eyes flutter to the ceiling and land on the vent above my head. Dots burst through the room, and I gasp at seeing an open tunnel running the length of the compound leading right over the observation room.

Lucas looks up and snaps his fingers. "Perfect. Dr. Graham, can you take me down to the server room in the basement?"

Dr. Graham nods, "What do you plan to do?"

"I don't know yet," Lucas says, running his hands through his short hair.

The smile on Dr. Graham's face makes Lucas shift his glance toward me. "I know for a fact Saber Corp's network is a bit on the outdated side. A certain computer virus might be able to wipe out the information in all the facilities across the country." He wags his eyebrows. Has he been planning this long before today?

"Where would we find such a--?"

Dr. Graham holds out a small thumb drive, disguised as a pen.

"This virus will even corrupt backup files. Any and every computer our network attaches to will be infected. This could very well take down the whole internet for a time."

"Where did you get this? And why haven't you used it before now."

He thumps the drive in his fingers, allowing the grin to slip from his face. "Fear. If Saber found out I'd infected his system, my whole family would die."

"But you're willing to take the risk now, why?"

"Braidan, I've been willing to take the risk for a long time but needed the opportunity to present itself. My family just needs one cryptic phone call from me, and they will disappear from the face of the earth, for all Saber knows. If what you say is true, this is the presenting opportunity, and it's time for me to make that phone call."

28

Dr. Graham holds the chair steady as Lucas helps me into the tunnel. It could be an air vent, though no air is flowing through it. We've stacked two tables and a chair on top of each other to get us close enough to reach the ceiling. I pull my body into the metal housing and slide on my belly along the three-foot-tall shaft. I soon feel a hand on my foot, and then Ian is in the pipe with me.

In my dot matrix, I see Dr. Graham balance himself on the wobbling chair, then replace the grate over the opening. I silently pray as I watch him climb from the chair down to the floor and head for the phone.

I refocus on the tubes in front of us and see the rat maze crossing over rooms where people sit, stand, work, and even sleep. The pale-green of the imprisoning material is in the rim of my sight as we crawl inch by inch through our metal confinement. I'm irritated to see each of the individual prison cells covered in this material.

A knife twists in my stomach when I envision one of these children acting out uncontrollably in the manner I have every day of my life since receiving the serum on the plane. I can't let this happen to these kids. I won't let this happen. My arms tremble as I pick up speed, knowing this is our only chance. If we can't break them free, we will die trying. The pale-green molecules inch closer, and my heart rate accelerates. I can't see through the material, but the wiggle in my chest is growing stronger, telling me they're in there.

Once on top of the familiar round observation room with the ten windows, I scan and rescan the area. No camera exists here due to the sensitivity of the program, or more likely, Saber's distrust in people, afraid someone will find out he kidnapped ten children on whom he is actively testing.

This side of the vent is plain metal, and with a flick of my mind, I unscrew the bolts, my fingers in the slats so it won't fall to the floor. I pull it up and slide it carefully away. Going headfirst into the hole, I hold onto the edges of the ceiling. When I'm far enough out, I flip my feet around, and drop to the ground with a soft thump.

The observation room is icy cold and sterile, bringing a familiar loathing. Dread leaches into my bones, like the chill of an early morning winter day. Every time I've been in a room such as this it's been to prepare for testing or to be ridiculed for acting out in a manner unfit for the hybrid program. Since I was eight, this room has bred terror in all of us, as if designed to break our spirits and show us we could not escape.

Ian drops to the ground behind me, and when he wraps his arm around my shoulders, I know he feels it too. The horror is so thick in this room it's almost a visible fog trapped in the stale air. I grab Ian's hand and walk to the closest window, anxious about what I will or won't see.

It's incredibly dark as I peer through the glass, so I press my face against the cold pane and hold my hand to shield the dim light inside the oval room. My heart catches in my chest at seeing a small redheaded girl lying there. Her hair flows over the side of the cot, and her skin is so pale she's almost glowing. You'd think she's never seen the light of day. She clutches herself because she has no pillow. No blanket. No security.

Anger laps at my insides, but I press it back and move on to the next window while Ian continues staring into the first. Another tiny redhead comes into focus, turning my blood cold. Tears collect in the corners of my eyes as I race to a third window to confirm my fears.

My feet speed me to the next window. And the next. The sight of the children nails a stake in my heart and fuels my motivation to get them out even stronger, thicker, more urgent. I cover my mouth as the realization seeps into every cell in my body. Ian, seeming to sense I'm about to lose it, rushes to my aid. He grasps my elbow, helping me stay upright.

"What's wrong?"

I gulp continuously, trying to formulate the words, but my body wants to break into sobs. Never in my life would I have considered this possibility. Never. This is insane.

"Braidan?"

I twist toward Ian and grab his shirt, begging for him to

make this nightmare go away. "They're... They're..." I swivel my head to the nearby window and press my forehead against the frigid glass, hoping they've magically changed into something else. But when I see the red waves of hair, I know it's true.

"They're me."

29

I'm numb as I peer through the glass at the child in room three. A cloned version of myself. The child looks only about eight, which means Saber cloned my cells eight years ago, before he gave me the second serum. He knew I was different. He knew I'd be the one the mutated vaccine would work on.

"How are we going to get them out?" I press my hands against the glass. "And after we do, what next? They don't have parents. They have no one. They've only ever known Saber."

Ian runs his hand through his hair. "I've got no clue. This is certainly not what I expected." He flops on the nearby chair and hangs his head between his legs. His body language says we've failed. The situation before us is bigger than we are and even more overwhelming than we could have prepared for.

"How long do you think we have?"

He glances at his watch. "It's midnight, so I assume we have five hours or so." A sigh escapes his lips. "You have a plan?"

My eyes roam over the pale-green material of the room the girls are sleeping in. The glass is way too thick for me to manipulate. I tried so many times in the past. It's made from a synthetic blend of minerals combined with the same material as the walls. "There has to be a way for me to get through this crap."

"Haven't you tried before?"

I stare at the substance on the wall and think about radio waves. The stats click through my mind's eye, and the specifics for microwave technology come into focus.

"Oh my goodness." I twist toward Ian, who's now on his feet. "My mind just came to the conclusion that if I can harness the radio waves in the room, I can microwave the material until it becomes pliable, then manipulate it and get the kids out." I'm so excited, I barely recognize the confusion on Ian's face.

"Your mind did what?"

I ignore him and turn toward the window again, evaluating the spaces. "You know, that whole CPU thing? When I come up with several ideas at once and my brain clicks back and forth and analyzes it for me?"

"It does what?" Ian is beside me at the glass now, staring at the second head I've apparently grown.

"You mean, you didn't know?"

Ian blinks and stutters through a few unintelligible words.

"I don't think anyone knows. Did you ever tell anyone you could do this?"

"Well, I don't know." Does he think I've been hiding some great secret? I reach back into the recesses of my memories. "No, I guess I haven't. Come to think of it, when it happened at Saber Corp, it shocked me, but I welcomed it, considering it normal for the epic hybrid I am. But now that you're making me think about it, I think it's a new trait."

"I wonder if your genes have mutated again, causing this new skill."

The gleam in his eye makes my heart thud against my chest. Michael had the same look on more than one occasion during our time together. And more recently, just before he tried to take my life. Is Ian with Saber? Oh God, please no.

"It's not a big deal. It's like thinking fast." I turn away and press my hand against the glass. My heart hammers against my chest as I peer into the darkness while my mind spins over everything that's happened since the rescue from the lab. I pick apart every phrase and comment Ian has thrown out at either myself or Lucas.

"Well? Are you going to try it?"

"Huh?" I take in his body language and feel like bursting out in relief. He's as nervous as I am, and his eyes scream with the same panic for these children that I feel.

"Yeah, I'll try it. It has to work."

I hesitate, still staring into his face, waiting for a missed step. Eventually, guilt rushes over me. Here this boy is, risking everything for me, for these kids, and I think he's up to no good. In essence, he allowed his father to die, maybe even killed him to save me. Yet, I'm doubting every motive he's ever exhibited.

I shake off my shame and steady my nerves. My vision blinks, and I see the molecules as diamonds as I press on the impenetrable glass. I focus on a section of the wall away from the door, afraid any movement there will alert security, then begin searching for radio waves in the small room. They enter my consciousness easily, and I coax them into the space on the wall I've chosen. They hit the wall, and most of them bounce off, but a few wiggle into the water particles. The color of the molecules changes as they start bouncing around. Before long, the particles are knocking into each other and rebounding off the material around them. Once I think I've excited them enough, I focus on the other material around the bouncing molecules. It bends with ease, and I push a hole right through.

"Ian, look!"

His eyes flutter to the floor. "No way." He kneels down in front of the growing hole and peers into the room.

I push my thoughts harder, and the hole grows even faster.

"I think it's big enough for me to fit through." He kneels to the floor and prepares to enter.

"Be careful. The edges are probably still really hot."

"I'll keep clear. You go to the next one while I wake her."

I'm on my way before the words are completely out of his mouth. I focus on the next wall, and again it melts like wax. I'm already working on the third hole by the time Ian emerges with a groggy redheaded girl close behind him.

"Sit here for me, okay?" He pats her arm, and she obeys without reason. He darts into the next hole and disappears.

My focus wavers when I notice the little girl is watching me. I wonder if she knows who I am or why she's here. My eyes flit over her face first, then her hair, and I realize she has no blonde streak. She hasn't been given the second serum. I release the pent-up breath from my lungs. A small victory. I'll take it.

When Ian shuffles from the hole, I realize I'm not even half done with the one in front of me. I bite the side of my cheek and twist away from the girl, refocusing my energy into the radio waves. I try hard to ignore the hurt I feel for these kids, but it explodes from my cells. I grab the feeling, almost literally, then force it into my resolve.

On the sixth hole my breathing becomes labored. It has everything to do with the three clones now huddled in the center of the room, staring at me. Only four more, Braidan. You can do it for... Oh my. Do they even have names? My head flips around, and my eyes roam over every identical face as I feel hatred for Saber licking at my mind, begging for release. No. No Braidan. Four more.

I move on to the next room, and the wall melts with practiced precision. Maybe it's the venom breeding in my veins enabling me to manipulate this material as if I've been doing it all my life. Whatever it is, I'm glad I can shift to the next one within seconds.

The tenth hole opens before I even realize I've begun. Ian is still two behind me, so I should go in. I slip my frame through the wide opening, fascinated I did this at all. The small girl is lying on the cot, tucked into a ball. I don't know how Ian wakes them, but my first thought is to kneel beside the bed and whisper. So I do.

"Wake up," I rasp, as if I haven't spoken in weeks. When the child doesn't move, I lean over her and push a few red locks from her face. "Wake up, Angel," I say, and my heart bursts in my chest. That's how my own mother woke me when I was younger. This child has no mother.

I fall back on my knees and cover my mouth, unable to hold back the enormity of the situation. I try to silence the sob that wants to escape, but I fail and startle the little girl awake.

She sits up slowly and glances around the room before connecting with me. Her eyes roam over my features, and they trace the bleach-blonde hair under the hat. She holds out her hand, and her blue ID bracelet dangles from her wrist. She takes hold of my braid and tugs it out of my collar. She fiddles with it for a moment before grasping a thick red strand we must have missed. She appears briefly confused, then her eyes light.

"Are you my mother?"

I stare at the child, unable to formulate a single syllable. I have no idea what to say or how to react.

"Braidan?"

I twist, and she releases the hair, which falls onto my shoulder.

"We have to get moving," Ian says, waving at us through the opening.

"Where are we going? And why didn't you just use the door?"

I grasp her arms and peer deep into her eyes. "A lot of things are about to change, but I need you to go with it. Ian and I are the good guys, and we're taking you somewhere safe. Okay?"

She nods, and her curls bounce around her head. She reaches out and takes hold of my face. "I'll follow you anywhere, Mommy."

My heart breaks as I turn my head and try not to choke on the emotion. "We have to go, Angel." I stand and pull her to her feet.

She steps toward the hole while I hesitate, fighting the urge to lash out, scream, cry, or be sick right there on the floor. Hold it in, Braidan. Save it for Adrien.

Standing in the observation room brings an eerie calm, in complete contrast to what I felt inside the cell. The girls sit huddled together in their thin nightshirts, all looking to Ian and myself for guidance. I only realize now that every girl has a different color ID bracelet on her wrists and ankles. I half expect them to be robots or some shell of a human, but in each of their eyes I see life.

"Do we go back through the shaft?" Ian asks in a quiet whisper.

"We're going to have to, aren't we? We can't very well sneak ten girls with fiery red hair through the halls of Saber Corp unnoticed."

He turns his back on them and leans closer. "It's spooky that they look almost exactly like you."

My eyes bulge. "Ian, what do you think they are?"

"I know what they are, but it's still spooky. It's like a whole army of Braidans." He grins, which I ignore, and then gulps. "Right. I guess that was the point." He flips around and tells the girls to stand. "Listen, we're going to need to be completely silent for the next twenty minutes. We don't have time for bathroom breaks or injury timeouts. We just need to press on and get to our goal." He motions with his hands like he's talking to a football team not a bunch of eight-year-olds.

I smack his arm and take a few steps toward the girls. My heart catches in my throat as they all stare at me, enamored. I push the breath from my lungs and pretend I'm talking to Tanner. "Okay girls. See that opening up there?" I point, and they all look up. "We're going to have to use that to get out of here, but when we get up there, we all have to be so quiet no one can even hear us breathe, okay?"

"Quiet like mice?" The girl with the blue bracelet speaks.

"Yes, Angel. Quiet like mice. Can you do that?"

They turn to each other and slowly begin to nod.

"Maybe you should take this." I unclip the gun belt from my waist and dangle it toward Ian. As it hangs in the negative space between us, my heart thuds against my chest, and I draw it back before he can grab it.

"Braidan?" He searches my face for understanding.

Complete hopelessness washes over me. But it's not for me, it's for him. If I hand him the belt and crawl into the shaft, it will be our last contact. I can't do that.

"You should go up first." I wrap the belt back around my waist and begin to buckle it.

Ian's hand covers mine, and I look up. "Absolutely not. You go in first. I will hang back and make sure everyone gets in."

"But Ian..." What am I going to tell him, that I feel he's going to die here? That I'm having some sort of premonition he won't make it out alive? No alarms have sounded. How can that even be possible? I'm just paranoid. I hand the belt over, and Ian clips it to his waist.

"Now, you need to get up there and get moving." Taking the gun out of the holster, he checks the barrel, and I know he feels it too.

It's been far too easy for us. Someone or something is prowling nearby. Before I can waste another minute, my arms are around Ian's neck and I bury my face in his shoulder.

"Thank you so much for coming for me."

He takes his unarmed hand and runs it over my back.

"Had I any idea why my Dad wanted you, I would have never tried to find you, Braidan." His voice is strangled. "It's my fault all this has escalated. I'm sorry."

I take a step back and place my hands on his cheeks. "It's not your fault. It's better this way. I had to know, right? Besides, look at these girls. We would have never known about them if all this hadn't happened."

Ian tugs from my grasp. "But my Dad was the enemy he claimed had found you. He wanted you out of the fog so the others would follow your lead and maybe even come to your rescue."

"Like Lucas did."

He nods.

"Are the others really dead?" I gulp at the answer even before he's said it.

"Yes. I thought my father tracked them to make sure they were okay, but..."

"Hindsight is 20/20, right? We can't beat ourselves up for something we didn't know."

"I should have known. It's so obvious now." He thumps his fingers against the gun handle.

I suck in a full breath. "You're a hero, Ian. I know it, and now so do these girls." I grab his face and force it toward the girls, who still wait quietly nearby, listening to our conversation. "These girls owe their lives to you, as do I. You've saved us all, and for that, I'll forever be in your debt."

His chest inflates as he gazes at every adoring face. He leans his forehead on mine and allows a smile to crawl across his lips. "Thanks, Braidan," he whispers, then places a kiss on my forehead and turns toward the girls. "Our time is running out. Let's move."

It only takes a small jump for me to catch hold of the edge of the vent and pull myself up. I position myself on the far side of the pipe so I can send the girls down the other.

"We need to hurry, so if everyone can get into a single file--" Seeing them, the words die on my tongue. Each girl is already neatly in a line, ready for their next command. A sorrowful sigh escapes my lips, but I motion the first girl forward.

Ian grabs her waist. "Ready?"

She nods, and he lifts her over his head. She grabs hold of the edge of the vent and wiggles her way in. I grasp her arms and help her the rest of the way into the tunnel.

"Go up just further, but remember, be as quiet as a mouse. Okay?"

She nods and pads slowly away from me.

Ian lifts each of the girls into the vent, and each does exactly what I've asked until nine are crowding the tube ahead, each face twisted toward me, waiting.

Only one remains, the girl with the blue bracelet, Angel.

"You ready?" Ian asks, wiping the perspiration from his brow.

She pinches one eye shut and tilts her head toward the tube. "Is there room up there for one more?"

I stifle my giggle and motion Ian onward. I can already tell this group of girls will be fireballs, just like I was rumored to be at the ripe age of eight.

Her fingers are grasping hold of the metal when a blast rocks the room, slamming me sideways against the edge of the vent. Smoke immediately fills the tunnel, and panic takes hold of my heart. I scramble to the hole and peer down.

Angel and Ian are gone.

My sight blinks over the room as I scan for any sign of life. Fire laps the sides of the once-sealed door, and when I broaden my vision, the terror in my chest grows. The whole facility is on fire. I have to get these girls out of the building before we are consumed by flames or die of asphyxiation.

I scan the room and find Ian and Angel crouching behind a large armchair as two other people amble into the room, both armed with guns and gas masks. I hold my breath as they step toward Ian and Angel's hiding place. They stalk forward, as if they can see them, and I panic. I have to get them out. Before I think better of it, I drop into the room, and at the *thump* of my feet hitting the floor, both men spin on their heels and fire.

Shots rocket through the room, but I tumble behind the couch before our attackers can take proper aim. Black smoke is filling the area, and flames lick the walls inside the door, melting the plastic and spreading toxic fumes into the air.

A slight cough breaks through the silence, and both men turn their attentions to the vent. One of them fires into the ceiling, and I dive for them, fury making my movements quick and calculated. He collapses under my weight, and I twist his body over the top of me before the second man fires multiple shots into his partner.

Ian screams and lunges, grabbing him around the neck and pulling him backward. His gun goes off into the ceiling again, and I hear the girls scream.

"Angel, come on baby!" I call for the scared girl, still behind the couch.

She runs to my arms, and I lift her over my head. She wiggles into the tube, and her feet are disappearing when two more men enter the room. My hands tremble as I dart to the floor and grab the gun out of the dead man's hand. Smoke billows through the room in great clouds as more shots echo around me. My heart stops when two bodies collapse to the floor nearby.

Ian pushes the man from off the top of him and crawls to me. "Braidan, get out of here. Get those girls to safety," he says, reloading the clip on his gun.

"I can't leave you."

He grabs my shirt and yanks me toward him, making my heart seize. Blood covers his right side, and he's blinking so hard he's trembling. "You have to save those girls. I'm not dying to have you all die."

My mind blinks into dots, and I see the blood seeping through multiple wounds on Ian's body. "Oh my... There's too many... Ian, you can't..." Hysteria is pumping through me. "No. No. I can still save you." I pivot toward the door and see three more men sneaking through.

"No, there's no time. You need to go, Braidan." He grasps my neck and pulls me to his forehead. "Get those kids to safety... you need to live."

Movement behind us makes me gasp, and with two more quick shots, two of the five men who just entered collapse to the ground. The three remaining hide themselves.

"Please, Braidan. I promised Lucas I'd get you out alive, and I don't intend to break that promise. I'll buy you time, but you have to go." His eyes are trained on mine now, and I see there's no way I can talk him out of this.

My lips find his, and I pour my soul into him, praying that despite my fears, he will live.

He pushes me away. "Please, Braidan. Go." His eyes plead with me. "Please," he rasps, begging.

I have to listen. I have to go. And it kills me.

"On my count, run as fast as you can to that vent and don't look back, okay?"

Tears tumble down my face, but I nod. "I love you, Ian."

He brushes his thumb against my cheek, taking in my face for probably the last time. "I know you do. Ready?"

I push out an unsteady breath.

"One... Two... Three!" He jumps to his feet and fires randomly into the smoke, scattering the three guards.

I dash toward the vent, and with a jump, I pull myself up into the housing. Tears streak every girl's face as they look to me for guidance. I scan them quickly for injury and allow a momentary sigh of relief at finding them unscathed.

"We've got to go as fast as you can. No more quiet as a mouse!"

I check in all directions as we crawl through the maze, my heart picking up speed as I see no signs of life, only flames, in every room below us.

"You can do it, girls. Keep going!" I call through the tube, hoping they can't hear the sobs that have overtaken my body.

The metal underneath us is suddenly searing hot, and the girls cry out in pain. They're trying to push through toward our freedom, but the coughing and slowed pace show they are succumbing to the inhalation.

We aren't going to make it.

"Braidan!" Lucas' hysterical voice echoes through the tunnel ahead, and I release a cry of relief.

"Lucas! Lucas! Help!" The urgency in my voice presses the girls further. Our palms are raw from the burns, but everyone moves with haste, following Lucas' calls.

The first girl reaches the outside vent. She kicks it, crying when it doesn't budge. I wrap my mind around the screws and yank, sending the grate tumbling to the ground.

"Jump!" Lucas tries to persuade the first girl out of the vent.

I realize it's nearly fifteen feet to the ground, and if these girls are like me, the height is paralyzing. The flames crawl up the wall of the building around the vent, framing the area we need to jump from.

"Girls, look at me. I know it's high, but we have to get out. We'll die in here if we don't jump." I scream over them. "I promise Lucas will catch you. He'll catch all of us."

The first shakes her head, terrified.

"Honey, I need you to jump, so we can save you and your sisters."

Tears trickle down her sooty cheeks as she turns back toward the opening. She wiggles her way to the edge then looks back to me once more.

"You can do it." I nod.

When she jumps, her scream ricochets through the tunnel, cracking my heart in two. Lucas bobbles under the weight of his load but sets her safely on her feet and motions for the next. She jumps without hesitation and doesn't even scream.

Smoke, thick as night, penetrates our hiding place now, and the girls moan under the lack of oxygen. The thought occurs to me that I can remove the smoke. I follow through and push it from the tube.

Flames rush through the tube behind me, engulfing my feet. I scream and flip on my back, patting the flames with my hands. The girls see the fire and press forward, forcing the girl up front out unwillingly. She flails through the air, but thankfully, Lucas grabs her before she hits the ground.

The fire tempers down at the end of the tube, but the extreme heat turns the metal to wax. Two girls remain in the tube, and with a quick jump, only one.

A body moves inside my mind's vision. I push past the last girl, putting my finger to my lips as I stick my head out the tube. Lucas peers up, confused, then counts the girls. I point first toward the approaching figure and then toward the trees, waving him off. He appears conflicted, but he shepherds the girls into the foliage, their red heads bobbing along. They vanish only seconds before a man enters the light.

I shrink back and hold Angel closer to protect her. I lift her nightdress over her nose and mouth and pull my shirt up to do the same, but I'm not sure how long we can remain like this. I already feel the carbon monoxide filtering through my blood, wreaking havoc on my mind. The metal is so hot now. Angel whimpers, and I draw her up onto my side, accepting the heat searing my senses.

The crunch of gravel below us mixes with the crackle of fire. The man stops to inspect the vent grate lying on the ground.

Angel gasps for air and lets out a slight cough. She'll die of asphyxiation if I don't get her out of here.

"We're going to be okay, Angel. I promise," I whisper to her and push back the hair from her face. "Just hold on."

The man peers up at the vent hole, then rotates on his

heels and dashes toward the direction Lucas and the kids went.

I scramble forward. "Listen, you have to jump, okay? I'll catch you. Can you do that?"

She nods, only half awake.

"Angel, look at me." I grasp her face, and her eyes barely open. She's going to die.

The idea comes to me as I feel the breeze at my back. I analyze the air around us, and my mind grabs the oxygen particles. I pull them together and shove them into her lungs. She shudders until she's able to pull in another breath, but once she docs, life returns to her eyes.

"Okay, you ready to jump?"

She nods.

I scan the landscape and see the man still running toward the truck. I have to get there. I push myself from the hole and fall to the ground with a thud. I hop to my feet and wave at Angel. She scoots her small body toward the opening and sits on the edge. She hesitates, then leaps from the burning vent.

Terror paralyzes me as she seemingly falls in slow motion. What if I can't catch her? What if Lucas and the others are caught? What if I can't save them? What if Ian died for nothing?

Her scream fills my ears, and I snap to, barely snatching her from the air. We both let out a sigh of relief, and she hugs my neck so hard I can barely breathe. I set her on the ground after she releases me and peer into her sooty face. "Are you okay?" I press her hair back, checking her for any injuries.

The building beside us groans. I know what comes next. The explosion rockets debris toward us faster than I can react, pelting us with hot cinders and sweltering rock. My mind responds and focuses on the air around us. It presses the air molecules outward, raising a force field of protection and sending the rubble bouncing to the ground.

My heart catches in my throat when the crunch of gravel slices through the night. I thrust Angel behind me as someone steps into the dim firelight. The blood immediately drains from my face when I see the tattered folders in his hand.

Adrien seems to be taking a stroll in the park rather than fleeing for his life, which makes me twitch with righteous anger. When his eyes land upon my face, he freezes midstep. "Braidan? However are you in my facility without my knowledge?" His eyes dart right and left, searching for his salvation.

"Don't even bother, Adrien. I know you knew I was here. It was all too easy to get in and destroy the lab." I stay very still as he steps closer, hoping he can't see the child hiding behind me.

"Find anything interesting in there?" He flicks his tongue on his teeth as he considers me. "No, probably not, because I don't allow sensitive information in other's hands. That just makes for a messy clean up."

"Well, I certainly hope you backed up your computer

system." His bulging eyes tell me this is a hot button. "What, is that a no?" I tilt my head to the side and raise my eyebrows. "Right now, a virus is infiltrating every computer in your network. And I'm sure, millions of others."

He curses and bites his lip. "You lie!" He grits his teeth and fights the trembles taking over his body.

I shake my head, trying to fight off the grin.

"You!" He points an unsteady finger at me. "You have ruined years of work with one stupid mistake. I should've killed you when we found you again!" he yells, stepping toward me.

I step back, knocking Angel to the ground.

His eyes widen. "How...? You..."

I pull her to her feet, then tuck her behind me again. "It doesn't matter, Adrien. I've got her, and that's all that matters."

"You really don't want to do this, Braidan." Greed filters through his eyes as he stares straight through me. "The breakthrough we've made with this program will revolutionize the world, and those children are proof that it's worked."

"Why did you need more of my blood, Adrien? Why did you even care where I was?"

He spits on the ground, barely considering me. "Because the second serum didn't work on them the way it worked on you. Countless calculations revealed that the only way to change them into true clones was to have the mutation only found in your blood. With the new blood we transfused into them from you, it's only a matter of time before it mutates. Imagine what this could do for the world." He grips the air in front of him with his fist.

"You are sick, Adrien."

His nostrils flare. "You just don't realize how valuable you are, Braidan. You could be a millionaire with just a vial of your blood."

"Did you get rich off my blood, Adrien? Or is that for next week?"

"What are you going to do with that child?" Aggravation coats his words. "It's not like she's a real person."

I've hardly registered his words before Angel flips out from behind my back. She stares at Adrien, the hurt on her face enough to shatter my heart.

The rage I've been holding to a simmer now boils. My brain is in a pressure cooker, and it's about to explode. The landscape blinks into dots, and in one motion I yank burning flames toward Adrien. They wrap around the folders and light them up.

"No! No! Braidan, don't!" he screams, refusing to release his grasp. He smacks the papers against his legs, then his torso, hoping to extinguish the flames.

I watch in horror as his clothes ignite almost as fast as the folders did, but he still clutches the burning documents.

Angel gasps. I spin her around and press her face into my soiled shirt, unwilling to let her live with such a nightmare.

Adrien continues to fight the flames. Part of me says to rush to his aid while the rest tells me to stand my ground. I only intended to burn the paperwork. He's the one who chose to burn with it. The human in me fights the tremors. Can I just let this man die, even as vile of a creature as he is? If he lives, he will hunt us down relentlessly. Though the tears stream down my cheeks, I resolve to do nothing.

With his body fully aflame now, I can't bear to watch as his screams go from panic to complete pain and horror. I dip my head and press my face against Angel's, squeezing my eyes so tightly the tears burn for release. As his torturous screams echo in my head I start to sing loud enough for us both to hear.

Hush, little angel, don't say a word, Mama's gonna buy you a mockingbird.

If that mockingbird don't sing, Mama's gonna buy you a diamond ring.

If that diamond ring turns brass, Mama's gonna buy you a looking glass.

If that looking glass gets broke, Mama's gonna buy you a billy goat.

If that billy goat doesn't pull, Mama's gonna buy you a cart and bull.

If that cart and bull turns over, Mama's gonna buy you a dog named Rover.

If that dog named Rover won't bark, Mama's gonna buy you a horse and cart.

If that horse and cart falls down, Well you'll still be the sweetest girl in town.

The last of the words roll off my tongue, and I hear Adrien no more.

Angel pushes back and looks up into my face. "Will you really get me a dog?"

Her eyes are so bright when she asks, I can't say no. "Yeah."

I glance to the fiery mess beside us, and my stomach turns. Any evidence of this program has been eliminated.

My mind flickers over the remains of the building, and my hopes are crushed when I clearly recognize the center room, obliterated by the fire.

"Mommy, was Ian a good guy?"

I stare at the burning, charred mess, still unwilling to release my hold on the precious little girl I've named Angel. "Yes. He was a very good guy."

"I wish I could tell him thank you," Angel says, peering at the flames still licking through the building.

My eyes shift toward the heavens, and a deep serenity passes over me. "He knows, Angel. He knows."

Epilogue

Eighteen Months Later

"Where did all the evidence go?" McCready's exasperated voice carries to every ear within twenty yards.

"We're still working on decoding the drive we found in Bailey's lab, but he was really good at encrypting and fail-safing," the soldier says, stepping back.

"What about the other Saber Corp laboratories? You can't tell me that you've found nothing in the past year and a half. Something has to exist!"

The soldier gulps back the lump in his throat. "We seized all records coming into and going out of the labs and we've combed through every piece of paperwork we could find. Several times. Everything seems to indicate normal business practices."

McCready isn't buying it. "What about their computer systems? Have they been checked again? Surely Saber used something besides folders to keep his research in. He had to have had some kind of backup or something." His face turns bright red as he speaks. "Anything?!"

The solider bites his lip, debating whether to continue. "The trail has gone cold, sir."

McCready sweeps his arm across the desk, sending his computer crashing to the floor. The soldier scrambles to pick it up.

Another one hurries into the room, barely saluting before he speaks. "Sir? Doctor O'Donnell is on the line for you."

McCready grabs the phone and straightens his uniform before putting it to his ear. "James, tell me you have good news for me. Tell me Braidan has finally established contact with you, and she's safe. From a father to a father, I'm concerned about her."

James sighs long and sorrowfully. "No, Colonel, no sign of her." He pauses and sucks in a deep, cumbersome breath. "The reason I've called is to notify you that we're leaving the program, effective immediately."

McCready curses under his breath. "Why would you do that, James?"

"We remained under your supervision and protection for eighteen months, McCready. A full six months longer than you requested of us." James pulls in a great breath and continues. "Our family has been through a lot. And with no trace of Braidan, we'd really like to start over and put this behind us once and for all. We've already taken the legal action to part ways, and I really hope you don't take it personally if this is our final contact."

"I'm sorry it's been such a difficult time for you, James, and I completely understand where you're coming from. However, I have one question for you before you go." McCready picks at his nail, mocking emotion. "We're still trying to figure out what the rooms were used for at the center of the two labs. They were lined with a synthetic material and appear to have been holding cells." He pauses to listen for a sign that James knows something he's not sharing. "Lab techs say they were used for night shift workers who needed to rest, but I'm not so sure. Seems like an awful lot of security for a hotel room. Any idea what else those rooms were used for?"

"When I worked for him, they were always available to our shift workers."

"Huh," McCready says, still not quite believing him. "Do you think that Braidan could have been right? Do you think Saber could have been testing on other children? That there were more like her in his facility?"

"I suppose anything is possible, Colonel. But it would be a downright tragedy to think that was even possible and that they too perished in the fire."

Colonel McCready tapped his chin and clicked his tongue on his teeth. "Yes. Yes, a tragedy."

"I wish you the best in your ongoing investigation into Saber. I don't mean to sound callous when I say this, after all, she was my daughter, but I'm glad this is over for us. All of us."

"Uh-huh."

James clears his throat. "I guess this is goodbye, then."

"Yes, well, goodbye James. I wish your family well. Give my best to your wife and boys."

"I will. Thank you, sir."

And with a click, the line goes dead, just before the trace can finish.

~

"Did he believe you?" Sheila asks, touching James's shoulder.

"There's no telling, but he sounded infuriated. Do you think we made the right choice?" He turns toward his wife and folds her into him.

Her happy sigh is his answer. She stares at him for a long time, then turns to admire the chaos of the wedding reception in the courtyard beside them.

Ten redheaded girls, dressed in all white with different color ribbons in their hair, race around playing tag with Tanner and the other children. Each time the girls zigzag, deep red petals fall from the flower girl baskets in their arms.

Their good friends, Doctor Graham and his wife, stand nearby, their own small children giggling with delight as they weave in and out of their parents' grasp. They'd been such a blessing to Braidan and the girls, taking them in for the time Sheila and James remained in the government's protection program. It was hard not to contact them, but everything has changed.

Sheila's eyes float to Drew, who holds Rover's leash and tries to keep him calm as the children rush past. He barks excitedly, but no one seems to care. The girls' laughter is contagious, and soon both James and Sheila join the chorus.

The once spotless wedding runner is now soiled, and the sight of it makes butterflies thump up against her belly. She's become a grandma in the blink of an eye as well as a mother-in-law and is loving every second of it.

It's fascinating how the children each have a piece of Braidan in them. Her eyes flicker across their pink cheeks and smiles.

Danielle has Braidan's compassion. She's already tried to save a spider from its untimely demise.

Bailey has Braidan's bravery. She was the one to step up and squash the spider with her finger when her sisters screamed at the horror of it.

Jasmine has her temper. She uses it to fight for what she believes is right and wrong, and boy is she good at it.

Faith has her strong belief in the one true God. Even with her unconventional life and being, she knows He has His hand on her and loves her.

Grace has her sense of movement. She seems to always be dancing. Even when she brushes her perfect white teeth before bed, she sways back and forth, moving to the music in her head.

Charity has her sweet spirit. She is always there to help one of her sisters, even if it means she has to sacrifice something in return.

Elisabeth has the adventurous piece of Braidan. We've already caught her wandering off to explore the corners of the earth. They may have to find a leash for that one.

Hayley has Braidan's cleverness. She can't stop asking questions but also quickly comes to accurate conclusions, which she shares with everyone within earshot.

Iris has Braidan's funny bone. She always tries to make everyone laugh and usually does.

Sheila's eyes move to the last child, who has blue ribbons in her hair, and can't hold back the sigh.

Angel. If it's actually possible to create an exact clone of a person, Angel is that child. Every word out of her mouth. Every movement. Every gesture. Every sigh. Completely, one hundred percent, Braidan. Down to the brand new blonde strip of hair in the front of her head.

The situation hasn't been anyone's notion of ideal, but everyone has accepted it. It is the right thing to do. And now Sheila and James' lives are blessed with ten giggling little girls and a new son-in-law.

And it makes her happy. Very happy.

"James?" she says, returning her attention to her husband. "Do you think the others are safe?"

Happiness seeps from his face as crow's feet appear around his eyes. "I hope so." His gaze is fixed somewhere off in the distance. "Let's not talk about it. I don't want anyone else to know."

"You did the right thing, you know?"

He nods and brings her in close again.

～

Lucas' eyes move out across the sea of fire bobbing around the courtyard, and he smiles. This wasn't exactly what he'd planned his wedding day to look like, but with his adoring bride by his side, it has been no less than perfect.

He wraps her tightly in his arms and releases a contented sigh. "It's absolutely amazing," he says, and he means it. "I can't believe I'm the new Mr. Braidan O'Donnell." He allows the grin to capture his face as she elbows him in the ribs.

"No way. No. Way. We are all Tresses now."

He pulls her around. "Braidan Tress. It has a nice ring to it." He bobs his head back and forth and pinches one eye closed, mocking her. "As does, Angel, Bailey, Charity, Danielle, Elisabeth, Faith, Grace, Hayley, Iris, and..." he pauses for a moment and says the ABCs in his head while Braidan taps her foot. "Hold on. Give me a second." He scrunches his face and laughs when she pokes him in the gut. "Just kidding... Jasmine." He pulls her back into his embrace and kisses her head. Their faces both turn to view the courtyard. "Can you believe it? We're parents. On our wedding day!"

"It is pretty amazing." She shifts her glance back to him. "And you're sure you're ready to deal with all this? There's still time to back out."

"What? And abandon my wife and children? No way. Besides, I think Hayley has my eyes." He grins and places a kiss right on her mouth.

"You know what I mean, Lucas. This is a big responsibility. You're now a father of ten!"

He stares down, taking in all her beautiful features. "I'd like to be a father of eleven."

One Month Later

The warm breeze filters through the sheer curtains on the window as I check on the girls one last time before sneaking from the large custom-built house. I softly pull the door shut and tiptoe down the hall, meeting my mom and dad in the kitchen.

"Are you sure you two are going to be okay?"

Sheila waves her hand over her face. "It's only one night. You two need some private time for once. Besides, how hard can ten sleeping nine-year-olds be?"

"Mommy?" Angel stands in the narrow hall, arms crossed in front of her.

"What's wrong, Angel?" I rush to her and kneel, pushing the two-toned section of hair from her face.

"I can't sleep." Her eyes shift to grandma, then back to me. "Will you sing me my song?"

"Of course. Let's go sit."

Angel climbs into my lap in the old-fashioned rocking chair. She lays her head on my shoulder and curls up like a toddler instead of the nine-year-old she is. I have to remind myself often that they're still toddlers in the affection category, and they still need as much love and attention as we can afford them.

While I sing, I'm moved with intense emotion at the entire situation.

I am a mother of ten girls. Ten girls who look up to me. Ten girls who will see me fail. Can I do this? Can I be the mother they need? I'm not perfect, not even close. Even with the hybrid strands floating through my body, I'm lacking. They deserve so much more than I can offer. So much more than this life of hiding in some foreign country where they can't even speak the language.

I continue to sing as my thoughts roam over Ian and the price he paid for me to share this moment with my daughter, rocking her to sleep. I keep a framed picture of Uncle Ian on each of the girl's nightstands, a reminder every day that they're loved beyond measure. That they're an important part of life, and no one can deny their existence in this world as anything but marvelous. They know Uncle Ian saved their lives and never have to be reminded to mention him in their nightly prayers.

Angel has fallen asleep in my lap, and I wrap my arms around her, listening to the small voice echo inside me, telling me that though I have doubts, everything will be okay. These girls will be okay. Maybe not because of who their mom is or who saved their lives or even how they came to be on this earth, but because they are pieces of me. And I love them.

CPSIA information can be obtained at www.ICGtesting.com
Printed in the USA
LVOW121600270613

340557LV00004B/487/P